He didn't know whether to be amused or angry.

"Where does that leave me?"

Rachel swung her eyes to meet his. She'd been wondering the same thing. "Where *does* it leave you, Justin? What is it you want from me? Everyone wants something. Tell me what it is, so we can get it out in the open."

He reminded himself that she'd been hurt badly and that none of that had been his doing. He wouldn't react angrily or defensively. He'd simply be honest. "I want your friendship, the chance to get to know you better and . . ." He paused, wondering how to phrase the rest.

Her eyes widened, became challenging. "Yes?"

"I can't deny that I'm attracted to you. I wonder if you'll be as honest with me."

"What do you mean?"

"Will you admit that you're attracted, too? That you're interested? And maybe that you're just as surprised by that attraction as I am?"

He'd hit the nail on the head. She could deny it until the cows came home, but there it was.

Dear Reader,

Each month, Silhouette **Special Edition** publishes six novels with you in mind—stories of love and life, tales that you can identify with—romance with that little "something special" added in.

August is a month for dreams...for hot, sunny days and warm, sultry nights. And with that in mind, don't miss these six sizzling Silhouette **Special Edition** novels! Curtiss Ann Matlock has given us *Last of the Good Guys*—Jesse Breen's story. You met him in *Annie in the Morning* (SE#695). And the duo BEYOND THE THRESHOLD from Linda Lael Miller continues with the book *Here and Then*—Rue's story.

Rounding out this month are more stories by some of your favorite authors: Laurey Bright, Ada Steward, Pamela Toth and Pat Warren.

In each Silhouette **Special Edition** novel, we're dedicated to bringing you stories that will delight as well as bring a tear to the eye. For me, good romance novels have always contained an element of hope, of optimism that life can be, and often is, very beautiful. I find a great deal of inspiration in that thought.

What do you consider essential in a good romance? I'd really like to hear your opinions on the books that we publish and on the romance genre in general. Please write to me c/o Silhouette Books, 300 East 42nd Street, 6th floor, New York, NY 10017.

I hope that you enjoy this book and all of the stories to come. I'm looking forward to hearing from you!

Sincerely,

Tara Gavin
Senior Editor
Silhouette Books

PAT WARREN
That Hathaway Woman

Silhouette Special Edition
Published by Silhouette Books New York
America's Publisher of Contemporary Romance

To Pat Reid, a good and loyal friend,
who tells jokes better than anyone I know

SILHOUETTE BOOKS
300 East 42nd St., New York, N.Y. 10017

THAT HATHAWAY WOMAN

Copyright © 1992 by Pat Warren

All rights reserved. Except for use in any review, the reproduction
or utilization of this work in whole or in part in any form by any
electronic, mechanical or other means, now known or hereafter
invented, including xerography, photocopying and recording, or in
any information storage or retrieval system, is forbidden without
the permission of the publisher, Silhouette Books, 300 E. 42nd St.,
New York, N.Y. 10017

ISBN: 0-373-09758-1

First Silhouette Books printing August 1992

All the characters in this book have no existence outside the
imagination of the author and have no relation whatsoever to
anyone bearing the same name or names. They are not even
distantly inspired by any individual known or unknown to the
author, and all incidents are pure invention.

®: Trademark used under license and registered in the United
States Patent and Trademark Office and in other countries.

Printed in the U.S.A.

PAT WARREN,

mother of four, lives in Arizona with her travel-agent husband and a lazy white cat. She's a former newspaper columnist whose lifetime dream was to become a novelist. A strong romantic streak, a sense of humor and a keen interest in developing relationships led her to try writing romance novels, with which she feels very much at home.

All underlined places are fictitious.

Chapter One

Sunrise was her favorite time of day. Rachel Hathaway stepped onto the apartment's covered porch, noting that the weathered boards could use a fresh coat of paint. The early-morning sky was a pale blue, with a golden flush just beginning to tint the far horizon. The humid air was warm, but without the heat that the August sun would soon be spreading. From the vantage point of the second floor, she gazed through the treetops, trying to catch sight of the Gulf of Mexico just two blocks straight ahead. Inhaling deeply, she caught the familiar salty scent of the sea.

The railroad tracks, overgrown now, were still visible. Years ago, the San Antonio Railroad had had daily runs along there. Beyond were the huge ranches and a smattering of stately southern homes. On the other side of the tracks—Rachel's side—were the older, seedier houses always in need of repair.

Moving to the far left, she leaned forward at the waist as far as she dared. Rachel could just barely make out Main Street stretching westward, the business district that nearly all of Schyler's residents visited at some time each day. Typical of most small Texas towns, the shops and public buildings were all clustered along that thoroughfare, a hodgepodge like so many colorful child's blocks arranged by an unskilled hand.

The morning breeze rearranged her long hair, and Rachel brushed it back from her face, her memory supplying what her eyes couldn't quite make out along Main Street. On the near corner was Herb's Gas Station, then the red brick library with the twin lion statues flanking the double doors, and the post office with the flag flying in front. Next to that was Edna's Diner with its long counter and red vinyl booths, probably not open yet, but it would be by seven. Then there was Hannah's Beauty Shop, the general store, the newspaper office, and across Main, the rest of the stores, most of which were owned by the powerful Quincy family—the Quincys who'd forced her to leave town ten years ago.

Turning, she saw that the old glider was still against the wall sporting new yellow corduroy cushions. With a sigh, Rachel settled onto the swing and pressed her bare feet to the floor to start the gentle swaying. She couldn't help thinking she wouldn't mind having a nickel for every time she'd sat here just like this. Sometimes dreaming, oftentimes crying. Rarely happy.

Around front she heard a car rumble down the road. Schyler was waking slowly, as it usually did in town. On the large cattle ranches, the hands had been up before the sun, she was certain. Just as she was certain nothing much had changed in Schyler during her absence.

Rachel drew her legs onto the swing, crossing her arms atop her bent knees. She'd slipped on terry-cloth shorts and a loose shirt when she'd crawled out of the tangled sheets of her childhood bed. She hadn't slept much, but then she'd known she wouldn't. She hated being here, hated Schyler, Texas, hated the reason that had brought her back to the town she'd vowed to never visit again.

But she'd had no choice. Her mother needed her today more than she ever had. Today they would bury Orrin Hathaway, her youngest brother.

She'd shed her tears two days ago when her mother had phoned her in California. Tears for the sweet retarded boy who'd died of pneumonia at age twenty-five. Orrin had never developed mentally beyond eight or nine; perhaps this was merciful, for he alone of all the Hathaways had never realized the scorn that Schyler had for his family. For Orrin, she'd broken her self-imposed exile and come back. And for her mother.

Rachel lay her cheek on her arms and closed her eyes, fighting a surge of emotion that threatened to have her weeping again. What was she going to do about her mother?

For all of Rachel's growing-up years, Gloria Hathaway had been a pillar of strength. Abandoned by her husband, the father Rachel scarcely remembered, Gloria had gone to work in the tavern, the town's only "beer garden and eatery," as the sign above the door boasted. Waitressing was hard work, but Gloria had managed in order to keep her children together, for along with the job had come the rental of the apartment above the tavern at an affordable rate.

And Gloria was still here in this dingy apartment, Rachel thought with dismay. Still waitressing, even though Bart Mitchell, the bartender who'd hired her, had died a few years ago and shocked everyone by leaving Gloria the saloon and building, such as they were. And Gloria was still smoking even though she had emphysema so severe that she had to sit on the top step after climbing the stairs to her apartment. Still stubbornly refusing to leave Schyler, where scarcely one of the Hathaways could remember having a truly happy day.

Why? Rachel asked herself as she gazed into the sky now bright with the rising sun. Why wouldn't her mother move with her to California now that Orrin was gone and her other son, Curt, was in the Navy? There'd never been anything much for her here in this nasty, unforgiving town, and there never would be.

"No one's going to drive me out of my home," Gloria had told her yesterday, when Rachel had flown in from Bakersfield. Then she'd lighted another cigarette, inhaled deeply and gone into a coughing fit that had turned her face a mottled reddish color. Before Rachel could say another word, Gloria had gone into her small bedroom to lie down, effectively calling a halt to the conversation.

Rachel ran both hands through her hair and let out a ragged sigh. Worried about her mother, she had steeled herself and walked down Main Street toward Doc Tremayne's tiny office located in a two-story building on Barlow Road. Doc, a round-faced man with a bent back and kind eyes, had delivered her twenty-seven years ago, and she'd never known him to hedge. He'd told her the truth she'd feared, that her mother was very ill.

Stunned, Rachel had walked back to Gloria's apartment above the tavern, hardly aware of the surreptitious glances from behind the windows of the stores and buildings she'd passed. Strangers and prodigal daughters were treated the same in Schyler—with suspicion. Rachel Hathaway's return had been duly noted the moment she'd stepped foot over the county line.

She could deal with Schyler's rejection, Rachel thought, rising to go stand by the railing again. She had for years. But she wasn't sure how to deal with the knowledge that her mother would soon be gone.

Gloria had always understood Rachel's reasons for leaving, for not returning all these years. They'd kept in touch by phone and mail, both unhappy that they couldn't be together but accepting the way things were. Rachel had harbored the hope that one day things would work out and she'd be able to convince Gloria and Orrin and even Curt to join her in California, to forget Schyler and begin life over. She'd known it would take time, but she hadn't once considered the possibility that at forty-six, time would be running out for Gloria.

"There you are," Gloria Hathaway said from the doorway.

Turning, Rachel smiled at her mother. "I was watching the sunrise. It was lovely."

The inevitable cigarette in her hand, Gloria took a drag and moved to the banister, her gaze taking in the morning sky. "I remember. You used to come out here a lot when you were little."

She's aged, Rachel thought sadly. The blond hair that had been long and thick like her own was thinner now, with strands of white lightening the once-rich color. About two inches shorter than Rachel's five-seven, Gloria still held herself erect, though her shoulders slumped wearily when she thought no one was watching. Her figure, always lush enough to invite admiring glances and more offers to share her bed than Gloria could count, was still good. But her skin had a sallow cast, and the green eyes that Rachel had inherited had lost their sparkle.

Swallowing around a lump, Rachel rose and slipped an arm around her mother's waist, pulling her close for a moment. In the distance, a train whistle could be heard, and somewhere below them, a dog barked in protest. "Remember the time I hid behind that old glider because I was so mad at you?"

Gloria released a stream of smoke, then smiled. "I'd refused to let you have a puppy for your fifth birthday, and I thought you'd run away. I grabbed the boys—they were just babies, really—and I searched all over for you. I was nearly frantic."

"And Edna found me."

"That's right. She'd closed the diner to help me look for you." Gloria's husky voice held a wistful note.

"Did she ever scold me for scaring you! Then she bought me a stuffed dog the next day and told me it would last longer than a real one and was much easier to care for."

Nodding at the memory, Gloria stubbed out her cigarette in a coffee can in the corner. "Doc Tremayne told me you were allergic, that I shouldn't allow a pet in the house. You never liked cats, but you wanted a dog so badly. How do you explain allergies to a five-year-old? But you grew to love that stuffed dog. You named him Rufus, remember?"

"Sure. I found him on the closet shelf last night." Rachel shifted her gaze toward the sea, deciding not to tell her mother that she'd lain awake for hours, clutching the scruffy animal and staring at the ceiling. She'd avoided walks down memory lane for years, but back here again, she was caught in its uneasy grip.

Gloria tightened the belt of her robe, then leaned her elbows on the ledge. "It's hard being back here for you, I know. I'm grateful you came."

"I'm sorry I didn't come sooner," Rachel answered, her voice thick with regret. "Orrin had had so many asthma attacks in the past. I never dreamed he'd . . . he'd . . ."

Gloria reached for her daughter's hand. "I know. The pneumonia struck so fast that even Doc was surprised. At least Orrin didn't suffer long."

Rachel squeezed her mother's fingers, nodding. "I suppose we ought to get dressed."

Gloria straightened. "I'll make some coffee while you shower. It's going to be a long, difficult day."

"We'll get through it, Mom. We always have." Squaring her shoulders and reaching for the cool reserve that had seen her through many difficult days, Rachel walked inside.

"Are you sure I can't go with you, Daddy?"

Justin Wheeler adjusted the rubber band on the end of his eight-year-old daughter's long, dark braid and smiled down into her round, freckled face. He'd walked her over to the sitter's house located four doors from their own small bungalow, and they'd been locking horns over the day's agenda every step of the way. "We've been over this, Katie. Funerals are no place for young girls."

"But Orrin was my friend, too," Katie Wheeler said, giving her voice that persuasive note that usually worked on her father.

"Yes, he was. And I want you to remember him as someone very special. But I also want you to stay with Mrs. Porter while Grandpa and I go to his funeral." Justin touched her chin and waited until she raised her blue eyes, startled as always at how much they resembled her mother's. "Will you do that for me?"

Katie's good nature never let her argue losing battles too long. She grinned up at him, revealing a gap where two teeth were still missing. Then she jammed her baseball cap sideways onto her head. "Okay, Daddy."

Feeling a rush of love for her, Justin gave her a quick hug and flipped her hat around until the bill faced the back. "That's how real ball players wear their hats."

"Not *girl* ball players, Daddy." Pulling from him, she adjusted her cap back to her preferred position and ran toward the porch of the neat gray house.

Justin saw Emily Porter open the screen door and wave to him, then turn her attention to welcoming Katie. He waited until the door closed behind them before strolling away. He was lucky to have Emily to watch his daughter after school and on summer days when he couldn't have her hanging around the newspaper office.

Emily's husband had died in a tractor accident several years back, leaving her with two small children. Not wanting to leave them and work outside the home, she'd begun taking in neighborhood kids to watch. Some days she had as many as half a dozen in a variety of ages along with her own two, filling the big house with cookie crumbs and noise.

He liked Emily, Justin thought, as he rounded the corner onto Main Street. She was attractive, good with kids, and kept a clean home. She'd also hinted more than once that she wouldn't mind seeing him aside from the times he dropped off or picked up Katie.

But Justin wasn't interested in pursuing a relationship with Emily, or anyone else for that matter. Finally, at thirty-three, he had his priorities straight. He had Katie and Pop, his work at the *Gazette,* a sandlot baseball game now and then and an occasional cold beer. What else was there?

Slowing his long-legged stride as he passed the building housing the *Schyler Gazette,* Justin glanced through the window. He could make out the bald head of their typesetter, Sid Lewis, bent over something on the front desk. The young college student they'd hired last year, Matt Russell, was on the phone, his lean hip braced on the other desk. They can get along without me for a while yet, Justin thought, as he headed for Edna's Diner. He wasn't scheduled to meet Pop for another hour, and he could use a cup or two of Edna's coffee. No matter how he tried, his brew never tasted as good as hers.

Entering the homey diner, Justin greeted two businessmen from the local insurance agency just leaving, and waved to Phil Crane, the barber, finishing up in a back booth. By eight-thirty, most of the regulars who breakfasted at Edna's had eaten and gone to open their businesses, so the place was relatively quiet, with only a few customers lingering. Sliding onto a red vinyl stool, Justin sat at the counter and waited for Edna to finish at the cash register.

Edna Ames had owned and operated her diner on Schyler's main street for as long as most residents could remember, or so Pop had told him. When Justin and Katie had moved here three years ago, she'd welcomed them warmly, saying that any kin of Pop Wheeler's was okay in her book. Somewhere in her fifties, Edna hit the scales at over two hundred pounds and had a heart as big as her waistline. She also knew everyone and everything that went on in town and on the surrounding ranches.

Stifling a yawn, Edna came over with a cup of coffee and her friendly smile. "Don't you look sharp today?" she commented, her intelligent gaze taking in Justin's gray suit.

Justin removed his tie from his pocket and set it on the counter. He'd always hated ties, but he supposed funerals and weddings demanded them. "I didn't want to embarrass Pop by going to the cemetery in jeans." He took a sip of the coffee and smiled up at Edna. "You sure you won't marry me? This is the best coffee I've ever tasted."

Pleased but determined to hide it, Edna waved a dismissing hand, then walked to the back where her short-order cook had rung the bell signaling another order ready to be picked up.

Justin glanced around and noticed a newspaper on the counter. Yesterday's paper from Dallas, probably discarded by someone passing through town. His practiced eye scanned the columns. The *Gazette* he and Pop published was a weekly paper, yet he felt it measured up to the best of even the daily offerings. And he'd worked on some of the finest—in Houston, San Antonio, and Dallas. He had even put in a year as foreign correspondent out of Chicago, based in London. But that had been in another lifetime.

"She's back, have you heard?"

Justin turned, realizing someone had taken the stool alongside him. Recognizing a clerk from across the street at Quincy Dry Goods, he nearly groaned aloud. Mel Stone was a case of arrested development. A short man in his thirties with a receding hairline and a flabby belly, Mel talked like a randy teenager, his conversation sprinkled with sexual innuendos. "Who's back?"

"That Hathaway woman. Rachel Hathaway." Mel's dark eyes were excited. "Have you seen her, Justin?"

"Can't say I have. But then, never having met Rachel Hathaway, I probably wouldn't recognize her." Justin sipped his coffee, hoping Mel would go bother someone else.

Mel chuckled as he gestured to get Edna's attention. "You'd know her, all right. She's stacked, man." His pudgy hands drew an exaggerated version of the female form in midair. "Nobody in this backwater town is built like Rachel, right, Edna?"

Edna set a cup of steaming coffee in front of Mel and poured Justin a refill, her blue eyes guarded. "Rachel Hathaway's not back two days and already her name's all I hear. She's come home to bury her brother. You'd think folks would have better things to do than gossip about a grieving woman."

"We're just talking, Edna," Mel went on in his slightly high-pitched voice. "You've got to admit she's got a body worth looking at, just like her mother. Customers at the store yesterday damn near fell through the plate glass window watching her strut down Main Street." He turned toward Justin. "You're going to her brother's funeral, I suppose, since Orrin worked for you and Pop."

Justin, too, had heard Rachel's name bandied about yesterday. Orrin, in his open, childlike way, had spoken often of his beautiful blond sister who lived far away and his brother in the Navy. Justin knew Gloria casually from stopping in to eat at the tavern occasionally, but she'd never mentioned anyone except Orrin. "Yes, we're attending the funeral. I liked Orrin, and I'm sorry he's gone."

Edna slid a cinnamon bun onto a plate and set it in front of Mel, long ago having memorized her regulars' eating habits—even customers she found as disagreeable as Mel. She addressed her remarks to Justin. "When his mother told me Orrin had pneumonia, I was afraid he wouldn't make it. Asthma had weakened his lungs. I feel sorry for Gloria. She's been a good mother."

Mel snickered. "That ain't all she was good at, I've heard." He elbowed Justin, one man to another, as if sharing a private joke.

Though not in on the joke, Justin found himself repulsed by Mel. "I've always found Gloria Hathaway to be a hardworking woman who minded her own business." The implication was obvious, but he was sure Mel wouldn't get it.

"That's exactly what she is," Edna said, narrowing her eyes at Mel. "And I don't want to hear no bad talk against her in my diner."

Undaunted, Mel licked icing from his fingers. "I'm only telling the truth. Everyone knows that whole family's nothing but bad news. Vern Hathaway was a drunk who walked out on his wife and three kids. Gloria went to work in a saloon, leaving those kids alone till all hours of the night. Small wonder Curt joined the Navy as soon as he was old enough. Orrin was too simple to understand, and Rachel killed a man when she was only seventeen. You call them good citizens?"

The color in Edna's face deepened as her blood pressure rose. "Rachel was cleared of that charge, and you know it."

Mel drained his cup. "Yeah, well, where there's smoke, there's fire. Just ask the Quincys. They sure as hell believe that that Hathaway woman is guilty as sin." He held out his mug. "Got any more coffee in that pot?"

Placing her hands on her ample hips, Edna stood her ground, having heard enough. "Sorry, I'm fresh out."

Finally Mel realized he'd gone too far. "Come on, Edna. I didn't mean any harm."

Edna inclined her chin toward Quincy Dry Goods across the street, clearly visible through the diner's picture window. "Isn't it time you got over there and opened up, Mel? It's past nine o'clock."

Red-faced and visibly annoyed but not about to take on Edna, Mel dug a bill from his pocket, tossed it on the counter, and left without another word.

Justin watched Edna clear away the dishes and wipe off the counter. "Looks like you lost a steady customer."

She shrugged as she topped off his coffee again. "He'll be back, not that I much care. I never liked that man. He's got a nasty mouth and, right or wrong, he sides with the Quincys every time.''

The Quincys. Roy and his son, Theo. Half the town sided with whatever the Quincys said, Justin was well aware, and the reason was simple. A majority of the townspeople depended on the Quincys for their livelihood. ''I suppose Mel's just trying to protect his job.'' A newspaperman had to look at both sides of every issue. But he didn't necessarily have to *like* both sides.

''Just because they own nearly everything in Schyler don't make 'em right always, now does it?''

''No, it doesn't.'' Not for the first time, Justin found himself admiring Edna Ames for taking an unpopular stand. Of course, she owned one of the few businesses that was independent of the Quincys. But loyalty to a friend was part of her makeup as much as her sharp blue eyes, the gray hair wrapped in a bun at her nape, and the shapeless pink uniform she always wore.

Justin knew he could get an honest, fair answer from her. ''I rarely heard Rachel Hathaway's name mentioned by anyone except Orrin until yesterday. Did she really kill a man when she was seventeen?''

Heaving a sigh, Edna glanced over at the only other two customers left in the diner, a young couple obviously wrapped up in each other in the corner booth. Reaching for a mug, she filled it with coffee for herself. ''You mean Pop hasn't told you that story?''

Pop Wheeler didn't care for gossip any more than Justin himself did. Having published the *Schyler Gazette* for over thirty years, Pop probably knew the history of every living soul in town—the good, the bad and the ugly. Yet he seldom had anything but positive things to say about anyone, a trait Justin admired in his grandfather. However, later this morning he'd be meeting Rachel Hathaway for the first time, and he had to admit he was curious about her. Edna, he knew, would give him facts, not gossip.

But he wasn't about to put her on the spot if she was reluctant to discuss the Hathaways. "I'm sorry I asked. I know you're a friend of Gloria's."

Edna absently rearranged the pie slices in the plastic-covered showcase on the counter. "I guess I just assumed Pop would have filled you in."

Justin finished his coffee and shrugged. "You know Pop. He's not one to talk much. He'd rather fish."

Which was lucky for him and Katie, Justin thought. Just when they'd badly needed a change of scenery from their life in Dallas, Pop had invited Justin to come help run the weekly paper so he could do more fishing. Hesitantly hopeful, Justin had moved them and was still amazed at how much he and his daughter had come to enjoy living in a small rural community.

"I suppose by the time you moved here, talk had pretty near died down," Edna said as she leaned against the back counter. "And thank goodness it had, because the whole thing took its toll on Gloria. We have a lot in common, you know, Gloria and me. Both of us married men who loved the bottle more than their wives. Mine left years ago, too, and good riddance. Only I didn't have kids to worry about like she did." Edna took a long swallow of her coffee.

Justin propped an elbow on the counter and leaned forward. It occurred to him that he'd often sat and talked like this to Edna, yet she'd rarely revealed much about herself.

"Women like us, young at that time and divorced, are easy marks in a small town. The ladies don't like you, always thinking you're after their men. And the men think you're lonely and desperate to have one of them in your bed." She shook her head with remembered disgust. "I was always a little pudgy, you know.'' With a lopsided smile, she patted her ample hip.

Justin smiled at her but knew better than to say anything.

"And I have a big mouth. But Gloria's a beautiful woman, even now. A lot of guys tried, but I don't think any got to second base with her. Gloria had learned her lesson about men, and only her kids were important to her.''

Justin could relate. He, too, had been burned, and decided that the only female he needed in his life was Katie. "She sounds like a good woman, Edna.''

"Yeah, she is. I wanted you to know that, going to the funeral and all. And her kids are great, too. Rachel was such a skinny little thing, all blond hair and big eyes. But by the time she was in her teens she was awfully pretty, and the boys wouldn't leave her alone. They used to call her *that Hathaway woman,* and she wasn't even out of high school.''

Thinking of his Katie and how he'd feel if she'd have to go through something like that, Justin frowned.

"And Curt, only a couple of years younger, was always getting in fights. He had to take on the guys who made slurs against his mother, then the boys who went drooling after Rachel and all the kids who made fun of Orrin because he was retarded.'' She looked at Justin. "You didn't know any of this?''

Justin shook his head. "I only knew the little Orrin told me. He was already working at the *Gazette* when I arrived. Pop kept him busy sweeping up, stacking papers, delivering bundles. Orrin missed Curt a lot, and he also fantasized about the day his sister would return. I used to help him write letters to both of them.''

Edna rubbed at her arthritic knee absently. "In Orrin's mind, I'm sure Rachel was probably still a teenager as she'd been when she left here ten years ago."

Justin frowned. "Rachel left Schyler when she was a teenager?" Why? he wondered. And why hadn't Edna explained about whether or not she'd killed a man?

As he waited for her answer, the door opened and four teenagers came in, noisily scrambling into a booth and picking up menus.

Edna pushed away from the counter and straightened. "I think you should find out the rest from Pop. Or maybe Rachel herself. I just wanted you to know that these are good people who had something bad happen to them. Because I know you're a fair man, Justin, and I didn't want you to leave here with Mel's opinion flavoring yours."

Justin stood. "Thanks, Edna." His smile told her his words were meant for more than just the coffee he'd had. He laid a bill on the counter. "I'll see you later."

Moving to wait on the kids, Edna gave him a wave.

Outside, Justin looked into a cloudless blue sky, feeling the August heat pour down, unaware he'd left his tie on the counter. No one should have to be buried on a beautiful, sunny day. Funerals should be held on dismal, rainy days. But then Orrin, with his guileless eyes and his innocence, had loved sunshine. So perhaps it was fitting after all.

Starting toward the office, Justin couldn't help thinking that his conversation with Edna had aroused more questions than it had answered. Maybe Pop could fill in the gaps.

"What is it you want to know?" Pop Wheeler asked, as he maneuvered his station wagon toward the cemetery south of town.

Justin could sense the older man's reluctance to discuss a family he obviously liked. Quickly he explained the conversation he'd had earlier that morning at Edna's Diner. "Mel said Rachel had killed a man at seventeen, and Edna jumped in to say she'd been cleared of the charge. I find it odd that in three years I've never heard a word about something that must have been big news around here."

Pop shrugged. "It happened a long time ago. I feel sorry for Gloria, having to listen to the gossip start up all over again while she's dealing with Orrin's sudden death."

Justin turned to look at his grandfather. At seventy-two, Pop was still tall, only a couple of inches under his own six-two. Where Justin's hair was black and curly, Pop's was white as snow, but just as thick. And they both had the same wide-set gray eyes. Justin had always been pleased that he'd resembled his grandfather more than anyone else in their family. His own father had been a head shorter, with thinning hair and a stocky build.

Pop also had a live-and-let-live philosophy that endeared him to many. Justin admired that but had yet to achieve it, he thought with chagrin. His ambition had contributed to the collapse of his marriage, and his reporter's need to ferret out the world's problems and solve them had gotten him into more than one jam. He was working on changing, but knew he had a ways to go.

Justin brought himself back to the conversation. "Why'd Rachel Hathaway leave ten years ago, Pop?"

Pop's lips became a thin line. "Because of the Quincys. They made it impossible for her to stay."

Though he never outright maligned the Quincy family, Justin was aware of a subtle change in his grandfather's voice whenever he spoke of them. Rumor had it that Roy Quincy traced his ancestry back to southern plantation owners and slave traders, and often bragged of the shady connection. Somehow his father and grandfather before him had acquired vast land holdings in and around Schyler, and Roy had built from that base.

The family owned the dry-goods store, the drugstore, Quincy Feed & Grain, other buildings, and land, plus their huge cattle ranch west of town. Money and power. It took a special man to handle both well. From what he'd heard, Justin suspected that Roy Quincy hadn't managed to rise above temptation.

"How was she involved with the Quincys?" he asked.

Pop drove through the open iron gates leading into the cemetery before answering. "Against her will. That Theo Quincy's bad news. Seems like he's always looking for trouble."

That about described the man. Theo was big and given to excesses that had him looking ten years older than the thirty he was. Though he was married with two children, it was a behind-the-scenes secret that Theo ran around every chance he got, but never in Schyler where good folks might get wind of it. The father was semiretired, and Theo ran most of the businesses while Roy kept busy overseeing the ranch where they all lived. Justin knew both men but had had little dealings with either. "Don't tell me Orrin's sister was involved with Theo?"

Shaking his head, Pop pulled to a stop behind a short line of cars. "Good Lord, no. Rachel's got more sense that that, even back then." He shut off the motor and turned to Justin. "Theo had a twin named Tyrone. Hell-raisers, the two of them. Muriel's quiet, not one to notice things, but Roy seemed to encourage the boys. Just sowing wild oats, he used to say. They were home from college that summer, and Tyrone was crazy to get Rachel to notice him. She was only seventeen, but she was mighty pretty, you know."

Justin nodded. "So I've heard." A car pulled up behind them, and the occupants got out and climbed the hill to where a cluster of people stood. He turned back to Pop. "Well, what happened?"

"Rachel was walking home through the woods near the tavern late one afternoon, and the story goes that Tyrone was waiting for her. He wasn't in the mood to take no for an answer. No one really knows what happened, but Tyrone wound up dead, and they put Rachel on trial. She was acquitted on reasonable doubt." Pop opened his door. "The details are in back issues of the *Gazette*. I wrote the story myself. You can look it up in our morgue files. We'd better go on up." He got out of the car.

Hands in his pants pockets, Justin, his thoughts racing, followed his grandfather up the hill.

The noonday sun shone down on the silver casket draped with a blanket of white carnations. The service was brief, the crowd sparse. Several regulars from the tavern were standing around looking uncomfortable. Matt Russell and Sid Lewis from the *Gazette* stood off to the side, listening to the solemn-faced minister read from his prayer book. Edna was there, of course, on Gloria Hathaway's left side. And on her right was the woman Justin had been hearing about for two days.

Standing a step behind Pop, he gazed across the bier and studied Rachel. All right, so she was attractive. Not the most beautiful woman he'd ever seen, but nice. A good body, noticeable even in a simple black dress with a little white collar.

Justin narrowed his eyes. Maybe even a great body, he decided. Her blond hair blew about in the breeze, and she raised slender fingers to brush it back. Her hand shook ever so slightly. He liked her mouth, generous, inviting. Her eyes were hidden behind huge sunglasses. He wanted to whip them off her pale face.

He became aware that the brief service had ended as the few people who'd gathered together to say goodbye to Orrin Hathaway made their way to Gloria's side to offer their sympathies. Neither she nor her daughter seemed aware of the lack of mourners. Or was it that they'd schooled themselves not to give a damn about the people of Schyler some years ago? Justin asked himself.

He hung back, watching Edna hug her friend and speak softly to Rachel. There was obvious respect and affection between the three women.

Pop touched his arm. "Come on. I'll introduce you."

He followed, seeing the sorrow etched on Gloria's face as she accepted Pop's hand.

"Orrin loved working for you, Pop," Gloria said, blinking back a fresh rush of tears. "Thanks for being so good to him."

"He was a fine boy, Gloria. If you need anything, you know where to reach me." Pop moved over to say a few words to Rachel.

Gloria looked up at Justin. "Thank you for coming."

Justin took her hand. "All of us at the *Gazette* are going to miss Orrin, Ms. Hathaway."

"It's nice of you to say so."

"I don't believe you've met my grandson," Pop was saying to Rachel. "Justin Wheeler, Rachel Hathaway."

She'd been smiling at Pop, but the cool look she'd worn during the service slipped back into place as she turned toward Justin. He wished she'd take off those damn glasses. He held out his hand. "I liked your brother, Rachel. Very much."

She'd noticed him walking up the hill with Pop and caught him staring at her during the service. His look had been one of curiosity and nothing more. The suit he wore looked as if it had been dragged out of storage for the occasion. He gave the appearance of a man more used to casual clothes. He'd stood apart and a bit back from the rest, silent and observant. There was something about him that had her feeling awkward and uncertain. Still, she had no choice but to put her hand in his.

She felt the warmth surround her cool fingers immediately, felt the flush of response to his touch. He held on when she would have pulled back. His brow furrowed as he tried to peer through her glasses at her eyes. Rachel was relieved she'd not removed them, for she didn't want to expose the vulnerability she was certain was there.

Gloria was speaking and she'd scarcely heard a word. "What did you say, Mom?"

"I said that Justin's the man who helped Orrin write his letters to you."

Rachel felt her expression soften hearing that and swung her gaze back to his face. There was a hint of sadness in his eyes that she didn't think was new. He had a small indentation by the corner of his mouth that wasn't quite a dimple, but was nonetheless intriguing. His chin was square, suggesting a stubborn streak, and perhaps strength. A man not easily summed up in a brief meeting. "That was kind of you." She felt him squeeze her fingers before she realized he still held her hand and tugged it free.

"I was glad to do it. He spoke of you often."

Rachel wondered fleetingly what Orrin had told this compelling man. She felt a trickle of nervous perspiration skitter down her back. It wasn't just the funeral. It was being here, in Schyler, on view again. She turned to her mother. "Are you ready to go?"

Gloria cast a last glance at the coffin, then nodded and let herself be led down the hill.

Justin watched them go. Pop was talking with Sid alongside the station wagon. Justin stood with his hands in his pockets, trying to sort out his impression of Rachel Hathaway.

Halfway to the gray limo, Rachel turned toward someone who'd called her name. Justin saw a man standing in the shade of a tree. He was tall and slim with brown hair and a neat beard. With a quick word to Gloria, she moved to greet the man.

Curious, Justin studied him as he took hold of Rachel's hands. They stood talking for several minutes, then Rachel glanced toward her mother and noticed that she was getting into the limo. She turned back, gave the man a hug that seemed overly long for a casual goodbye, and hurried off to join Gloria.

As the limo pulled away from the curb, Justin saw the bearded man walk over to a late-model silver BMW and climb in. Strolling down to Pop's car, he wondered who the stranger was. Had that been comfort he'd witnessed or friendly affection? Or a lover's embrace?

"Did you notice that bearded fellow, Pop?" he asked as he got in beside his grandfather.

Pop started the car. "I don't see a bearded fellow. Where is he?"

"Gone, now. Never mind." As they left the cemetery, Justin wasn't seeing the green hills or the winding road. He saw instead a lovely woman with hair like raw silk who'd tried to look cool and disdainful, but hadn't been able to pull it off. He could still feel the light pressure of her fingers resting in his, the quick jolt of awareness her touch had evoked.

The truth of the matter was that Rachel Hathaway was not a woman easily dismissed from a man's mind, he thought ruefully.

Chapter Two

"I wish Curt could have been here today," Gloria said, as she sat back on the couch and studied her bare feet. "It doesn't seem right that the Navy wouldn't allow him leave time to attend his brother's funeral."

"He's under the sea, Mom, in a sub-tender, on a six-month tour of duty." Rachel handed her mother a glass of iced tea. "They can't be surfacing every time one of the sailors has a family crisis." The late-afternoon sun had the small apartment practically steaming, she thought, as she settled in the rocker and rubbed the back of her damp neck. She'd changed into cotton shorts and top, put her hair in a ponytail, turned on the overhead fan, and still felt sticky and uncomfortable.

Gloria lighted a cigarette, inhaling deeply, then exhaling into the already-smoky atmosphere. "The Navy Department should know how much it would have meant to Orrin to have Curt home with us."

Rachel sipped her tea, realizing that grief had made Gloria more than a little unreasonable. And the oppressive humidity didn't help either of their tempers, she thought, as she fanned herself with a magazine. Since returning from the graveside service, they'd already quarreled twice—once about Gloria's insistent smoking and lack of concern over her health, and then about Gloria's refusal to consider leaving Schyler.

She hadn't gotten her mother to budge on either issue.

"Are you hungry?" Rachel asked. "How would it be if I make us a big fruit salad? I notice you've got lots of fresh fruit in the refrigerator."

"Why would you cook when I own the restaurant downstairs?"

Rachel didn't think she should mention that she'd grown up with the pervasive smell of fried onions and greasy hamburgers drifting upstairs and permeating even her clothing, making the menu choices of the tavern not the least appealing. "Making a salad can't be classified as cooking."

"You go ahead, honey. I'm not hungry." Drawing on her cigarette, she coughed once. Then the cough took over and she struggled for breath, wheezing through the seizure.

"Mom, are you all right?" Rachel was up and at her side, frightened at the sound of her mother's deep-chested cough.

Gloria waved her away, coughed a bit more, then took a sip of tea. "I'm fine, fine." But she put out the cigarette and stood somewhat shakily. "I was going to go down and see how things are going at the tavern. But I think I'll lie down for a few minutes first."

"Yes, you rest." Pointedly Rachel picked up her mother's pack of cigarettes and stuffed them in the pocket of her shorts.

Gloria crossed her arms over her chest and eyed her daughter a long moment. "I know you mean well, Rachel, but the last person who tried to boss me around was your father and I sent him packing. Now I live the way I want to live and nobody—not this town and not my own kids—is going to tell me different. I love you, honey, but I'm not going to change for you."

Rachel couldn't prevent her shoulders from sagging. "I know, Mom. But I just lost Orrin. I can't bear the possibility of losing you, too."

Gloria gave a dismissive grunt. "I've just got a smoker's cough. Had it for years."

Bright green eyes met faded green. "That's not what Doc Tremayne says."

The information that her daughter had visited her doctor registered slowly on Gloria's face, then was replaced by a determined look. "All doctors are alarmists. I'll probably outlive him."

"You'd have a better chance of doing that if you'd come to California with me."

Running a shaky hand through her hair, Gloria shook her head. "And let the fine folks of Schyler think they've won, that I'm running away like a dog with its tail between its legs? Never. I'll be fine. You wait and see." Back straight as a ramrod, she walked to her bedroom and closed the door firmly.

Rachel let out a frustrated sigh and went onto the porch, hoping to catch a breeze stirring. Leaning over the railing, she gazed down toward Main Street. A couple of parked cars and only a few people out and about. A skinny dog strolling along, tongue out and panting. The flag hanging limply in front of the post office.

The large thermometer displayed at Herb's Gas Station just across the road registered ninety-six degrees. Two people at the air pump caught her attention, and she shielded her eyes against the sun, trying to see more clearly.

Sure enough, it was Justin Wheeler, only he looked so different than he had earlier that she almost didn't recognize him. Gone was the rumpled suit and white shirt. He wore jogging shoes, jeans that clung comfortably to his long legs and a blue pullover shirt. Haphazardly plopped on his head was a red baseball cap.

He was squatting, checking the tires of a blue bicycle held upright by a young girl also wearing a baseball cap. She looked to be around eight or nine with the same black hair as his, only worn in a long braid down her back. He must have said something funny, for she laughed, the sound carrying up to Rachel on the still summer air.

So Justin was a family man. Carefully Rachel pulled out the memory of her hand in his earlier today, that quick flash of nonverbal communication she was certain they'd shared. The male-female message that was difficult to ignore and impossible to fake. She'd had enough practice in her lifetime to recognize it from across a crowded room. And enough experience to rebuff it easily.

It was when a married man sent that signal that she really became incensed.

Funny, but she'd expected more from Pop Wheeler's grandson. Not that Justin had done anything wrong. But she knew she wasn't mistaken about the interest she'd seen in those wide gray eyes. However, it took two to tango, and she certainly wasn't interested. No one on God's green earth could convince her that *anyone* in Schyler was worth her interest, even a newcomer. And certainly not a married one.

Rachel saw the little girl climb onto her bike, bounce-test the tires, then grin approvingly at her father. Justin grabbed the child's cap and swiveled it backward on her head, causing her to protest loudly. Smiling, he watched her ride around the station's apron. Then, inexplicably, he looked up in her direction, his eyes colliding with hers.

Caught studying him, Rachel felt unnerved. Slowly she straightened, but her eyes never left his. Justin didn't smile, just stared for what seemed a long minute. She had the feeling that he could see right through her, into her troubled mind.

At last he turned and started walking down Main Street, the girl on the bike backtracking to ride alongside him. Rachel let out a long breath, then heard a car pull to a stop and shifted her gaze in the other direction.

The moment she did, she wished she hadn't.

The man slowly got out of a long white Cadillac, then lazily leaned his tall, solid frame against the driver's door. Mirrored sunglasses hid his eyes, but she'd have known him anywhere. For years, she'd seen him in her nightmares.

Theo Quincy reached into the pocket of his white Western shirt with the pearl buttons and drew out a cigarette, flicked his gold lighter and bent to the flame. Pocketing the lighter, he drew deeply, his eyes returning to the wooden porch railing above the tavern.

Heart pounding, Rachel stood her ground, though she longed to run and hide. She'd hoped to leave Schyler before running into any of the Quincys, but luck wasn't with her. When had luck ever been with her in this godforsaken town?

She narrowed her eyes, watching Theo blow smoke through his thick nostrils. White car, white shirt, white jeans hugging his heavy thighs, shiny leather boots. Probably a big white Stetson sitting on the car seat, one like his father always wore. Did Theo wrap himself in white to convince the world he was one of the good guys? Too bad he had a black heart, as did all the other Quincys.

Well, maybe not Muriel Quincy, his mother. Ineffectual and somewhat pitiful, Muriel had no say-so in that family and never had. Gloria had written that Theo had married some years ago. A farm girl named Mary-something. She'd given him the obligatory two children and was probably relegated to remaining on the ranch and keeping her mouth shut along with Muriel. Great family, the Quincys.

Unflinchingly she stood watching Theo until he dropped his cigarette onto the pavement and crushed it underfoot with one of his undoubtedly expensive leather boots, his eyes never leaving hers. Rachel kept her face expressionless as he opened the car door. Suddenly he tipped two fingers to his forehead in a mock salute. Or was it his idea of a warning?

Trembling deep inside, Rachel watched the Cadillac pull away in a swirl of dust, engine roaring. Hugging herself, she walked over and sat in the corner of the glider.

Three days back in town and she felt anxious, exposed, trapped. She simply couldn't stay in Schyler. It hurt to breathe the air here, to walk the streets, to try to sleep.

Yet how could she leave her mother who was stubbornly courting death with each cigarette? Could she go back to California and wait for another phone call, this time from a stranger most likely, telling her that one of the two people left on earth about whom she gave a damn was dead?

Rachel felt like screaming. She had a good life in California, one she'd painstakingly made for herself the hard way. Bakersfield wasn't nearly as small as Schyler, but it wasn't a *big* city, either. She'd run there ten years ago because that had been the farthest her bus money had stretched.

She'd gotten a job waiting tables, taken a room in the home of a widow who needed company more than the small rent, and enrolled in a community college. It had taken her six years of hard work and study to get her teaching degree. But she'd done it. She had her own apartment now, a nice place she'd decorated slowly herself, only two blocks from the elementary school where she'd been teaching third grade for four years.

She had a life she was comfortable with, if not the most exciting existence one could imagine. She loved working with the children, and she'd made friends with a couple of the teachers. She dated sparingly, cautiously, wary of men in general. She thought she'd outgrow her distrust of men in time. She hadn't yet.

No one in California knew the truth about her background. She'd escaped her past and felt safe there.

Until Orrin's death had called her back.

Rachel rubbed her forehead, fighting the beginning of a headache. All right, it was decision time. Earlier, Gloria had told her that Curt would be coming home in three months, finished with his tour of duty in the Navy. She hadn't seen her youngest brother since he'd stopped in Bakersfield on his way to enlist eight years ago. She had no idea what career goals he had in mind, for his letters had been sporadic and unrevealing.

Suppose she stayed in Schyler with Gloria until Curt returned along about mid-November? Oh, Lord, Rachel thought, groaning aloud. Could she do it? She could call her principal in Bakersfield and arrange for a long-term substitution. Katherine Fielding was a good administrator and an understanding woman who would help, she was certain. She could even find out if they had any openings at Schyler Elementary and work here temporarily, as a fill-in perhaps. Anything to make the days and weeks hurry by.

Then, when Curt returned, together they'd figure out what to do about Gloria, depending on how her condition was by that time. She didn't want to do any of this, Rachel reminded herself. But she had so few choices.

From inside, she heard Gloria coughing through her closed bedroom door. She would never forgive herself if she left her mother alone and ill. Rising, before she could change her mind, Rachel went to the phone to call her principal in Bakersfield.

It was the top of the ninth, one man on second, the score tied three all as the Brown City Badgers faced the Schyler Red Sox. The count was one strike and three balls. The pitcher for the Red Sox, the sandlot baseball team organized three short years ago, was hot, harried and distracted. Taking off his cap and wiping his damp forehead on his sleeve, Justin Wheeler knew exactly why he was having trouble concentrating on his pitching.

A short time ago, Rachel Hathaway had happened along and now stood in the shade of a big citrus tree just behind the cyclone-fenced backdrop at home plate.

Picking up the signal from the catcher, Justin went into his stretch, then the windup, and gave the next pitch his best shot.

"Ball four!" the umpire called out. "You walk."

Damn! With two men on base, Justin wasn't a bit surprised to see Randy Lloyd, the catcher, come strolling out toward him for a chat. Cramming the ball in his mitt, he waited.

"Game's a mite off today, Justin," Randy said cautiously.

It hadn't been, until she showed up.

Justin looked into Randy's boyish face and nodded. "Some days are like that. You want to replace me?"

"Nah." Chewing his ever-present wad of gum, Randy squinted toward the backdrop, then back at Justin. "I saw her, too. I'm lucky, though. My back's to her."

He felt like he was back in high school, comparing notes over the new cheerleader. "It's not what you think...."

"Yeah." Randy adjusted his cap over his damp hair. "What I think is I'd like to get this ball game over and go get a cold one. Neville's up next. Strike him out, will ya?"

Kicking at the pitcher's mound with his toe, Justin nodded, as Randy ambled back to home plate. The wives and children of many players sat around on folding chairs or stood behind the fenced barrier. Rolling his shoulders to loosen the tension, Justin looked up and nearly dropped the ball. Katie had gone over and was talking with Rachel.

It had been a week since Orrin's funeral. He hadn't seen Rachel since the afternoon he'd looked up from the gas station and caught her watching him from Gloria's porch. But he'd heard about her from nearly everyone. At the *Gazette,* at Edna's, even at the barbershop. Folks said she'd soon be leaving. Others said she'd decided to stay. Rumor had it she'd applied for a teaching job. Scuttlebutt hinted she wouldn't last, and that the Quincys were annoyed as hell she was still around.

Frankly Justin didn't care. Not really. Oh, he was as curious as the next person. And, gazing at her now through lowered lashes, he had to admit she looked good in any damn thing she chose to wear. But beautiful women held no appeal to him. They had once. He'd dated them, bedded them, and even married one. Leona had cured him, but good. No one man could hold on to a really beautiful woman, Justin was convinced.

Watching Rachel Hathaway break into a genuine smile as she looked at Katie, he was doubly convinced he was right. And the way he'd chosen to handle beautiful women the past few years was to let them know early on that he wasn't in the least influenced by looks. No, sir, it took a whole lot more than that to impress Justin Wheeler.

Neville stepped up to the plate, peering toward Justin through his glasses.

Justin decided to show Rachel how cool he could be under pressure. Winding up for the pitch, concentrating now, he threw the ball.

Neville hit the first home run of his life.

Amid the cheers of the Brown City Badgers, Justin walked off the field, finding it a bit difficult to keep his head high under the circumstances. He avoided looking at Randy as the catcher signaled the replacement pitcher to take over.

Katie wordlessly handed him a cold can of pop.

Justin drank deeply, then turned to gaze at Rachel standing several feet away by the tree. It was the first time he'd been close enough to look into the vivid green of her eyes without her dark glasses. He tried not to let the impact of them show as he forced a smile. "Looks like you caught me on a less than perfect day."

Rachel struggled with a smile that was tugging at the corners of her mouth. "Are you sure this is your game?"

He smiled as Katie jumped to her father's defense.

"Daddy organized the Schyler Red Sox and he's the first-string pitcher. He even raised the money for the jerseys and caps." She adjusted her matching cap proudly.

Rachel pushed back from the tree she'd been leaning against and came two steps closer. Since discovering from her mother that Justin was a widower, she'd again had to rearrange her opinion of him. She hadn't really intended to stop at the ball field today. But she'd spent a week cooped up in Gloria's apartment, fighting cabin fever.

So she'd set out for a walk after dinner while her mother insisted on checking on things at the tavern. When she'd seen the crowd gathered, she'd drifted over, and soon Katie Wheeler's friendliness had charmed her. She smiled now at the chatty little girl.

"I coach a girls' baseball team during the school year in Bakersfield." She looked up at Justin. "Your daughter's filled me in on nearly everyone here."

He'd just bet she had and would have given a hefty sum to know what, exactly, Katie had revealed. Flopping down on the grass, he tilted his head back and drained the can.

"Want a drink, Rachel?" Katie asked, seating herself alongside her father and pulling another can out of her insulated sack. "I'm the refreshment person around here."

"No, thanks, Katie." Feeling oddly comfortable with the child between them, Rachel sat and turned to watch the game.

"We're losing big-time, Daddy," Katie announced unnecessarily.

"This ain't about winning, sweetheart," Justin said in a dreadful imitation of Bogie with his lips twitching, "it's—"

"...about having a good time," Katie finished with him. Then they both laughed. "But who said losers have a good time?"

Justin reached to pull at her hat, but she spun away laughing again, moving to join a friend by the backdrop. He turned to Rachel and found her watching Katie, on her face a melancholy look. "My worst critic," he said, indicating his daughter.

"She's lovely," Rachel said softly. She envied the warm relationship she sensed between the two of them, and wished she didn't. She didn't want to feel good toward the Wheelers or anyone else in Schyler. She was only here temporarily. She kept her eyes on the game, but she could feel Justin studying her. Perhaps she shouldn't have stopped by.

She looked young and uncertain today, Justin decided. Her hair was hanging down her back in a long braid just like Katie's, and she wore tennis shoes, blue jeans and an oversize cotton shirt, her face free of makeup. This was not a woman trying to be a femme fatale, yet the beauty was there. In those incredible eyes that seemed too old for her oval face, in the honey color of her skin, in the unconsciously feminine way she moved.

"So what is it you do in Bakersfield when you're not coaching girls' baseball teams?" Justin asked, folding his legs Indian fashion and facing her. Orrin had told him that his sister was a teacher, but he'd heard half a dozen other versions of her occupation this week alone, some none too flattering.

"I teach the third grade." Her face was wistful. "I miss the kids." Then, as if she'd revealed too much, she shifted her gaze in time to see one of the Red Sox hit a high fly ball that was easily caught.

"School starts in about two weeks. Will you be going back?" The newspaperman in him zeroed in with pointed questions. He wondered if she'd tell him to mind his own business. There was a reserve about Rachel Hathaway, a closed-in look that discouraged inquiries, but he chose to ignore it.

"Not right away." A part of her wanted to pour out the whole story about her mother's condition and her own reluctance to remain even temporarily in this town that had never truly accepted her. But the other part—the sensible part—warned her that although Justin Wheeler was seemingly friendly, he could just be pumping her for information. He might even dredge up her whole miserable past and do a follow-up story in the *Gazette* in case there was a living soul in Schyler who didn't already know far too much about her. After all, that sort of thing sold papers.

Justin wondered why she seemed almost defensive in answer to a rather innocuous question. "Schyler's not such a bad little town," he said, offering her the opinion he'd finally settled on himself after three years.

Her head turned and her dark green gaze studied him a long moment. "Isn't it?"

Edna had told him she hadn't been happy growing up here, but that had been years ago. Was she still holding a grudge against the whole town? "Maybe you should give the town another chance." He wasn't sure why he was trying to convince her. Perhaps it didn't sit well with him that some people in Schyler had made it uncomfortable for her to remain here, and he wanted to make it up to her.

Rachel looked unconvinced. "Maybe. We'll see. I've applied for a teaching position at Schyler Elementary."

Justin nodded. "Good. I know that Gloria will be happy to have you with her."

Suddenly the Badgers applauded wildly as another Red Sox player struck out. "Shouldn't you be going up to bat and helping out your team?" Rachel suggested.

"Nah. When you're a dynamite pitcher like me, you're not expected to bat a thousand as well." He smiled at her, sharing the joke on himself.

He had a nice smile, Rachel thought. And a nice daughter and probably a nice life here. She wondered how his wife had died and how long ago. Gloria knew none of the details. But what difference did it make, anyhow? Rachel asked herself. She wouldn't be around long enough to get to know Justin or his daughter.

It was time to start back. Rachel stood just as a big cheer broke out. Glancing over, she saw the Badgers congratulating one another as the dejected Red Sox muttered predictions about *next time*. "Can't win them all, I guess," she offered Justin by way of consolation.

Justin watched his daughter distributing cold drinks to the players as he rose to his feet. "Winning's fun, of course. But playing's the thing. If you love baseball, you just like to play. And these guys need something to do, you know." He swung back to Rachel. "We don't have golf courses nearby. Not even a bowling alley. This is healthy exercise."

"Is that why you organized the team?"

"More or less. Baseball's a good outlet for energy. But it's more than that. A man can play a little ball, impress his kids, get closer to them. Every kid needs a hero to look up to. Kind of nice if their first one's Dad." He smiled, feeling a little foolish having said all that. "Why do you coach?"

She couldn't tell him it was because her social life was sadly lacking and that she felt more comfortable being with children than adults. "I guess because I like baseball and kids."

All around them, players were gathering up equipment, saying their goodbyes, walking off in two and threes. On the other side of the tree where they stood, two men stopped as one bent to tie his shoe, unaware of their voices carrying.

"I'm surprised she came back and even more surprised she's still hanging around," the taller, upright man said.

"Maybe she's going after Theo this time," the squatting player suggested. "Hell, it wouldn't take much to get him into her bed."

"How'd you like to find her waiting for you in the woods?" The tall man make a smacking sound.

Finished tying his shoe, the other man stood. "You think she was putting out when Tyrone got killed?"

Growing angrier by the minute, Justin took a step toward them, but Rachel's hand on his arm stopped him in his tracks.

"Sure I do," the tall one went on. "My brother went to school with the Hathaways. Rachel was as wild as her mother."

"Maybe I'll start cutting through those woods by the tavern on my way home," the shorter man commented. "Might get lucky." Laughing, the two men walked on.

His mouth a thin line, Justin saw that the blood had drained from Rachel's face, making her look impossibly pale. He wanted to reach out, but instinctively knew she wouldn't welcome his touch. "Look, Rachel..."

"I have to go." She glanced over at Katie, grateful that the child was caught up in distributing cold drinks and hadn't heard.

"If you'll wait a minute, I'll walk you home." It was the least he could do. Damn insensitive clods.

About to turn away, she swung back to look at him. "You'd better watch the company you keep, Justin. Small-town reputations tarnish easily." With that, she walked off, her back straight, her steps unhurried.

Justin stood watching her, wondering what he could do. Go after those guys and make them apologize? Rearrange their faces a bit so maybe next time they'd think before they spoke? But what good would it do? From what he'd been hearing, half the town, if not more, felt the same way about Rachel Hathaway.

Yet he had the feeling every last one of them was wrong.

"Daddy," Katie said at his elbow, "did Rachel leave without saying goodbye?"

Absently he put his arm around his daughter's shoulders. "Yes, honey. She needed to get home."

"I wish she could have stayed longer. She's nice."

"Yeah," he said, watching Rachel disappear around the far corner. "I think so, too."

Rachel opened the door to Gloria's Volkswagen and got behind the wheel. The end of summer didn't bring cooling temperatures to southern Texas. It was sweltering inside the car that her mother had bought used ten years ago. But it wasn't the heat that had her hands trembling. She'd just left a meeting of the Schyler District School Board.

They'd turned down her application for a teaching position.

All six men and one woman had looked at her as if she were a fly who'd had the nerve to land in their soup. She should have known better than to apply, Rachel thought, as she wearily brushed back a lock of hair. Roy Quincy was on the board and had been for years.

Floyd Upton, the president, had given her the news, his pudgy face smug with righteous indignation. Roy's beady eyes had narrowed, daring her to challenge them. Even Ilona Cates, the unmarried lady who'd been Schyler's librarian for over thirty years, had looked down her hawk-like nose at Rachel.

She'd learned from the secretary that there were two openings, yet they'd turned Rachel down on the basis that she didn't meet their exacting criteria. In a pig's eye, she thought, with a flush of anger. If anything, she was over-qualified. She could, as Floyd told her, appeal. But appeals took time and she needed a job now.

She couldn't bear just sitting in Gloria's apartment for three months. Besides, her rent back in Bakersfield would go on, as would most of her other expenses. She had some savings, but dipping into them would make her truly nervous. The last thing she would do would be to work in the tavern, which seemed her only other option. Who else but her own mother would hire her in this town?

So now what? Rachel asked herself, as she cranked down the car windows. Listlessly she turned on the engine and headed for Main Street. Maybe she'd stop in at Edna's Diner for a cold drink. Edna, at least, offered a friendly face.

Lunchtime was always the busiest at Edna's. People came and went between eleven and two—working folks, teenagers, and shoppers, as well as those passing through town. Because he invariably caught up on the reading of his trade journals at lunch, Justin preferred the back booth along the right side.

It was almost one o'clock when he finished his chicken sandwich and glanced up to see Rachel Hathaway walk in. Busy as she was, Edna stopped for a conversation with her friend's daughter. Justin noticed her frown at something Rachel said, then lay a heavy arm about the young woman's shoulders and lead her to a just-vacated booth on the opposite side. In moments, Edna placed a frosted glass of tea in front of her and lingered for a few more words. He saw Rachel shake her head dejectedly and wondered what they were discussing.

Closing his magazine, Justin studied Rachel across the crowd, and noted he wasn't the only male who'd observed her arrival. A couple of guys at the counter were sending her interested looks. She wore a simple long-sleeved ivory blouse with a row of buttons running up to her throat and a slim black skirt with heels. Yet, dressed up or down, Rachel Hathaway drew the attention of men even though she sat quietly, her eyes staring into her glass.

Why was that? Justin wondered. She was attractive, but not enough to stop traffic. Probably in New York or L.A., she'd be given no more than a perfunctory appreciative glance. It had to be her reputation in this town.

What had she done to earn such blatant, unsavory regard? Had Tyrone Quincy been so beloved that her involvement in his death ten years ago in whatever capacity elicited such disdain, even today? If Tyrone had been anything like Roy or Theo, Justin doubted that had been the case. How had Tyrone died and why had Rachel been accused, then acquitted? *Had* she been a loose teenager as many suggested and only Pop and Edna protested?

Justin didn't think so. She seemed intelligent, almost shy, and certainly downplayed her looks. Not even her enemies could label her flirtatious in the least from what he'd seen. She was a teacher of young children Katie's age, certainly not an occupation to attract a woman who was wild in any sense of the word. At the ball field several days ago when those two men had slurred her, she'd seemed more hurt than angry. Yet if it was so uncomfortable for her here, why was she remaining?

Perhaps he'd walk over and join her, see if he could discover a few of the missing pieces to the puzzle that was Rachel Hathaway. But before he could slide off the seat, a tall man from the counter sauntered over to Rachel.

Justin recognized Joe Bob Gilliam, one of the ranchers who worked the Quincy spread. Sporting a beer belly, Joe Bob was single and known to like his women long-legged and loose. Watching, he saw the slightly bowlegged cowhand lean down and say something to Rachel that caused her to almost reel, then quickly replace the sunglasses she'd removed.

Rising, Justin started toward her booth.

Unaware he was being observed, Joe Bob laughed nastily, then reached to touch Rachel's hair. Quickly she slapped his hand away. In knee-jerk reaction, he raised his arm to strike back, but not quickly enough.

Justin grabbed Joe Bob's arm, twisting it viciously behind him and angling him away from the booth.

"What the hell?" Joe Bob yelled.

Edna appeared faster than anyone could have predicted, two-hundred pounds of angry woman facing Joe Bob. "Get out of my place. Now."

Justin gave the big man a shove toward the door to start him on his way as the diner fell into silence, all eyes on the fracas.

Joe Bob rubbed his arm and rolled his shoulders, narrowing his pale eyes at Justin. "I won't forget this," he snarled.

"See that you don't," Justin said, his voice low and menacing. He watched through the window as the hulking rancher got into his pickup and sped off.

Edna touched his arm. "Thanks." She turned back to her customers. "Excitement's over, folks." Back behind her counter, she called to her cook to get moving with the orders. People returned to their lunches, whispering among themselves.

Justin turned around to see Rachel slide out of the booth and toss a bill onto the table. Gathering her shoulder bag, she moved toward the door. "Wait," he said, touching her arm.

Her hands trembled as she fingered her keys. "Thank you, but I've got to go." And she hurried out the door.

Swearing under his breath, Justin dug in his pocket for his money clip, placed a couple of bills and his check on top of the ancient cash register, and rushed out after her.

But Gloria's Volkswagen was already turned and jolting out onto Main Street, scooting in front of a large produce truck.

Hands in his pants pockets, Justin watched her head toward the tavern and Gloria's apartment. He could follow her, but it was obvious she wanted to be alone.

He'd give a lot to know what Joe Bob Gilliam had said that had upset her so. Or maybe it was better that he didn't know. It had been a long while since he'd hit a man in anger, and though he wouldn't run from a fight, he didn't seek it, either.

Maybe it was time he took Pop's advice and dug into the back files of the *Gazette*—to read for himself the account of what had happened between Tyrone Quincy and Rachel Hathaway that fateful day in the woods.

Chapter Three

Reasonable doubt. Many an accused had been released by a jury because of reasonable doubt. Some unquestionably had been innocent; others were likely guilty. Justin spent most of the afternoon rummaging through the *Gazette*'s morgue, reading Pop's painstakingly unbiased version of Rachel Hathaway's trial, detailing how she'd been freed on reasonable doubt. Then he'd gone to the library a few doors up the street on Main and read dozens of microfiche pages of other newspaper accounts of the murder and acquittal.

Back at his office, he sat thoughtfully at his desk, sorting through his impressions of all that he'd learned. The public defender who'd represented Rachel had been Ray Brewster, who was now a practicing attorney in Schyler and doing quite well, Justin knew. Ray had based his defense on three points.

One had been that a forensics expert who'd examined the body had testified that it was extremely doubtful that a hundred-and-ten-pound woman could have delivered the single savage blow that had killed Tyrone Quincy, a large, muscular man who'd weighed one-eighty. The second had been that no murder weapon had been found on or around the scene, even though Theo had entered the woods and found his brother lying still and Rachel dazed and glassy-eyed. And the third point had been that investigators had found *four* sets of footprints in the soft, damp earth.

Naturally one set had been Rachel's, another Tyrone's, and the third, Theo's. But the fourth imprint had been made by shoes with a tire-tread sole, shoes which later had been determined to have been worn by a heavy-set individual, probably a man. Neither the shoes nor their owner had been found—thus, the reasonable doubt. Despite the district attorney, known to be a Quincy sympathizer and friend, who had viciously tried to discredit her reputation as well as that of her family, the jury had let Rachel go.

Toying with his pen as he leaned back in his chair, Justin could well imagine how unbearable the Quincys and their allies had made life for Rachel in Schyler after that acquittal. So at seventeen, scarcely out of high school, she'd left home. Projecting his Katie into such a scenario, he grimaced.

How had Rachel managed to live, to get her education, to survive without some support system? Justin remembered all too well having left the country once years ago over a serious problem that left most of his family and friends powerless to help. He was alone and hurting, and it had taken him a long while and a lot of courage to rebound. And he'd been a grown man, ten years or so older than Rachel had been during her ordeal.

He was filled with admiration for her courage and the deep-down feeling that she was innocent of any wrongdoing.

Which left him with his investigative-reporter's antenna twitching. If Rachel hadn't killed Tyrone, who had? Whose shoes had made that fourth set of prints? Was the murderer still here in Schyler, living among them? And was he a little nervous now that Rachel was back, reviving the talk, the memories?

Hearing the door open and close, Justin swiveled about in his chair and looked up to see Pop coming toward him.

With a wave to Sid working in the back room through the archway, the old man sat at his desk facing Justin's. "Heard tell you almost got into it with Joe Bob Gilliam over at the diner."

It always amazed Justin how fast word traveled in Schyler. "Edna tell you?" he asked.

"Edna and Sara at the post office and two or three others." Pop picked up the pipe he often toyed with but no longer was able to enjoy. "You want to tell me about it?"

Justin shrugged. "Rachel Hathaway didn't want him touching her, and Joe Bob isn't good at rejection. I gave him a little assist out the diner's door."

Pop's eyes twinkled in amusement at the mental picture. "He's got fifty pounds on you. You might want to watch your back with that ornery fellow carrying a grudge."

"I always watch my back. Where've you been?"

"I stopped in after the school board meeting. I wanted to talk with Floyd Upton about the bond issue they want to put on the ballot for this fall's election. Found out more than I went in to learn."

"That so?" Justin knew that there was no rushing Pop. He said what he had to say in his own way, in his own time. Patiently he watched his grandfather disassemble his pipe, then search his desk drawer for pipe cleaners.

"You know, I've been thinking," Pop said, his eyes roaming the room and landing on a pile of folders stacked on a cabinet, waiting to be filed. "We're going to need more help around here. Matt's going back to part-time in another week when college starts, and I don't think I want to come in every day. Getting lazy, you know."

Lazy like a fox, Justin thought, knowing full well that Pop was as sharp as a man his age could hope to be. But, as always, he played along, knowing he'd discover the reason behind Pop's unexpected suggestion in due time. "You might be right. Have anyone in mind?"

Pop blew into his pipe stem, studying the cavity with avid interest. "Just so happens I do. It appears that Rachel's going to be staying in Schyler awhile. She's a teacher, you know. Quick and bright. Thought we could offer her a job proofing and filing, maybe teach her layout work. Sid's got more than he can handle with the bookkeeping and typesetting and all."

There was more here than met the eye, Justin was certain. "I thought she'd applied to teach at Schyler Elementary?"

"She did. Board turned her down in a special session this morning. Told her she wasn't qualified. A lot of hogwash, and we all know it."

So that was where she'd been before she'd stopped at the diner. And the fine, upstanding citizens of Schyler turned her down. "This is Roy Quincy's doing, right?"

"Most likely, his and his friends."

"What I can't understand is why Rachel wants to stay. This town probably isn't going to accept her ever."

Pop put his pipe back together, then tested it with a couple of airy puffs. "Because her mother's quite ill, and she can't face leaving Gloria alone."

Justin was surprised at that news. "What's wrong with Gloria?"

"Emphysema. Doc Tremayne diagnosed it more than a year ago. Stubborn woman refuses to stop smoking." He gazed longingly at the pipe he'd given up a good while ago. "I understand how she feels, but I can't condone it."

Justin hadn't seen enough of Gloria to realize she was ill, though he'd been aware of her cough since he'd known her. "Helluva situation for Rachel to come home to, her brother's death and her mother's illness."

Pop nodded. "Yes. And Curt's on Navy maneuvers and won't be back for another couple of months. He hasn't been home in years, probably doesn't know. So it's all up to Rachel."

Justin found himself admiring Rachel for not abandoning her mother, especially since staying here was costing her dearly.

Pop stood, brushing a speck of ash off his leather vest. "So what do you say? Do you think we need help around here?"

So that's what he was up to. Justin smiled up at the old softie. "Yeah, I think we do."

"Good. Go on over and offer her the job." Turning, Pop headed for the back door.

"*Me* ask her? I thought you'd want to do that."

"Nope," Pop called over his shoulder. "I'm going to collect my granddaughter over at Emily Porter's, and we're going fishing. And if you're a good lad, we just might share our catch with you."

Smiling, Justin watched his grandfather stop to have a word with Sid, then go out the back way. He was lucky to have Pop, and so was Katie, who adored the old man.

Turning back to his desk, he slid the article he'd been editing into his top drawer. Could he handle having Rachel here daily, those cool, sea green eyes watching him without seeming to? The attraction between them was real, yet each seemed determined not to acknowledge it, much less act upon it. There was an air of sophistication about Rachel that seemed to indicate she wanted much more from life than small-town living. For his part, Justin wanted no complications in his neat, orderly world.

And Rachel Hathaway could certainly be a complication.

Then again, maybe she wouldn't take him up on their offer, Justin thought, as he pocketed his keys. No time like the present to find out. With a wave to Sid, he left the *Gazette*.

The best way to work off anger was physical activity, Rachel had learned years ago. On her knees in her mother's fenced backyard, she ripped weeds from the soil with a viciousness that yanked out every speck of root. Truth be known, if she pulled out every flower and green thing in the garden, she probably still wouldn't be rid of her inner rage.

Ever since she'd stepped over the county line into Schyler, she'd been angry. Angry with the gods for taking her sweet brother, and for the fact that her mother was seriously ill. Irate this morning that those smug, self-righteous members of the school board hadn't hired her. Furious with Joe Bob Gilliam whose lewd suggestions had shocked and embarrassed her, proving again that wherever Rachel Hathaway walked in this town, trouble walked with her.

Moving on her knees to the next row, she bent to clean out the marigold bed. Oddly enough, though she didn't take much interest in the house, Gloria loved her flower garden. Each season, she prepared the soil and planted a variety of seeds, mostly without regard to any prescribed form. As a child, Rachel remembered her mother digging in the dirt, thinning, replanting, clipping blossoms for the table. Perhaps Gloria, too, had used physical activity to rid herself of anger. But these days and in this heat, Gloria wasn't up to tending her garden, a limitation that frustrated her.

Frustration was becoming her daily companion, too, Rachel realized. Teaching was the only thing she was trained to do. How would she support herself if she remained here? She could have worked at the library, if that sour old pickle, Ilona Cates, had been halfway human. But no, Roy Quincy had nearly everyone in his pocket.

Except Pop Wheeler and his grandson.

Sitting back on her haunches, Rachel paused, wiping her damp brow with the back of her hand. Justin Wheeler had sprung to her defense in the diner so swiftly, so surely that he'd surprised everyone, most especially her. To her recollection, no man had ever done that for her before.

Still, she mustn't make too much of it, Rachel reminded herself, as she went back to her weeding. Justin was a Schyler resident and a newspaperman. Maybe he'd done it because he thought there was a story there somewhere in her return to town. It had been Rachel's experience that most men had motives for their actions, and that most of those motives were self-serving.

Finishing, she straightened, rubbing her tired back. She'd been at it all afternoon but at least the garden looked fairly good. Quickly she tied the trash bag stuffed full of weeds and dragged it alongside the aluminum shed. Then she bent to pick up the hose, turned on the water and moved to the far end to sprinkle the flowers no longer being crowded by the creeping weeds.

Sweat was running down her back, and her cotton blouse was sticky against her skin; her knees were black from the soil, and her face red from more sun than she was used to getting. But she felt better than when she'd come outside,

Rachel thought, turning the water into a fine spray so as not to injure the smaller plants.

Back in California, she often ran in the cooler mornings and the quiet evening hours before dark. But here, she dared not do even that for fear of running into some crazed friend of the Quincys, out to prove he was a man by throwing her to the ground and having his way with her. If that happened in the center of Main Street, Rachel felt certain most of the townspeople would just stand around watching and perhaps cheering.

"Rachel?"

Startled, she turned at the sound of her name, swinging the hose and its spray forward. The water hit Justin broad in the chest, dousing even his slacks before he could jump back out of the way.

"Oh, I'm sorry." She angled the hose off to the side. "You startled me." It was disconcerting to see the man she'd been thinking of only moments before.

Patting his wet shirt, Justin smiled. "That's all right. I was too hot anyway."

She stared up into his eyes, finding them calm and amused. A man who could laugh at an accident. Would wonders never cease?

"I knocked at the gate and even called your name from there. Gloria told me I could find you back here."

Getting herself under control, she aimed the water back onto the flowers. "I guess I didn't hear you. I apologize for getting you wet."

"No problem. I'll dry in no time." He let his gaze roam over the garden, finding it neat and inviting. "It's nice out here."

She pointed to a lounge chair on a small patio. "My mother likes to sit out here when it's too hot upstairs." Carefully she shut off the spray, wondering if she could guess why he'd come. "I should have thanked you back at the diner. I appreciate what you did."

"You did thank me, but then you ran off."

Rachel turned the spigot off, then coiled the hose into its holder. "It would have been a bit awkward to stay, didn't you think?"

"Joe Bob's bad news, but I think he'll steer clear of you now." He wanted to say something that would take that haunted, defensive look from her face. "Rachel, there are people in this town who are on your side."

Wiping her hands on a rag she removed from the pocket of her shorts, she raised her head to look up at him. "Is that a fact? I never thought a newspaperman would be that naive."

"Things have changed since you left," Justin said, wondering why he was persisting, since he wasn't utterly convinced he was right. Perhaps it was because he *wanted* things to be as he claimed they were.

She raised a quizzical brow. "In Schyler? I seriously doubt it. You heard those men at the ball field and their wonderfully unbiased opinion of me. Then there's Joe Bob, who thinks that I'm dying for his attention. The fathers of these same men were propositioning my mother when I was barely older than Katie. So where's the change?"

She had a point, but he wanted her to see the whole picture. "Some guys are sleazes, but not everyone in Schyler is. There are some fine people here who—"

"Oh, yes. You mean the pillars of the community, like the seven people on the school board who turned down my request for a teaching position, saying I wasn't qualified?" Hands on her slender hips, she regarded him challengingly.

"I heard about that, and I'm sorry."

Rachel ran out of steam. "I'm not. I wouldn't work in this damn town if they paid me in gold bricks." Gathering up her gardening tools, she shoved them into a basket.

"That's too bad, because I've come to offer you a job." He let his words sink in and watched her suspicions mount. He wondered if she knew how expressive her eyes were. If she did, she'd probably keep her sunglasses on night and day.

Slowly Rachel took a step back, giving herself a moment. This had truly come out of left field. "Now, why would you want me working for you, Mr. Wheeler?"

"Because one of our employees is going back to part-time while he finishes college. My grandfather's semi-retired and doesn't come in every day, which leaves only Sid and me. We could use some help. But the main reason is that Pop likes you." There was wariness written all over her face, but there was a spark of reluctant interest as well.

"I don't know a thing about the newspaper business."

"Pop told me that you're quick and bright, his very words."

"Did he talk you into this?"

For the first time, his eyes cooled. "Nobody talks me into doing what I don't want to do, Rachel."

She studied him a moment, then nodded. "I believe you. I'm sorry, but being in Schyler brings out my skeptical side."

"I understand that you wouldn't trust anyone in this town easily. But I've been here barely three years, and I didn't arrive with preconceived opinions. I like to form my own. So, what do you say?"

He smiled, and she saw again that small indentation at the left corner of his mouth. She wanted to take a chance, yet she was hesitant, too. But she did need to stay for a couple of months, and it wasn't as if she had an assortment of offers from which to choose.

"It would have to be temporary," she told him honestly. "I've taken a leave of absence from my teaching job in Bakersfield, and I'll be going back there when . . . when my brother returns, and we can make some family decisions."

"I have no problem with that."

She might as well tell him all of it. "I have to fly back and arrange to sublease my apartment. And pick up my car."

"Fine. Would a week be long enough?"

"Yes."

"Then let's say you'll start after the Labor Day weekend is over, on Tuesday morning. All right?"

He was being awfully nice, awfully cooperative. She longed to trust him, but she needed to go slowly here. Trusting men was foreign to her experience. Nodding in agreement, she picked up the gardening basket and walked him to the gate.

Opening the latch, Justin paused. "Maybe you'll be back in time to go to the county fair on Labor Day. Katie would like that."

He'd spotted her weakness, his daughter. She had to let him know that she wasn't easily manipulated. "I doubt it," she said, putting a cool edge to her voice.

Slowly he raised a hand and laid it on her shoulder, somewhat surprised when she didn't shrug it off. "Don't you get tired, carrying that heavy chip around?" He watched the shifting emotions reflect in her eyes. Then, because he'd been wanting to for so long, he trailed his fingers along the silk of her cheek. "You don't have to be afraid of me."

She blinked up at him in the waning sunlight. "Don't I?"

Justin shook his head, then turned and walked out the gate.

Rachel stared after him, uncertain whether to be pleased she had a job or worried about her new employer.

He was a man who didn't particularly enjoy county fairs. He'd grown up in the Dallas area and had never even attended one until the year he'd moved to Schyler. But Justin knew the value of PR, of strolling among people and shaking a hand here and there and of buying a jar of homemade preserves from a neighbor who'd just won a blue ribbon. He also knew how good it made him feel to spend a day watching his daughter have fun.

"Daddy, there's Marissa," Katie said, tugging on his arm and pointing to her best friend. "Is it okay if we go on the Ferris wheel together?"

Returning from the ticket booth with another strip, Justin handed her one. "Go get in line. I'll wait for you here."

He stood back alongside the caramel-corn stand, which was doing a thriving business, the sweet smell somewhat cloying in the late-afternoon heat. They'd arrived about noon, filled up on hot dogs and soft drinks, then they'd wandered over to the animal barns.

Katie had loved seeing the baby lambs, the calves, and the piglets. They'd admired the prize-winning bulls and pigs until Katie had announced that the barn odors in the heated building were turning her stomach. Pop had been with them, but he'd lingered to talk with some of the ranchers while Justin and Katie had strolled to the midway.

Leaning against a pole, Justin decided it was a good thing he enjoyed people-watching, for it seemed as if Katie would not soon tire of being jostled about by a variety of rides. Tomorrow would be her first day back to school so he decided to indulge her in this last vacation fling.

His eyes scanned the crowd, and he nodded occasionally to someone he knew, saying a few words to a passerby now and then. The adults were mostly strolling, taking in the carnival atmosphere, with one eye on their children. Barkers were coaxing people to their games of chance, and little ones were eating too much cotton candy and peanuts. Shy boys were walking hand in hand with young girls wearing shorts and halter tops. A slice of Americana, he thought.

Straightening, he caught sight of a woman with long blond hair walking along by herself. But when she turned, Justin realized it wasn't Rachel Hathaway after all, and he felt a stab of disappointment.

He knew she'd flown back to California and had returned on Saturday driving a compact yellow Toyota, which had been parked alongside Gloria's old Volkswagen ever since. After she'd told him she probably wouldn't be coming to the fair, he'd decided not to call and repeat the invitation. But that didn't prevent him from searching the crowd for a sign of her. People changed their minds all the time.

"Hello, Justin. Enjoying yourself?"

He turned toward the husky voice, surprised to see Gloria Hathaway beside him, a cigarette burning between her fingers. He hadn't thought her the county-fair type any more than he was. Smiling at her, he pointed toward the Ferris wheel where Katie's car was climbing upward. "I enjoy watching Katie. She's nuts about these rides."

Gloria's laugh was reminiscent. "I was, too, when I was a kid. Then I'd go home with a bellyache every time."

Justin nodded. "She'll probably have one, too. Did you come alone?"

"No, Rachel dragged me. Told me I needed a little sun and fun. She's a terrible nag." Her voice filled with affection, Gloria took a last drag on her cigarette, then ground it out underfoot. "I want to thank you for offering her a job. That was mighty nice of you and Pop."

He shrugged off her thanks. "We can use her help."

Gloria eyed him knowingly. "Yeah, sure."

Justin craned his neck, looking around. "You say Rachel's here?"

"She saw someone she knew and stopped to talk a minute. She'll be along. Tell her I went into the tent to check out the white elephant sale, will you?"

"Right." He checked Katie's progress again, noting she was still circling, then raised a hand to shade his eyes, inspecting the passing faces. At last he saw her.

She was wearing white slacks and a black top, her hair hanging loose and wind-tossed. And she was smiling up at the tall, bearded man she'd spoken to at the cemetery.

Thrusting his hands into his pockets, Justin stared, struggling with battling emotions: curiosity, and, he realized, a flash of jealousy.

Feeling sad, Rachel watched the man walk away, heading for the parking lot, a quiet dignity in his bearing. Seeing him again was just another frustration added to the many that being in Schyler brought to mind. But she'd be staying for at least a couple more months, and she'd have to concentrate on making the best of things.

Turning, she looked across the hordes of people, trying to locate her mother, when she noticed Justin Wheeler standing near the Ferris wheel watching her. She'd known he'd be here, of course. She started toward him, wondering if that was the subconscious reason she'd insisted Gloria come to the fair.

Though she'd tried not to think of him, Justin's image had been on her mind during the long drive from Bakersfield to Schyler. And the memory of the touch of his long tanned fingers on her face had disturbed her sleep more than once.

Actually she'd been worried about attending the fair, concerned that someone might be provoked into an incident by her very presence. But, if she had to be working in town for weeks to come, she'd have to learn to coexist with the residents in some manner. Adjusting her sunglasses, she stopped in front of Justin.

"Nice day for a fair," she said. Not the greatest of openings, but it was all she could think of.

Justin wished that just looking at her didn't warm him, that finding her here didn't please him. "Yes, it is."

Bounding off the Ferris wheel, Katie rushed up to them. "Rachel, hi! Want to go on a ride with me and my dad?"

Rachel touched Katie's long braid, unable not to, envying the child's confident spontaneity. "Sure. Which one?"

"Don't let her persuade you if you don't want to," Justin said quietly, as Katie looked around eagerly, trying to choose the perfect ride.

"Nobody talks me into doing what I don't want to do," Rachel said, tossing his own words back at him.

"Touché," Justin answered with a smile.

There was something about Rachel Hathaway that set off warning bells inside him. She would only be here a short time, a woman who hated Schyler and would leave as soon as she fulfilled her obligation to her mother. He didn't want to let himself be interested in someone who would be around only temporarily, nor did he want Katie to grow fond of her, only to have Rachel walk away. His daughter had already lost too many people important to her in her short lifetime.

Yet, as he watched Katie happily draw both of them toward the Tilt-A-Whirl, he wondered how he could stop things already set in motion.

When it was their turn, they climbed into the red car, Katie seating herself between the two adults. Justin slammed the protective bar in place and stretched his arm along the back of the vinyl seat. "I hope you have a strong stomach," he said to Rachel.

Tossing her hair back over her shoulder, she gripped the bar. "I hope so, too. I haven't been on one of these in over fifteen years."

"This is one of the milder rides," Katie announced. She pointed toward a wire cagelike structure that shook its occupants every which way including upside down, all the while spinning around its axle. "*That's* the really scary ride."

"And one I think I'll stay clear of," Rachel added.

Then they were moving around the wildly hilly track, faster and faster, tilting first one way, then the other. Laughing, they slid into one another, then the car would whirl them in the other direction and they'd scoot nearly off the shiny seats.

"Isn't this fun?" Katie yelled above the screams coming from the other cars.

Justin wasn't sure it was, but he shouted agreement anyway. Rachel, her hair flying, seemed to be enjoying herself as much as his daughter. Eagerly Katie leaned forward, bringing Justin's hand into contact with Rachel's shoulder, forcing her to shift closer. Though they were whirling, she turned to face him, her expression hidden behind the dark glasses. He didn't remove his hand, and she didn't shrug it off. His touch was quite casual, and yet awareness had leaped between them immediately. He knew she felt it as much as he. He also knew that she didn't know what to do about it any more than he did.

At ride's end, Katie jumped out and ran down the ramp. Justin offered Rachel his hand, and she took it long enough to climb out, then let go. "Wonderful to be a child," Justin commented.

Rachel threaded her fingers through her hair, trying for some semblance of order. "I suppose it can be."

"Daddy, Marissa's in line for the haunted house," Katie said, not in the least ready to call it a day. "Can I go?"

Justin handed her a ticket, then pointed to a vacant bench. "I'll wait for you right there." Quite naturally, he touched Rachel's elbow and guided her to the bench. "I don't mean to monopolize you," he said, knowing full well it was a lie, "but I thought you might want to sit down a minute."

Monopolize her? That was a good one, Rachel thought. Not a single, solitary citizen of Schyler had even spoken a greeting to her since she'd entered the park. But there was no use whining about that. And it wasn't fair to Justin, who was simply being polite to her, she was certain. "Do you come to this every year?"

Angling toward her on the bench, Justin nodded. "Katie loves the rides, and Pop likes to examine the prize-winning steer. I understand they've had a county fair in Schyler for thirty years or more. Did you used to come when you were young and living here?"

"A couple of times. My mother was always working so I'd bring my brothers." It occurred to her that she knew very little about Justin other than that he was Pop's grandson and his wife had died. She told herself her interest was simply because he was going to be her employer starting tomorrow. "Do you have brothers or sisters?"

"No. I don't think my mother was cut out to raise a brood. She always seemed a bit shocked that she had me." He felt comfortable sitting quietly chatting with her, isolated from the people passing by. Perhaps if he opened up a little about himself, she'd do the same and satisfy his growing curiosity.

"I think I heard that your folks live in Dallas. Is that right?"

"Originally. My father died ten years ago. He was a heart surgeon. My mother married one of his patients and moved to London, where she still lives." He didn't add that she sent a birthday gift and Christmas present to her granddaughter each year and felt that her grandmotherly concern ended there. Even back when he could have used her moral support, when he was battling in the courts for Katie's custody, his mother hadn't shown much interest. Instead she'd left on a round-the-world cruise with her retired husband.

"I'll bet she's proud of Katie," Rachel said, waving to the child as she neared the entrance to the haunted house.

"She hasn't seen her since Katie was two." At least she'd attended Leona's funeral and visited him in the hospital after the accident.

Except for the times when he was genuinely amused, there was a lingering sadness in Justin's gray eyes, Rachel noticed, not for the first time. The tone of his words seemed to imply that something had been lacking during his growing-up years. Perhaps because of Pop's warmth and the loving relationship he had with his daughter, she'd assumed that Justin had come from a caring background. Wrong again.

"I guess very few people have an ideal childhood, except in books." She became aware that he'd stretched his arm along the bench behind her, and concentrated on ignoring it.

"How about ideal adulthoods?"

She crossed her legs as she shook her head. "I don't know anyone who has that, either. Do you?"

"Pop always says that it isn't what happens to you that matters. It's how you handle it."

Three teenage boys trooped on by, sending surreptitious glances toward Rachel. One made a remark, and then all three burst into laughter as they scrambled past.

Justin felt Rachel visibly tense up.

"I guess some of us aren't as good at handling things as others." Glancing about, she wondered where Gloria was. Perhaps it was time to go.

"Are you looking for your friend?" Justin asked.

Frowning, she turned back to him. "What friend?"

"The fellow with the beard."

Rachel removed her glasses and thoughtfully stared up at him a long moment.

But Justin's curiosity wouldn't let it be. "You two seemed quite friendly. An old boyfriend?"

Rachel felt a rush of disappointment. Somehow, she'd thought Justin was different, not like everyone else in this town, who seemed to think she'd been lovers with every man she smiled at. "Someone I used to know," she finally said in a halfhearted explanation. "Satisfied?"

He wasn't, but he shrugged. "Occupational hazard in the newspaper business, asking questions."

"I hope you'll fight the urge in the future. I'm not used to explaining my every move." She stood, hoping she'd made her point. "Please tell Katie goodbye for me." Her back straight, she walked away in search of her mother.

Puzzled by her quick defensiveness, Justin stood watching her. Was his curiosity cloaked in jealousy? he asked himself. Or was it more than that?

Did the investigative reporter in him wonder if the mysterious man with the beard owned a pair of shoes with tire-tread soles?

Chapter Four

It was amazing what a difference the arrival of an attractive woman in an all-male office could make. Justin sat at his desk trying to work on this week's editorial while listening to the voices across the room.

"The thing you have to remember about doing pasteboards is that if you mess up, it's no big deal to fix," Sid Lewis said, as he wiped his hands and looked at Rachel. "We just run it out again, hang up the galley strip to dry, wax it, and then paste it on the board."

"Doesn't sound difficult. Can I give it a try?"

"Sure, sure." He handed her several galley strips. "Here you go, and there's the board."

Rachel sent him her quick smile, then leaned over the table and went to work.

"If you need anything, I'll be right back there." Somewhat reluctantly Sid walked back to where he had his bookkeeping ledgers spread out.

Justin smiled into the hand he had cupped over his mouth. He'd been doing a lot of that since Rachel had started working at the *Gazette* a week ago. Smiling to himself and damn near laughing out loud a couple of times.

He'd wondered how the staff would respond to Rachel, and he'd found out quickly enough. Sid had not only begun shaving regularly—something he'd only done when pressed before—but he smelled suspiciously like some godawful musk cologne that made Justin's eyes water if he got too close to the man. Sid was also talking more, grabbing every opportunity to explain things to Rachel, from the filing of the morgue records to bookkeeping, and today the pasteups. In his slow, methodical way, drawing his chair up close beside hers, Sid was teaching her more than she probably wanted to know. And far more than she needed to know in her temporary position.

Then there was Matt Russell, the twenty-year-old part-timer. Matt's usually wild and often-unkempt red hair was now in a respectable cut worthy of Peter Jennings, a journalist the boy greatly admired. He was neatly dressed, maddeningly effusive, and hanging around almost as many hours as he had on full-time. Rachel treated him much as she would her kid brother, wisely refusing to acknowledge his crush on her, fully aware he'd outgrow it in another week. Instead she got him to talk about his girl, Annie, whose father owned the local cleaners and thought his daughter was too young to date a college junior.

And every day after school, before going on to Emily Porter's, Katie stopped in, ostensibly to see her father, but finding half a dozen questions to ask Rachel before Justin would shoo her off to the sitter. There hadn't been many women in Katie's life who'd lasted, and this new attachment worried Justin, for he knew she'd be crushed when Rachel left.

Pop was probably the only one who hadn't altered his behavior much since Rachel had started work at the *Gazette*. He'd stop in for brief visits several times a day, polite and friendly to one and all. But Justin noticed a particular warmth in his grandfather's greetings to Rachel, and he knew that Pop regarded her with affection. She knew it, too, and thrived under his caring eye.

Watching Rachel's reaction to Pop's obvious fondness, it occurred to Justin that although she'd undoubtedly had a carload of male attention all her life, she probably hadn't had much genuine warmth from adult males. She was like a flower who'd survived the drought, eager for water, yet afraid to believe it was freely available.

Justin tossed aside the pencil he'd been using, realizing his mind was wandering too far afield to complete the task today. He, too, had been affected by Rachel's presence, a fact that didn't sit well with him.

The Tuesday morning after the Labor Day fair, she'd arrived bright and early and with a smile. It didn't quite reach her eyes, but it did indicate she was willing to forgive if not to totally forget their mild skirmish. In an effort to make her feel welcome, he'd introduced her around, shown her the ropes, given her real tasks to do so she'd feel useful, and kept her supplied with cold drinks when she began to look warm and weary.

She caught on fast and fit in well. She dressed conservatively, minded her own business, was considerate, courteous and tactful. Yet she bothered him, and he was well aware of the reason why.

He was attracted to her and did not want to be.

He hadn't been deeply attracted to a woman since college, when he'd met Leona. Perhaps if their courtship, marriage and subsequent parting hadn't been so tumultuous and eventually destructive, he would have had more interest in an active love life. But his work and his lengthy battle to regain his daughter had left him drained and with little energy to pursue anyone romantically. And, truth be known, he hadn't met anyone in ages who'd accelerated his heartbeat significantly.

Until Rachel.

Swiveling his chair, he glanced over at her working at the paste table. She was bent over and concentrating, her long hair tied back from her face with a piece of yellow yarn, dressed casually in blue jeans and a cotton blouse as he'd suggested, since parts of her job could get quite messy. As he watched, he saw that her tongue was methodically tracing her upper lip as she fastened her attention on the piece she was pasting in place.

Irrationally he wondered what she'd do if he stepped over and pulled her close so he could taste her, as he'd been wanting to do since he'd first set eyes on those full lips. Probably slap him a good one, Justin thought, returning his gaze to his editorial.

Yes, there'd been changes at the *Gazette* since Rachel's arrival. Yet, except for his increased mental meanderings, things were working out, Justin decided.

Across the room, finished with the first board, Rachel picked up a damp cloth to wipe her hands on, as she mused that things really weren't working out as she'd hoped on this job.

Oh, the work was easy enough, the little she'd been given to do. Mostly busywork, she thought, since she'd been hired because Pop liked her and felt sorry for her rather than the fact that she'd really been needed. But she could even put up with that since her stay was temporary.

The staff hadn't been the problem she'd feared, readily accepting her, which had almost brought tears to her eyes. Sid was such a sweet, fatherly type that she certainly couldn't fault him for his often tongue-tied efforts to teach her his version of the newspaper business. Then there was Matt, who with his boyish enthusiasm reminded her of Curt who'd always tried to please. Pop's gentle affection had been unexpected since she'd scarcely known him before she'd left, but it was most welcome, for she felt he was one man she could trust.

Setting the pasteboard on the far end of the table, she stood back a moment to admire the page. Not bad. Of course, Katie probably could have done just as good a job.

Katie. Rachel smiled. She was the real bonus to working here. Katie was lovely, bright and filled with mischief, a wonderful little girl. She was open and trusting and had a wondrous curiosity about everything. She was the way Rachel, raised as she had been with a drinking father and an overworked mother, had had so little chance to be. The time she spent with Katie made up for any negative aspects of her job. She would miss the child terribly when the time came to leave.

And she would miss Katie's father.

Walking over to stand by the window, Rachel looked out on a sunny September afternoon. There, she'd come to the crux of why she knew things weren't working out as she'd planned. She'd hoped she could work alongside Justin and ignore him. She'd prayed that her thoughts about him would diminish, her desire to see him disappear, her pleasure in his company dissipate.

If anything, the attraction had increased. But that wasn't the worst of it. The surprise was that she honestly liked Justin Wheeler.

He was kind to everyone who came into the office—from newsboys to bank presidents—in a thoroughly masculine way that earned their respect. He was fun and funny, a man who could laugh at himself, which Rachel thought a rare trait. He was sensitive—to his daughter's feelings, his co-workers moods, his readers' needs. He was sexy in a low-key way, yet it was enough to make her nights restive and her dreams vividly sensual.

Because of her early maturity, Rachel had had men coming on to her for years. She'd learned how to coolly turn them off. What she'd never learned was how to be friends with a man. Frankly she'd pretty well convinced herself that friendship between a man and a woman was a foolish fantasy—until this past week, spent working alongside Justin.

But that didn't mean the attraction wasn't there. Even now, she could feel his eyes on her back. If she turned, she knew she'd see in his pewter-gray gaze the same longing she'd seen in her own.

This *thing* between them had nowhere to go. She would be leaving just as soon as she, in all good conscience, could. Wild horses wouldn't make her stay in this narrow-minded, judgmental town. Yet this was Justin's home now, and Katie's. They were entrenched, settled, part of the establishment. They could no more leave than she could stay.

A woman who sought a relationship that would surely end badly was a fool or a masochist. Rachel had never thought herself either. Yet here she stood, wondering what it would be like to know him, *really* know him.

But she had to put thoughts like that aside, she told herself. She would have to be careful not to let Justin see the effect he had on her. She would keep their conversations brief, their eye contact to a minimum, and the time they spent alone together down to almost nil. She might not be able to control her feelings, but she could master her own behavior. She had to stop longing for him before someone got hurt. She could be that someone.

But she could be friends with him. That decided, Rachel turned and found Justin staring at her, in his eyes such a look of abject yearning that it took her breath away. Gripping the table's edge with trembling hands, she returned the look.

How was she going to get through the next several months?

Tuesday evenings were hellish at the *Gazette.* It was the day they "put the paper to bed," a journalistic expression that meant everything had to be finished before Matt would drive the pasteboards thirty miles to the neighboring town of Kingsville and the small print shop that serviced many weekly papers. Though Justin was usually calm under pressure, this particular Tuesday he was hot and frazzled and running behind.

"Matt, where's that ad you brought in from the Nickelodeon?" he yelled toward the back office.

His red hair disheveled by his nervous fingers, Matt searched among the papers on his desk. "It's here somewhere. Coming right up."

Justin turned back to his computer and the graphic layout he had nearly finished. When he'd first joined Pop at the *Gazette,* they'd still been using typewriters. With some heavy talking and by investing some of his own capital, he'd convinced his grandfather that though they were a small paper, they didn't need to use archaic equipment. They had four computer terminals now, two with color capabilities and infinite graphic possibilities.

Completing his layout, he pressed the "save" key, then switched over to program the printer. "Rachel," he called over his shoulder, "you finished proofing that back section yet?"

"In a minute," she answered from her desk, her red pen hovering over each line as she read.

Her teacher's eye rarely missed a thing, he knew. Leaving her, he walked toward the back to see how Sid was coming on their newest acquisition, a typesetter. For years, they'd leased a typesetting machine, and Justin had vacillated over purchasing one. When he'd run across a barely used machine offered by a bankrupt paper in Brownsville, he'd driven down personally to grab it. "How goes it, Sid?" he asked, looking over the older man's shoulder.

"Coming along fine, Justin. I should have the rest of the galleys for you in about ten minutes."

He clapped him on the shoulder. "Great."

Back at the front, Justin removed the sheets from the printer box and added them to the growing stack. The issue this week would be thirty-six pages, a respectable edition. Their circulation was hovering around fifteen thousand—nothing grand, but not shabby, either. The split of sixty percent ads and forty percent editorial was a good mix. Scanning the pasteboard of the front page, he nodded with satisfaction.

"Here are the proofed pages you wanted, Justin," Rachel said, as she handed them to him. "Are the rest ready for me to go over?"

He picked up the next group of four and held them out but didn't hand them right over. "Wait a minute." With a knuckle, he wiped an ink smudge from her cheek just under her left eye. "Occupational hazard," he said, with a smile.

This was the first day she'd spent at the *Gazette* working really hard, and Rachel felt pleasantly tired, but very useful. She reached up to swipe at a spot on his chin. "You, too, boss," she told him.

It was the first time she'd voluntarily touched him, Justin thought, as he got lost in the green of her eyes. "Thanks."

"You're welcome," she answered, her voice husky.

"Damn!" The uncharacteristic curse came from Sid.

All three of them hurried to his side.

"Our new typesetter's jammed, and just when I was nearly finished." Sid ran an ink-stained hand over his balding head.

By the time they fixed the machine and all the galleys were dry and pasted up, it was past seven. Almost at a run, Matt jumped in his pickup truck and set out for Kingsville and the print shop, where Justin had alerted them that he was on his way. Mumbling wearily, Sid, who'd been in since eight that morning, bid them good-night and headed for home. Justin turned to Rachel who was examining the wax on her hands.

"Why don't you wash up, and I'll take you out for a sandwich or something? You were a big help today."

Rachel looked down at her rumpled clothes and knew that she wasn't dressed for fine dining and in no mood to eat at the tavern, where too many curious eyes waited. And there was her resolution to avoid being alone with Justin. "I don't think so, but thanks."

"Come on. A booth at Edna's, a cold beer, and a BLT." He touched her arm, wanting to, needing to. "If you're afraid to be alone with me, I could call Katie from Pop's and have her join us."

Now he was reading her mind. Actually it was more that she was afraid of how she felt when she was with him. Still, she was hungry, and the diner would have other guests. She turned toward the rest room. "I'll be right out."

With a victory smile, Justin called to check on his daughter while Rachel washed up.

* * *

Seated across from Justin in the last booth along the back wall, Rachel sipped from her beer glass while he tipped his head back and drank straight from the bottle. It was still in the seventies outside, but fall brought an early dusk that had the streetlights already on. An elderly couple sat finishing up at a windowed booth, and two teenage girls were at the counter toying with chocolate sodas.

"I don't know how she manages these long hours at her age," Rachel commented, as Edna left them to turn in their order to her cook.

"She's amazing, all right," Justin said sincerely. "And loyal to a fault. If Edna decides you're worthwhile, she'll stick with you forever."

"Like Pop. He's a wonderful man. How long has his wife been dead?"

"About twenty years. I was just a boy, maybe twelve, when my grandmother died. A heart attack. They'd been together thirty years or so."

She ran her finger around the rim of the glass absently, her eyes on his face. "Must be hard to lose a mate." She let the thought hang in the air, wondering if he'd pick up on it. Though she hated to ask, she was curious about his marriage. In all her chatterings, Katie had never mentioned her mother.

"Sometimes."

All right, so she'd have to nudge him. What could he do but tell her to mind her own business? "Tell me about Katie's mother."

He'd sensed this coming. It wasn't that he didn't want to talk about his past, but rather that no one had asked in a very long time, and he had to gather his thoughts. "It was one of those college elopements that never should have taken place. Leona was very beautiful with dark hair and eyes as blue as Katie's. Her family, the Stewarts, is very wealthy. Oil, silver, newspapers, and even a television station or two. My family had a few bucks, but nothing to compare to hers. She was an only child, and they'd spoiled her rotten, but I was twenty-one when we met, and I couldn't see it then. Neither side wanted us to marry, but right after graduation, we ran off to a justice of the peace. Sometimes, we should listen to our families." He took another swallow of his beer.

"Not a marriage made in heaven, eh?" Rachel wasn't surprised. It was the only kind she'd ever witnessed up close.

Justin went on, gazing at the brown bottle in his hand but seeing the past. "Hardly that. I was determined to make something of myself so that Leona's parents wouldn't feel she'd married beneath herself. I got a job on one of my father-in-law's Texas newspapers, worked my way up to investigative reporter, and then foreign correspondent. That meant a lot of traveling, a lot of nights away from home, which didn't please Leona at all. Especially after Katie was born."

"You were living in Dallas?"

"Yes. Her daddy had built us a big house that I hated. But I wasn't in it much, and when I did come home, we quarreled most of the time. Katie was my only bright spot. Leona complained that she hated being left alone, but I didn't listen. I had this burning need to make my mark in the world. I didn't see and wouldn't acknowledge that she had needs, too."

Edna chose that moment to deliver their sandwiches, but noticing that they were involved in a serious conversation, she quickly withdrew.

Rachel saw Justin's hand curl tightly around the beer bottle and thought she ought to prod him to finish. "So what happened?"

Justin drained the bottle and leaned back. "I came home unexpectedly one night and found she'd hired a sitter and was out. I waited and she finally came home, all drunk and messed up. She told me that she'd been going out a lot, but that it was my fault for leaving her alone so much. She started crying, bolted out the door, and jumped into her car. I ran after her, barely made it inside before she pulled away. I tried to get her to stop, but she wouldn't listen. There was a crash."

Instinctively Rachel reached for his hand, feeling his remembered pain. She'd imagined that his wife had died of an illness. What she was hearing was much harder to live with.

"Leona died, and I wound up in the hospital for six weeks. Ruptured spleen, broken clavicle, internal injuries. The Stewarts came to see me and told me not to worry, that they'd take care of Katie while I recovered. She was a baby, only two. I relaxed. I shouldn't have."

"Why, what did they do?" Rachel withdrew her hand and waited for the rest.

"I found out the day I was released from the hospital that they were fighting me for custody of Katie, and they have pots of money." Noticing the sandwich as if for the first time, Justin picked up a quarter and took a disinterested taste.

She could only imagine the horror of that. "But you obviously won."

He shook his head. "Not at first. They claimed I was an unfit father, always gone, even hinting that I'd caused Leona's death. My own father was dead, my mother already remarried and living out of the country. I had very little money or support. So I did something I'm ashamed of. I ran.''

Rachel swallowed bacon and toast and tasted a familiar unease. She, too, had run away from trouble once, and had her own regrets to live with.

Justin went on. ''I left the country, free-lancing in England. I tried to bury myself in work, but Katie's little face wouldn't leave my mind. I'd been too young to spot Leona's immaturity and too self-centered to see that my marriage was falling apart. And I'd been far too trusting of the Stewarts. I'd always ignored my problems, or run from them. But I couldn't keep running from Katie. I couldn't let those people raise her.''

''So you came back,'' she guessed, giving him time to pause and eat.

Swallowing, he nodded. ''Right. Pop helped me get my act together, sent me money and gave me moral support. It took two years, but I won her back. Then Pop coaxed us to move to Schyler, saying he was ready to do less work and more fishing.'' Justin shook his head affectionately. ''The old rascal.''

Pushing her near-empty plate away, Rachel smiled. ''He has a way of offering things and making it seem as if you'd be doing him the favor, when in fact, he's doing you one.''

He'd thought she'd seen through Pop's job offer. ''But he only does that for people he really cares for.''

Rachel dropped her eyes and fussed with her spoon. ''I care about him, too.''

He decided she didn't say that about many people. He reached for her hand, wanting to say something more. But when she looked up, he couldn't. So he just held on, letting his eyes speak for him.

''How about another beer, folks? Or maybe a piece of pie?'' Edna asked, coming up to their booth.

Rachel quickly pulled her hand free. "Not for me, Edna. It was delicious."

Justin was surprised to see he'd eaten everything on his plate. He glanced up and saw that while they'd been eating and talking, everyone else had left. "I think we'll just pay our check and let you close up, Edna."

Rachel stood looking out the window while Justin was busy at the register. She heard the loud roar of an engine before the car came into view. Instantly she recognized Theo Quincy's big white Cadillac as it paused in front of the diner. Motor idling, Theo leaned an elbow out the open window and stared directly into her eyes. Her heart leaped to her throat.

Justin came up behind her, his solid presence a comfort. Yet she couldn't prevent the shiver that raced up her spine, not even when he touched her shoulder reassuringly.

Theo yanked the cigarette from between his lips and hurled it through the window, the lighted end arcing as it hit the ground. His eyes narrowed, and his lips twisted into an unflattering leer, before he stepped on the gas. The big car roared down Main Street.

Heart thumping, Rachel watched the Cadillac's tail-lights disappear from sight. She hadn't realized she'd been hugging herself in reaction. Slowly she relaxed her grip on her arms and felt like sagging to the floor. The menacing way Theo had looked at her had drained the blood from her face. What more did he want from her?

Justin was well aware of the effect that seeing Theo had had on her. Saying good-night to Edna, he took Rachel's elbow and walked outside with her. "Come on. I'll walk you home."

Ordinarily she'd have refused. But she was too un-nerved to protest and suddenly grateful for his company.

The evening hadn't cooled off much since they'd entered, Justin thought. The shops on Main Street were all closed, and even Herb's Gas Station was dark and quiet. But as they approached the parking lot of the tavern, he saw a half-dozen cars angling this way and that. "Looks like Gloria's place is still going strong," he said, hoping a little normal conversation would relax Rachel's nerves.

"Every night until two," Rachel commented, needing to talk about something so she could block out her black thoughts. "She's put in this wide-screen TV since Bart died and added that huge antenna that drags in sporting events from all over. Keeps the place packed."

"Gloria isn't still waitressing?"

"She's down there nearly every night till closing. Probably not carrying trays, but she can't seem to stay away. A habit, I guess."

They walked around the side of the tavern to the wooden stairs that led up to the apartment. Rachel turned to thank him, but he placed a hand at her back and started up. "You really don't have to see me right inside the door." She'd always fought her battles alone. She wanted his protection but was afraid to trust his motives.

Justin glanced around but couldn't see the white Cadillac anywhere. "I'll feel better if I do." He waited until she came alongside him on the narrow stairwell. "Theo hasn't been bothering you, has he?"

"I've only seen him once before tonight, parked across the street over there, staring up at our porch." The remembered incident caused her hands to be less than steady as she unlocked the door and stepped inside.

Justin followed. Someone had left a lamp turned on low on an end table. The room was small, sparsely furnished. Through the arch, he could see flowers in a vase on the kitchen table. The place smelled of onions and beer, probably had for years. Music drifted up, thrumming with a heavy beat.

On top of the television set was a framed photo of a younger Gloria, her arm around two small boys. Off to the side and back a bit was a thin girl of about ten with long, blond hair. Funny how even then, Rachel had stood apart.

Tossing her keys and purse on the couch, Rachel stood with her back to him. She wanted him to go; she wanted him to stay.

"Why is Theo Quincy trying to rattle you, Rachel?" he asked softly. It wasn't the reporter questioning this time. It was the man inexplicably drawn to protect a fragile woman.

"I wish I knew." Her hands at her sides clenched and unclenched, despair etched in her words.

He touched her shoulders and turned her to face him. "Tell me what happened that day in the woods. I want to help you shake him, to take away the reason he keeps hounding you. And I can't do that unless I know."

Closing her eyes, she shook her head wearily. "He won't stop, not ever. He blames me for his brother's death, no matter that the jury freed me. You can't help. No one can."

He tightened his fingers on her arms. "You're letting him get to you. That's just what he wants, for you to break down." He'd covered enough cases to know that that was how bullies worked. And this particular bully had the backing of half the town.

"I don't know what to do. I've got to stay until Curt comes home, and yet, I don't know if I can stand it. He did this last time, before I left. He and his father followed me everywhere, harassed me, made it impossible for me to stay. They want to drive me away again." She was trembling now, trying to stop but unable to.

He gentled his hands on her, rubbing her arms. "I wish you'd let yourself trust me. I won't let anything happen to you."

She raised her eyes to his, blinking to keep back the tears so ready to fall. "Even you can't stop Theo Quincy with all his family's money and power."

He tried for a bit of levity. "Haven't you heard that the pen is mightier than the sword?"

But Rachel was in no mood for humor. "But he doesn't do anything you can write about or have him arrested for. He just *watches and waits.*" Her mouth quivered with her effort at control. "Why won't he let me be?"

Justin had no answer so he gave her none. Instead he slowly gathered her close to the warmth of his body, touching her hair as he cradled her head on his shoulder.

She was rigid, her skin cold, her hands balled into fists. She trembled, blinking back tears, fighting her demons. She closed her eyes, willing the memories to recede, the fears to lessen.

He stroked her back, his voice low and reassuring. "It's all right. Hang on to me. You're safe with me."

Safe with him. She'd been safe with no man, ever. Yet there was something about Justin Wheeler that made her relax. Slowly, hesitantly, her fists unclenched, and her hands moved up to rest on his chest. The fear clutching at her stomach muscles gradually disappeared. She eased back to look up at him.

Here was patience and gentleness and compassion. She'd not experienced any of those up close in a man before. Here was tenderness cloaked in strength, an irresistible combination. Too moved to resist, she opened to him.

Justin brushed his lips across hers in what could barely be called a kiss. There was no demand, only a soothing warmth that slowly spread through her. There was no pressure, even as his tongue hesitantly traced the outline of her lips. Sighing, she melted into him as she'd never done before.

His blood heating, Justin forced himself to take it slow, to keep it gentle. Since meeting her, he'd wanted her here in his arms, he'd admitted to himself days ago. But passion was not what she needed now. She was offering him something more valuable than her surrender, more fragile than her kiss. She was offering her trust, which he felt certain she seldom had done. He would push back his own pounding needs and give her the comfort she sought and no more. For now.

Her hands moved to his shoulders, then crept around to touch the nape of his neck. Her soft body molded to his as he struggled with the jolt of reaction. He inhaled the sweet, womanly scent of her as her mouth clung to his. She was using him to distract herself, and he was a willing victim. But, as he lifted his head and edged back from her, he realized something he hadn't known before tonight.

He wanted to be far more than a distraction to Rachel Hathaway.

Drawing in a shaky breath, Rachel brushed back her hair and struggled with a wave of embarrassment. She'd all but begged the man to comfort her, to kiss her. Where was her cool detachment, her stiff pride, her resolutions about noninvolvement? She stepped back, trying to recall her firm resolve.

"I'm sorry," she whispered into the stillness of the room. "That shouldn't have happened. It was a mistake."

He'd watched her fight off the effects of the kiss, to come up with a reasonable explanation she could live with. But he wasn't buying it. He'd felt her dormant passion just un-

der the surface and knew that it would have taken only another, deeper kiss, another lingering moment, and he could
have set it free. And she knew it, too.

Justin placed his hand on the doorknob before giving her
a crooked smile. "No, Rachel. A mistake is something you
regret."

Chapter Five

"The quality of the *Gazette* isn't in question here," Pop said, as he leaned back in his leather swivel chair. "The paper doesn't need improving, nor would more people buy it if you did find a way. Advertising's at the highest peak we can expect from this limited area. So there's only one other way to up our income."

"And what would that be?" Justin asked from his desk across the room. It was four o'clock on a lazy Thursday afternoon, and they were brainstorming, trying to come up with new ideas on how to make more money. He had a lot of respect for his grandfather's opinions and methods. Though he'd never published more than a small-town weekly, Pop knew more about marketing and honorable journalism than any ten men on big-city newspapers.

"More distribution to stores. I say we order more glass newsstand dumps and get Matt to go around, say in a fifty-mile radius, and see how many more gas stations and fast-food stops and barbershops and such places we can sign up to offer the *Gazette* each Wednesday."

"At the same commission rate?"

"Bump it up if you have to for those beyond a certain radius. A piece of the pie is better than none, and it's still cheaper than mailings."

Justin nodded his agreement. "We've cut the mailing list way down. Only a few go out to special-interest ..."

The front door opened noisily, cutting Justin off and causing both men to look up. Roy Quincy stood there, his Stetson pushed back on his balding head, his florid face redder than ever. "Where is she?" he bellowed.

Justin braced himself. Roy was obviously upset, and he wasn't the sort who discussed his gripes calmly. Slowly he got to his feet and leaned a hip against the side of his desk. "Where's who?" Only he and Pop were in the office, but he had a pretty good idea who Roy was seeking.

"That Hathaway woman. Heard tell you hired her. Damn fool thing to do. Why didn't you just let her go back where she belongs?"

Pop's voice in contrast to Roy's was low and composed. "What would you be wanting with Rachel Hathaway, Roy?"

"She's making trouble again, and I've come to tell you. We need to run that woman right out of Schyler." Roy's beefy hand as he swabbed at his sweaty brow was shaking with anger.

"Suppose you tell us what she's done," Justin suggested.

"I just come from a school board meeting. Afterward I talked with Floyd Upton, the president. Man was pale as a ghost, and I asked him why." Roy grabbed a chair and pulled it out, easing his large frame into it before continuing. "Floyd got a threatening note in the mail yesterday, and it sure as hell came from Rachel Hathaway."

Justin tried for a reasonable tone, though he had trouble imagining Rachel pleading with the school board president to reconsider her for that teaching position, and certainly not in a threatening manner. "What did the note say?"

"That Floyd's close friendship with a certain young lady would be spread all over the front page of the *Gazette* unless he persuaded the board to hire a recent teacher applicant. Hell, there's only been one recent applicant."

Something is very fishy here, Justin thought. "Do you have the note?"

"Floyd showed it to me, then we burned it. He's been married thirty years. If his wife ever got wind of Floyd messing around, no telling what she'd do. You got to stop that Hathaway woman."

Pop had had enough. "Roy, most of Schyler knows that Floyd's been messing with Ella Mae Ferguson for years, and if his wife doesn't know it then it's because she chooses to look the other way. But to suggest that we'd print something so outlandish on the front page of the *Gazette* is ridiculous."

"Rachel wouldn't resort to blackmail to get a job," Justin told Roy. "Someone else wrote that note."

Roy shook his head, then his fist. "Ain't nobody had anything to gain 'cept Rachel. Mark my words, that woman's trouble."

"It would seem someone wants us to think so," Justin said absently.

Roy's pale eyes narrowed. "Listen, Justin Wheeler. You're new here, and you don't know that woman like the rest of us do. She killed my boy, Tyrone, did you know that? I heard you been spending time with her, but you best watch yourself.''

Justin straightened, his anger rising. "I don't want to hear any more. You can't produce a note, so how do we even know there was one? I suggest you tell Floyd to calm down, and you do the same. As to who I spend time with, that's *my* business. Rachel Hathaway is a good person who..."

The door opened a second time, and a child's laughter could be heard as Rachel and Katie walked in, ice-cream cones in hand.

Even above Katie's laughter, Rachel had heard the last part of what Justin had said. Her eyes flicked from him to Roy and she turned pale, her arm slipping automatically about Katie to keep her from getting too close to a Quincy.

In the sudden silence, Roy got to his feet, shoving his chair back with a loud, scraping sound, followed by his sharp grunt of disapproval. "You two crazy, letting that little girl stroll around with that woman? No telling what she's telling her, what she's teaching her."

"That's enough." Justin's voice wasn't loud, but it was strong and firm enough to get Roy's attention. "I think you'd better leave."

As Rachel and Katie backed away from the door, Roy moved to it, fuming. "You wait and see. You're going to regret giving that woman a job, keeping her here." He strode out, his booted feet loud on the wood floor, and slammed the door behind him.

An uncomfortable silence resumed as Rachel looked at both men in turn, her eyes demanding an explanation.

Pop cleared his throat. "Katie, let's you and me go for a walk, what do you say?" He took the confused child's hand.

"What's wrong, Grandpa?" Katie asked.

"Nothing we can't fix." He opened the door and scooted her out, following close behind her.

Rachel's eyes hadn't left Justin's face. "Tell me what he said," she asked coolly.

Justin told her, quickly and unemotionally, aware of her rigid control as she listened. It was the same way she'd held herself a week ago when he'd walked her home and kissed that mouth that she was now struggling to keep from quivering. And he wished he could pull her into his arms again and relieve her distress. But he knew she wouldn't welcome his touch at the moment.

"Do you believe Roy and Floyd Upton?"

"No. Maybe there was a note, maybe not. But I certainly don't believe you sent it if there was." He ran a hand through his hair thoughtfully. "But except for the Quincys, I just don't know who would have anything to gain by sending such a note to Floyd."

"Except me, you mean?" It was happening again. The memories came rushing back, of another time, in this very town. No one had believed her then, either. Rachel felt as if she were suffocating.

Suddenly aware that she was still holding a dripping cone, she wrapped the messy confection in the napkin she held and tossed it into the nearest wastebasket, her appetite gone. From her desk, she picked up her purse and moved to the door.

"Wait." Justin was at her side, his hands on her arms, turning her around. "Where are you going? I told you I believed you."

Her eyes as she looked up at him were dark green and filled with pain. "Do you?"

"Yes. Why can't you trust me?"

"I think that's my line. Let me go, Justin."

He dropped his hands and watched her walk out the door. He felt a childish desire to hit something very hard. Instead he stood with his hands balled in his pockets, wondering what else he could have said to ease her mind.

The atmosphere in the offices of the *Gazette* had shifted to chilly by Friday morning. Matt wasn't in, nor was Pop, but Sid noticed it almost immediately. And Justin certainly did.

It wasn't that Rachel was sulking or uncooperative. She went about her work quietly, answered when spoken to and, to the undiscerning eye, she was the same as always. Only the light had gone out of her eyes, and she'd lost her smile somewhere between yesterday afternoon and this morning.

Try as he would, Justin couldn't think of a way to bring her around without rehashing the whole scene. Instead he chose to work on an article he'd been putting together on the upcoming election, to be available if she wanted to talk, but to not pressure her. He pretended not to notice her sudden formality. However, by late afternoon, when the only person she'd been friendly to had been Katie during the child's brief visit, it was getting to him.

So he decided to do something about it.

Along about four o'clock, after Sid had left for the day, he sauntered over to her desk. "Have you seen this?" he asked as he placed a flyer in front of her.

Rachel studied the leaflet inviting one and all to a political rally tonight at the town hall, where Theo Quincy would be announcing that he was running for sheriff. The sheet went on to list all the civic organizations Theo belonged to and described his interest in making Schyler into the best little town in the Southwest. In the corner was a picture of Theo, his arm around a small, unsmiling woman, with two young children seated in front of them. Schyler had to be really hard up for political aspirants, she thought. Keeping her expression even, Rachel looked up at Justin. "Interesting."

"Sheriff Duncan's retiring, and so far Theo's the only one who's announced that he wants the job."

"Not too many will be brave enough to run against a Quincy."

"I'm going tonight to cover the rally for our next issue. I was wondering if you'd like to go along."

She sat back and regarded him. Was he testing her, or did he have another reason behind the request? "You don't think you can handle taking notes on his speech all by yourself?"

Justin sat on the edge of her desk. At least she was talking, and she was interested. "Sure I can. But it'd be nice to have a fresh viewpoint. There'll probably be a question-and-answer session. I want to see if Theo will be provoked into expressing his real opinions—if he has any—and I want to gauge how the people of Schyler feel about him. I always think two heads are better than one."

"If I go with you, the very sight of me might provoke Theo into saying all kinds of things." She shook her head. "I don't think I'd enjoy being at the center of a three-ring circus."

"Then again, your presence might be just the thing that would expose Theo and show the town what he's really like. Bigoted, judgmental, biased, pompous. Certainly not the sort we want wearing a badge around here." Justin touched her arm, a little surprised when she didn't pull back. "I can't promise it won't be upsetting, but I can promise that I'll be right there with you."

She wouldn't tell him again that merely being in the same town as Theo Quincy upset her. Maybe Justin was right. If she could do one small thing to keep that man out of office, it would be worth a little aggravation. And there was the way Justin's words—that he would be right there with her—made her feel. Warm all over, despite all her well-intentioned resolutions to stay away from him. "All right. I'll go."

He nodded. "I'll stop by for you at seven."

The rally was already under way as Justin and Rachel slipped in the back door of the town hall. About thirty people sat in the theaterlike arena facing the front. Four men were seated on folding chairs on the small stage, while a fifth—Schyler's current sheriff, a man named Duncan—was up at the podium extolling the virtues of the man who was hoping to replace him. In the front row, in an obvious show of support, was Theo's mother, Muriel Quincy, looking older and more frail than she remembered, Rachel thought. The thin woman next to her was undoubtedly Theo's wife, accompanied by his two young children.

"Sounds like Duncan's a buddy of the Quincys," Rachel whispered, as they took seats in the last row and listened for a few minutes.

"He is. Quincy money got Duncan elected years ago and kept him in office. In return, the sheriff makes sure what Roy wants Roy gets." The disgust in Justin's voice was evident even in his low tones. "I've hinted as much in several editorials—especially when Duncan was instrumental in getting some land Roy owns rezoned in order to reduce the tax assessment—but I've never been able to get solid proof."

Rachel found her stomach muscles quivering from tension as she sat listening to the forum. Roy Quincy sat on the end, his gray Stetson worn the way she remembered he always wore it—shoved back on his head. She was aware the moment his roaming gaze spotted her, and felt her blood run cold as he leaned over to point her out to Theo.

Again dressed in white, Theo's beefy face reddened as he stared at her, then at Justin. Coming here might have been a mistake, she thought, as memories flooded her mind. Memories of when father and son had sat side by side in a courtroom and looked at her with the same barely repressed hatred.

She sat very still as the other two men—Nathan Fredericks, the chairman of the board of directors of Schyler Bank and Trust, and Floyd Upton, head of the school board—took their turns endorsing Theo's candidacy. Only Justin's solid presence next to her kept her from bolting out the door and away from this charade.

Then Theo was lumbering up to the podium amid a smattering of applause. He began by thanking the speakers for their support and kind words. Next he rambled on about how much the town of Schyler meant to him and his family and how dedicated a public servant he would be, if elected. Pausing, his small eyes scanned the crowd, finally narrowing in Rachel's direction.

Here it comes, she thought, bracing herself.

Theo cleared his throat noisily. "Being sheriff of my hometown means more to me than catching an occasional speeding car passing through and keeping our security protection high so our businesses won't be broken into. It means keeping our community safe from outside influences for the sake of our kids—yours and mine." Here, he paused and smiled pointedly to where his two children sat squirming in boredom.

"Allowing riffraff to move here and take up residency among good people is a mistake," Theo's voice boomed out.

Justin felt more than saw Rachel tense up. His eyes never leaving Theo's face, he reached to take her hand in his, finding her fingers damp and trembling.

"Permitting murderers and undesirables to live among us and poison the minds and morals of our kids is a mistake. We need to speak up, to band together, to rid our town of these men—*or women*—who aren't fit to reside alongside decent folks." His heavy fist came down on the podium to emphasize his point as he warmed to his message. "If we have to ride them out of town at gunpoint, so be it."

Justin saw several people in the audience look around uncomfortably as if wondering who and what Theo was discussing, while a handful of others applauded in approval. His hand tightened on Rachel's as he waited for Theo to finish.

"I promise you when I become sheriff, nobody who has committed a crime and not been made to pay for it will be allowed to stay in Schyler. I promise you no man or woman who threatens one of our own to gain personal favors will be accepted here. And nobody who hires such individuals and encourages them will be looked upon with favor, either."

Floyd Upton started the applause, which rapidly caught on and continued, in spite of the fact that very few attendees were in on Theo's veiled references. After all, Justin thought, the man was promising to rid their town of every evil, real or imagined, so what was not to applaud? He risked a glance toward Rachel and saw she was tight-lipped but composed.

"Do you want to leave?" he asked quietly.

What more could he say at this point? "No. Let's hear the questions."

The questions, Justin realized, were oddly unrelated to Theo's speech. As fervent as Theo had been in his quest to rid Schyler of nebulous undesirables, the people gathered together wanted to know about more tangible issues, such as the allotted number of deputies to police the area, and the proposed rerouting of Highway 77, which would cut down on traffic but eat into local business revenue. But the hottest local debate was between environmentalists advocating the continued protection of the wildlife sanctuary on the outskirts of town, and developers who saw a chance to throw up a batch of condos and make a pile of quick money.

"That sort of thing would change the whole flavor of our town." Chet Jennings who owned a nearby cattle ranch stood up to have his say. "I don't want Schyler to expand and have a lot of city folks build second homes around us. I moved my family here years ago to get away from that. That sanctuary's next to Quincy land, Theo, and I want to know if you become sheriff which side you're on—the developers or those of us who like things just the way they are."

Justin leaned close to Rachel. "Let's see how Theo plans to keep those two opposing forces happy."

The discussion grew heated as a representative of a developer chimed in with his opinion.

"I'll bet the Quincys don't give a hang about preserving wildlife if there's a buck to be made otherwise," Rachel whispered back.

Trying to juggle both sides, Theo wiped his damp face with a white handkerchief. "When the time comes, we'll work this out to the satisfaction of all parties." Nervously he dug for his gold case and drew out one of his imported cigarettes, lighting it quickly and drawing in deeply. Again, his gaze shifted toward Rachel. "My first project is going to be cleaning up this town, as I mentioned earlier. For instance, there's that eyesore, the tavern. I'm all for shutting it down. A wild bunch of drunks hang out there. Those Hathaways cater to every form of lowlife, getting rich on the hard-earned money our ranch hands dish out for watered-down drinks, greasy hamburgers, and Lord-knows-what-all. My main priority's going to be to rid Schyler of drinkers and loose women. I'm going to see to it. Trust me."

The applause was hesitant at first, then louder.

"I never trust a man who says *trust me*," Justin said to Rachel. "Have you had enough yet?"

"More than enough." The anger inside her was like a living, breathing thing. It was one thing to attack her, which she'd rather expected Theo to do, but it was quite another to pick on Gloria's respectable little saloon. She stood, only then noticing that her hand was still clutching Justin's. Pulling free, she turned, made her way to the door and outside, and took a long, steadying breath of clean air.

Justin came up alongside her. "Pretty funny. Theo's been a drinker and womanizer since his teens, or so I've heard, and he wants to clean up the town."

"I think Schyler's in for trouble." If she said more, she'd say too much, Rachel decided. "Look, I hope you won't mind, but I've got to go back to the apartment and change into my running shoes. I've found through the years that running's about the only thing that helps when I feel the way I do right now." Angry, hurt, frustrated, impotent. The look on his face told her he understood when she hadn't expected him to, surprising her.

"Where do you like to run?"

Her favorite route locally had once been a zigzag path through Kemper Woods near Gloria's apartment. But after Tyrone's death, she hadn't stepped into the woods. "I don't care. Anywhere. Along Lake Willow, maybe."

He knew the area. A tree-lined path that bordered the grassy bank of the lake. Dark and deserted. "I'll go with you."

"You needn't, really." The need to run, to rid herself of angry energy, was greater than her need for caution right now. Surely Theo wouldn't leave his rally and go looking for her.

Justin took her elbow, leading them toward Gloria's apartment. He'd run in less suitable outfits than the cotton shirt, jeans and deck shoes he had on. "I'll wait while you change. I don't want you running alone tonight, not with the Quincys all over the place."

The Quincys again. Always the Quincys, wrecking her life, messing up her plans. But she couldn't afford another incident, so she went along with Justin's suggestion.

It took her only a couple of minutes to run upstairs, change into a loose top, jogging pants and shoes, and meet him at the bottom of the stairwell. Silently they set out at a comfortable pace as a rumble of thunder warned of a possible storm approaching. It wasn't until the lake was in sight that Rachel increased her speed and moved ahead, leaving him to follow on the narrow path.

It was twilight, a time of transition, when shadows deepen and night birds come out of hiding. Rachel kept her eyes on the unfamiliar ground, watching for tree roots or large rocks as she ran. Trying to empty her mind, she concentrated only on putting one foot in front of the other, on the pull of muscles growing lax from several weeks of missed exercise. It felt good. Yes, this is what she'd needed to cleanse her mind and loosen her limbs.

She could hear Justin's heavier footsteps not far behind her and took comfort in his protective presence. She was beginning to lean a bit too much on his protection and disliked the circumstances that had made it so. Yet running here alone would be as foolishly naive as the shortcuts she used to take through the woods as a trusting teenager, when she'd believed the world was basically a safe place. She knew better now, and the lesson had been hard won.

The hooting of an owl high in a tree startled Rachel, but she kept on going. A flash of lightning slashed through the darkening sky over the restless lake waters. The pungent smell of decayed oranges long ago fallen from overhead trees wafted on the wind as it picked up in volume. She'd been in too big a hurry to tie back her hair and tossed her head now, swirling the strands from her face.

She couldn't have said how long she ran, only that by the time she reached the far rim of the lake, she was tired and breathing hard, yet she felt better. Slowing, she finally stopped and dropped onto the damp grass, sucking in gulps of air as she let her heart rate slow.

Justin flopped down beside her, equally winded. He'd watched her run off her rage and could see in the waning light that most of the tension had slipped from her face. She'd been like a loose-limbed young colt, her feet hitting the ground in steady thumps, her slender form streaking along with scarcely a pause. He'd thought her too softly rounded to look athletic, yet it would seem she was no stranger to exercise. "You do this quite often?" he asked.

Rachel rolled onto her stomach in a protective gesture, feeling too vulnerable to his penetrating eyes while lying on her back. "Not lately, but regularly at home." She glanced over and saw him stretch his arms up over his head. "You're in pretty good shape. Do you run?"

"I used to years ago when I worked in London. I hate living in big cities, and I didn't feel comfortable joining one of those English clubs with exercise equipment. So I'd take the underground to some small town, like Hampstead Heath, and run up into the hills. Sometimes I'd stop and get bread and fruit and cheese and spend the afternoon poking around. The English have these great little walled gardens. Then when I returned to my cramped little apartment, I could stand it for another week.''

The moon was playing hide-and-seek among the clouds, and in its shifting light, she saw the strong line of his square chin with its day's growth of beard. Inexplicably she wanted to reach over and touch him, to run her hands over his face. Reaching instead to pull at a blade of grass, she struggled to keep her voice level. ''You were all alone?''

''Mostly. I was a married man back then, and Leona was in Texas.''

''Didn't you have male friends?''

He shrugged. ''It's hard making friends when you're always going off on assignments, leaving the city, returning weeks later. Foreign correspondents and free-lancers lead a transient existence. The nomadic life doesn't lend itself to deep friendships.''

Talking about him was safer than thinking about herself. ''But you've been in Schyler three years, and I'm sure you have many friends here now.''

''I suppose. Business friends and social acquaintances.'' He rose to lean on an elbow closer to where she lay, as another crack of thunder sounded overhead. ''What about you? Lots of friends in California, another reason you're anxious to return?''

Far fewer than he'd probably believe, after living there ten years. ''Like you, a couple.''

''Many men friends?'' He could almost see her stiffen visibly.

''Yes, hundreds.'' Her voice was clipped and cool.

"You don't like men?" He found the thought inconceivable in a woman as attractive as Rachel, yet he'd noticed a wariness about her in the presence of most men.

"I've never felt men were essential to my life." Until recently, she'd not thought overly long about any one man in a romantic sense. Now, it seemed there was one who dominated her thoughts all too much, and the knowledge didn't please her. The kiss they'd shared last week, while not exactly devoid of passion, had been initiated as a comforting gesture. Yet she'd lain awake nights, imagining what it would be like to touch and be touched, to give in to that smoldering desire she'd only just sampled.

If he hadn't kissed her the other evening, hadn't felt that quick rush of response, he might have believed she meant it. "Isn't there any one special man back in California?" Justin knew he was being blunt and somewhat rude, but he badly wanted to know.

Rachel kept her eyes on her fingers busily tearing up the grass as she shook her head.

"Why, Rachel? A woman as lovely as you must attract many men."

"It takes two, and I'm simply not interested. Men aren't—"

"Essential. So you said. That's not the real reason. What is?"

Rachel looked out across the shimmering water, wondering how much to tell this persistent man. "I suppose the real reason is that I don't trust men. Except maybe your grandfather."

"Because your father walked away?"

She shrugged. "That's probably when it started. I remember the wonderful promises he made when he was sober. But he forgot them all when he drank. Then when all that happened with Tyrone Quincy, my mother insisted I stay, that I'd be proven innocent and the people would know I'd been a victim, not a criminal. But the Quincy men saw to it that the people who live here and rely on them for jobs didn't forgive my so-called transgression. You heard Theo tonight. To him and most everyone here, I'm an undesirable, a murderer, a loose woman.''

''You surely aren't judging all men by the yardstick of an alcoholic father and the Quincys, are you?''

Rachel sighed. ''You want to hear about others? How about the professor I had in college, the one I went to when I knew I was in danger of failing economics to ask for help? He told me, in no uncertain terms, that if I would be *cooperative* I could expect to pass and even bring up my grade-point average.''

''There's always a few men like that around who—''

''A few? I've run into more than a dozen since I left home. So please don't try to defend the male population to me. As I said earlier, your grandfather is about the only man I know who is truly trustworthy with no ulterior motives. And a teacher I had years ago in high school. That about sums it up.''

He didn't know whether to be amused or angry. ''Where does that leave me?''

She swung her eyes to meet his. She'd been wondering the same thing. ''Where *does* it leave you, Justin? What is it you want from me? Everyone wants something. Tell me what it is so we can get it out in the open.''

He reminded himself that she'd been hurt badly, and that none of that had been his doing. He wouldn't react in anger or defensively. He'd simply be honest. ''I want your friendship, the chance to get to know you better, and...'' He paused, wondering how to phrase the rest.

Her eyes widened, became challenging. ''Yes?''

"I can't deny that I'm attracted to you." She released a whoosh of air, as if she'd been holding her breath, and he'd finally said exactly what she'd been expecting. "I wonder if you'll be as honest with me."

"What do you mean?"

"Will you admit that you're attracted, too? That you're interested? And maybe that you're just as surprised by that attraction as I am?"

He'd hit the nail on the head. She could deny it till the cows came home, but there it was. And she wanted to run from the thought, from him.

Rachel felt the first of the raindrops. Just in the nick of time, she thought, and scrambled to her feet. "It's going to storm. We'd better get back."

A vivid streak of lightning flashed above the windswept lake as Justin rose. The clap of thunder that followed had Rachel wincing, then ducking her head as the heavens opened up, and a sudden torrent of rain came rushing down to almost instantly soak them. Turning, she began to run.

She had to get away, to put the guards back up, to protect herself. She had to straighten out the mess her life had become. So many days and nights to get through until she could do something about Gloria, until she could return to the safety of the life she'd built for herself in California.

Her sodden shoes hit the ground with spiraling splashes, and she ran as if the devil himself were after her. And maybe he was. She was all wrong for Justin, couldn't he see that? He had a good life here and she would ruin it, ruin his reputation, his credibility in this town.

It was true that he'd managed to touch something in her that no one else had ever touched. But she would have to steel herself and walk away, before it got out of hand. In less than three months, she'd be leaving, and he'd be staying. What she felt for him was born of desperation for a kind word, a tender gesture. But hadn't she learned the hard way that few men ever meant what they said? She would go, and she would forget him.

She almost believed it.

Justin ran closely behind, annoyed that whenever possible, Rachel chose to run away. Didn't she know that everyone has to stop running sometime? What could he do to convince her that *he* was the one she should be running toward, not away from?

He'd meant it when he'd said he wouldn't let anything happen to her. He would find out what was pushing Theo Quincy to persecute her, and he'd take care of the man one way or another. He wanted to erase the nightmares of her past, to vindicate her, to let her walk unafraid in the streets, head held high. He wanted her to stay in this town, in his life.

Suddenly the storm turned freakish, a torrential downpour that made the path they were following barely visible.

Justin caught up with Rachel, his fingers closing over her arm as he shouted to be heard. "Let's duck over there under the trees until the worst of this passes."

She went, protesting. "You're not supposed to take cover under trees when it's lightning."

He pulled her into the thicket and stopped under a leafy overhang.

"Did you hear me?" Rachel asked, gazing around worriedly.

She was wet, with rainwater beading on her eyelashes and her hair sticking to her head. She was annoyed, she was a little frightened, and she was incredibly beautiful. "I heard you. I'm not supposed to do a lot of things. High on that list, I'm sure, is this." Dipping his head, he pulled her to him and touched his mouth to hers.

"No," Rachel murmured against his mouth. She couldn't let herself slide down that steep tunnel of desire she'd merely glimpsed before. Not tonight. She was too vulnerable out here alone with him and the thundering elements. "I don't want this. I..."

He slanted his mouth to again capture hers, using not the slightest force in the hands that crept up her back. He felt her shudder, felt her lips part a fraction, and he sent his tongue in to taste her more thoroughly.

Feeling herself slipping, Rachel twisted her head, freeing her mouth from his. "No, no!" But the hands that should have been pushing him away were instead restlessly roaming his chest, feeling his heart beat beneath her fingers. She shook her head, her emotions in a jumble of confusion. "I don't want..."

Water dripped from the ends of his hair. His eyes in the dusky darkness were boring into hers, waiting, watching. Rachel felt the ground beneath her tilt. "You don't understand. I don't want you...."

She felt his hands slip under her shirt and skim up the skin of her back, and her knees nearly buckled. Who was she trying to convince? Rachel asked herself as she released a trembling sigh. "Oh, God," she admitted at last, "I *do* want you, and I *wish* I didn't." Rising on tiptoe, she reached for his kiss.

She needed him. What else was there at this moment? Desire suffused her inside as surely as the rain soaked her outside. The force of it struck her as deeply as a lightning bolt might have, taking her out of the realm of all previous experience. She should have dated more, Rachel thought hazily. Should have experienced more so she'd be better able to handle this, to fight this.

But there was no fighting the needs that clawed at her much the same as her hands on his chest gripped his shirt, aching to get closer. She inhaled the dark male scent of him as if she'd been seeking that fascinating aroma all her life. Edgy with awakening passion, she let his mouth make love to hers.

Had he been without the softness of a woman too long? Justin asked himself. Or was it *this* woman and no other who could bring about such an astounding reaction? He'd been isolated in Schyler too long, concentrating on Katie and Pop and the paper, burying his needs. But they were screamingly alive tonight as she leaned into him, her sweet curves settling against him, causing him to moan, half in pain, half in pleasure.

Shaking, Rachel eased back to look into his eyes. Because she'd longed to, she reached up and traced the contours of his face, then shook her head. "This is crazy. This has nowhere to go."

He nodded and felt the moisture drip from his chin. "I know. You don't have to say it. I know you can hardly wait to leave Schyler."

She shifted soggy feet, yet was scarcely aware of the rain still falling on them. "I don't belong here."

"That's not a reason, it's an excuse."

"I don't mix well with men. I'll only hurt you." Why now, with this one man whose loneliness and longing seemed equal to hers?

"I'll risk it." His fingers brushed damp hair from her face, loving the texture of her skin, the desire he could see still simmering in her eyes.

She ran a hand over her wet face. "I never should have come back here."

"I didn't plan this, Rachel, but it's happened."

She tried to muster up some anger. "We can damn well make it un-happen. We can ignore it. I can stop working at the *Gazette.* I can stay away from you."

He trailed a finger down her cheek. "Can you?"

She stood silent, her huge eyes dark on his.

"Can you tell me you don't feel anything for me?"

She let out a trembling sigh. "Wouldn't that be stupid? The question is what to do about it." Absently she saw that the rain was slowing, the storm having run out of steam.

Justin cupped her chin, forcing her eyes to meet his. "Come home with me."

"No." If she let her mind rush ahead with that thought, she'd never be able to stand her ground.

"But you've already said there's no one else in California. So, why not?"

"I can't go with you. I shouldn't even be seen with you." Rachel averted her gaze so he couldn't read her heart's choice in her eyes. She couldn't afford the luxury of doing what she wanted, not in this town. Wordlessly she started back along the path, walking fast but with little energy left for running.

Back at the worn wooden stairs that led to Gloria's apartment, he walked with her up to the covered landing. Ever the gentleman, Justin thought. Only the way he felt about Rachel Hathaway tonight wasn't exactly gentlemanly.

They were both soaking, so she led him inside and hurriedly found a towel for each of them. The jukebox downstairs at the tavern beat out a country-western tune as she turned to look at him. She felt a shiver take her as she became aware of her wet shirt clinging to her breasts, which she was certain he had noticed. She should have stepped away from him right then, but she couldn't seem to move.

There was a dim light burning in the kitchen. Justin caught the faint scent of cigarette smoke and wondered if Gloria was in her room. He took a step closer. Rachel smelled like the autumn rain, like the dark, mysterious night. He brushed a damp strand of hair from her face. "How do you feel about seashells?"

She blinked in surprise. "Seashells?"

"Yeah. The kind you walk along a beach and gather. Katie and I are going to Padre Island tomorrow to hunt some. I know she'd be pleased if you'd come along." He was using his daughter unashamedly, and he didn't even feel guilty.

As invitations went, it wasn't romantic or touching. It was much more. It was so damn *normal,* a day gathering seashells with his daughter. She smiled at him as she took the towel from her hair and tossed it aside. "That sounds like fun."

He nodded toward the kitchen. "That drawing on the side of your refrigerator—I think I know the artist."

"Katie gave it to me."

He'd thought so. "Think she's got the makings of a child prodigy?"

"I wouldn't know. But I love the drawing."

"She's nuts about you, my Katie is." He leaned down to her, vaguely aware of the rain still splashing onto the wooden porch outside the screen door, extremely aware that something was happening here that was as exciting as anything that had ever happened to him. Her warm breath whispered across his face.

"Is that right," she asked, her voice husky.

"Yeah. And so's her father." He leaned closer. "May I kiss you, Rachel?"

No man had ever asked. The few who had dared had taken, not asked. In lieu of what they'd shared back by the lake, it was almost a laughable request. But Rachel wasn't laughing. She understood what he was doing and why. He was asking her to make a conscious choice. More than anything, the plea in his eyes won her over. "Yes," she whispered.

Her lips were cool, but his warmed them quickly. His hands were warm, too, as they slipped under her wet shirt and skimmed along her back. When she moaned low in her throat, he deepened the kiss, wanting her to want him as much as he wanted her.

She felt this kiss down to her toes, felt her blood heat and race through her veins. When his restless hands moved to the front and closed over her chilled breasts, she gripped his shoulders to keep from falling. She felt her flesh grow warm under his loving touch and reached to draw him closer, suddenly filled with an almost painful longing.

From the adjacent bedroom, they heard the unmistakable click of a cigarette lighter. Hastily they pulled apart, both breathing hard.

Justin stepped back slowly, leaving her shaken and breathless. "We'll be by for you around ten. All right?"

Rachel was surprised she could nod without shattering. She waited until he'd gone out and down the slippery steps, then turned and locked the door. Leaning against the painted wood frame, she closed her eyes, touching her swollen lips with trembling fingers. He certainly knew how to make a woman ache.

She smelled cigarette smoke before she heard Gloria come out of her room. Straightening, Rachel opened her eyes and knew there was no hiding her feelings from her mother.

Gloria pulled her robe tighter about her slender frame and stepped closer to her daughter, squinting through the smoke. "He's a good man, one who's been all over the world and decided to live in Schyler. Do you know what you're doing, getting involved with him?"

"Probably not."

Gloria frowned. "It's not too late. You can still walk away."

Rachel's smile was tinged with sadness. "Can I, Mom?" Knowing no answer was coming, she walked to the bathroom and closed the door.

Chapter Six

"The problem is that although Rachel probably knows a lot of men, she hasn't gotten to know any one man very well." Edna eased her wide hips into the booth across from Justin. It was nearly eleven on a cloudy Friday morning, a slow period when the breakfast guests had long gone, and the luncheon crowd hadn't yet arrived.

"That's pretty much how I figured it," Justin replied. He'd stopped in for a cup of Edna's coffee after going through some records at the courthouse for an article he was working on, and she'd come over to chat. In no time, she'd maneuvered the conversation around to Rachel Hathaway. Of course, Rachel had been on his mind more often than not since the evening of the rainstorm a week ago. But he was curious why Edna suddenly seemed anxious to talk about her.

"See, Rachel's basically quite shy," Edna went on, trying to explain, wanting at least one person in this town to understand. "She was around twelve when her body developed all those curves, and she didn't know what to do about it. Gloria was busy trying to keep food on the table, so Rachel'd come to me, confused and crying." Edna shook her head. "The poor little thing insisted on wearing these shapeless, baggy tops, trying to hide herself."

"I didn't know you were that close to her."

"Hell, yes. All three of them kids seemed like my own. Orrin used to eat here more often than home. And little Curt used to come to me after getting one of his countless bloody noses, wanting me to fix him up so his mama wouldn't know he'd been fighting again." She took a sip of her coffee. "But Rachel was always my favorite."

In a relatively short time, she'd become his favorite, too, Justin was well aware. The morning after the storm, he and Katie had picked Rachel up and taken the ferryboat across to North Padre Island. The day had been sunshine perfect. Endless stretches of natural sand dunes, beach morning glories in bloom, shells aplenty to gather, as well as piles of driftwood. They'd even found several flint points from the Karankawa Indians who'd lived there years ago. He'd been hard put to say who'd been more pleased with their findings, Katie or Rachel.

Katie had played in the lazy surf, then they'd spread out a blanket and devoured the picnic lunch Rachel had packed. They'd talked and smiled and laughed. He'd watched Rachel and Katie toss a Frisbee back and forth. He'd watched Rachel teach Katie how to braid her own long hair. He'd watched Rachel because he so enjoyed watching Rachel.

For the first time ever, Justin had felt he'd been on a family outing, something he'd never experienced. As a child, his parents had never taken him, his father too busy, his mother too social. Certainly, when Katie had been a baby, he and Leona had never gone anywhere together to just enjoy the day.

It had felt good. It had felt right.

Yes, Justin thought, he could understand why Rachel was Edna's favorite. "Did you keep in touch with her after she moved?"

"Oh, sure. I'd fly to California a couple of times a year to make sure she was all right. I offered to pay Gloria's way if she'd come with me, but she never did."

Justin had wondered how Rachel had survived on her own, leaving home at the tender age of seventeen, getting a degree, and so on. Now he knew. "You financed Rachel's education, right?"

Edna signaled the cook, who'd been leaning on the counter reading the newspaper, to refill their cups. She waited until he poured and walked away before answering. "I loaned her the money, but she's repaid every cent. Rachel's got a lot of pride."

He still wasn't certain why Edna was telling him all this, unless it was to gain Rachel some allies. However, she was preaching to the converted. "I agree with you. Rachel's a fine person who's been treated badly by many in this town. And now, Theo Quincy seems to be making it his personal project to run her out of town again."

Edna's face turned grim. "Someone should do something about that man."

"Someone's trying to."

Edna's eyebrows rose. "You? Hot damn! Are you on to something? Something you can get him for?"

"Maybe."

"Good, because if Theo becomes sheriff, I just might move the hell away from here, too." She touched Justin's hand, an uncharacteristic gesture. "Rachel needs someone in her corner, someone to clear her name so she can move back here and live in peace.''

Justin shook his head. ''I doubt if she'd ever do that. Too many bad memories. Even if I get something on Theo, his family will still be here.''

''Rachel's not going to be able to leave Gloria, and that woman won't leave Schyler. A hell of a mess.'' She studied her freckled hands a long minute. ''What we need here is the cavalry, the guys in the white hats rushing in.'' She raised her eyes to Justin's face. ''The knight in shining armor to save the day.''

As her message sunk in, a slow grin spread across Justin's face. ''Why, you old romantic, you. And just what makes you think I can make a difference?''

The door opened and a young couple came in, laughing and holding hands, seating themselves at the counter.

Edna's rest period was over, but first she'd give him her answer. ''Because I've got eyes and I see how you look at her. For years I've watched men look at Rachel Hathaway, but your look's different. It's all soft and dreamy. As I said earlier, what she needs is to get to know one man, *one special man,* who wants more than her body.'' Smiling at him, Edna slid her bulky frame off the seat and stood. ''Face it, Justin Wheeler, you're hooked.'' She gave his shoulder an affectionate pat and walked back behind her counter to wait on her customers.

Justin stared after her, feeling like a fish that had been neatly reeled in.

Friday afternoon was dragging, Justin thought, as he sat at his desk trying to focus on an article regarding a recent city-council decision to add more traffic lights to Main Street and its bordering thoroughfares. The material was dry and couldn't seem to hold his attention. By four o'clock, he gave it up and decided to finish the story later.

Leaning back, he did what he'd been struggling to keep from doing all afternoon. He angled his chair so he could study Rachel while pretending to be contemplating his article. Toying with his pen, his eyes drifted across the room to where she sat typing at her computer. Her eyes were glued to the monitor and her brow was furrowed in concentration.

Edna's words from that morning echoed in his mind. She'd said that when he looked at Rachel, he became all soft and dreamy. Hell, he'd never looked at *anyone* soft and dreamy, except maybe Katie when she was a baby. Fighting that thought, he rearranged his features, trying for cool and disinterested.

He missed by a mile. Though he didn't have a mirror, he just knew he did.

At least, Justin thought, no one else was around to see him looking like a love-struck teenager. Love-struck. No, he wasn't quite that. He didn't love anyone but Katie and Pop, Justin reminded himself. Those were *safe* loves, loves that wouldn't walk away and leave him. He *liked* Rachel, and he certainly was attracted to her. But he wasn't, as Edna had stated, hooked. He could back away anytime and . . .

Suddenly, sensing his eyes on her, Rachel looked up directly at him. For a moment, she just stared, then she smiled almost shyly. Her face deepened in color, as if she were remembering the kisses they'd shared last week, the tenderness they'd drawn from each other that stormy night. Then, just as abruptly, she glanced back to her screen and resumed typing.

Justin swallowed hard. Yeah, he could back away anytime. Sure he could.

Needing to move around, he rose and went to the bulletin board. Notices were posted there, work schedules, announcements. They accumulated rapidly and became an eyesore. Removing thumbtacks, he pulled notes off, attempting to restore order, throwing away outdated material and rearranging the current items. Anything to keep his mind busy and his hands occupied.

So absorbed was he that when the door opened, he didn't even turn around. Not until he heard and recognized the voice.

"You've gone too far this time, little lady," Theo Quincy's booming voice bellowed. He moved to Rachel's desk and tossed down a shoebox. "It's one thing to try to hurt me, but how could you do this to my little girl?"

Justin walked to the front as Rachel rolled her chair back and away from Theo and whatever it was he'd placed on her desk. Stopping inches from their uninvited guest, Justin cleared his throat to get the man's attention. "What do you want, Theo?" he asked, his voice deceptively soft.

Theo's eyes never left Rachel's face. "I want this... this *woman* to stop bothering my family. I want her out of our town and, by God, I mean to get her out." Reaching down, he yanked the lid from the shoebox. "There. Even you can see how sick she is to do this."

A strangled cry came from Rachel's throat as the blood drained from her face.

Justin looked inside and saw a small white kitten's body, the rope still around his neck. "What makes you think Rachel had anything to do with that?"

Theo let out a nasty laugh. "Everyone in Schyler knows she hates cats, always has. Used to throw stones at them when she cut through the woods. I got this here kitten for my Diane a month ago and just now, we found it hanging from Mama's favorite grapefruit tree by the side of our drive. Diane's still hysterical.'' Finally he swung around and looked at Justin. ''You better get that woman out of here. We've been trying to warn you. Any woman who'd kill a man the way she killed my brother sure wouldn't think twice about killing a child's kitten.''

Justin carefully replaced the lid on the box, picked it up, and held it out to Theo. ''Take this home and bury it. Rachel hasn't left my sight all day.'' Which wasn't quite true, but it might as well have been. He was as certain that she hadn't hung that kitten as he was that he himself hadn't.

Theo's dark eyes narrowed in anger. ''No one else in this town would've done it 'cept her. None of this was going on those years she was gone.'' Suddenly a knowing look crept over his fleshy features, and he glanced back and forth between Rachel and Justin. ''Oh, that's how it is, eh? Your brains slipped below your belt, Justin?''

His one empty fist clenched at his side, Justin stepped closer, his voice menacing. ''I told you to get out of here, and I meant it. You going on your own or do you need some help?''

Grabbing the box from him, Theo glared. ''You're going to be sorry you took sides with her. You wait and see.'' Turning, he stomped out the door, slamming it behind him hard enough to rattle the glass.

In three strides, Justin was in front of Rachel, his arms sliding around her and drawing her close. She let out a whoosh of air as he settled her against his chest and smoothed her hair. For long moments they stood like that, and finally he felt some of the tension drain from her, felt her breathing steady.

When she thought she could speak without shattering, Rachel eased back from him. ''You lied to him. I wasn't with you all morning.''

''It doesn't matter. You didn't do it.''

"Are you so sure? You hardly know me."

"I know you well enough to know you couldn't kill a kitten."

"You honestly believe that I didn't do it, without knowing where I was this morning?"

"Yes. You're incapable of that kind of violence."

She shuddered, then laid her cheek against his chest again, her whole body trembling. Could he mean it? Could he really believe her *just because?* Only her mother and Edna had ever believed her without question. No man ever had, with the possible exception of one of her old high school teachers. She wanted so badly to trust Justin, but she was afraid. Afraid of another disappointment. It was far easier to withhold trust than to be continually disappointed.

He rubbed her back almost absently, his touch light. "What are you thinking?" he asked after a while.

She didn't have to contemplate her answer. "That I want to run away. Right now. Today. And never come back. But..." She let the thought drift.

But there was Gloria, he finished for her mentally. Or had she been going to say something more? He angled his head so he could see her expression. "But what? Is it your mother?"

"Yes, my mother."

"And someone else, too?" he persisted.

"Someone else, yes." She craned her neck to check the clock. "Katie. I promised I'd go to her baseball game this afternoon." She pulled away from him.

Well, what had he expected? Justin asked himself. A declaration that she didn't want to leave him? Fool, he chided himself as he grabbed his keys. "Come on. I'll go with you."

* * *

The Redbirds were beating the pants off the Blue Jays. Literally, Justin thought, as he watched an eight-year-old girl in the outfield struggle to keep up her uniform pants that seemed about two sizes too large. Leading Rachel to a mound of grass under a shady tree behind the backdrop, he sat and waited for her to join him.

"These girls seem taller than the girls I coach in California," Rachel commented.

"You know how it is," Justin answered, his eyes on the field. "Everything grows bigger in Texas." He watched his daughter, one of the dejected Blue Jays, swinging her bat, testing the weight as her turn up to bat neared. "Actually, this group is kind of a jumble—the girls range from age seven to nine. Pop formed the team because the girls were annoyed they couldn't play football. With our weather, Pop decided they could play baseball year-round."

Rachel saw Pop turn his Blue Jays hat sideways like his granddaughter wore hers, then grin down at her. Whatever he said finally got a smile from her. "I see that Katie hates to lose."

"Positively loathes to lose. She puts her whole heart and soul into whatever she does."

Like her father, Rachel thought. No halfway measures for the Wheelers. She heard the pride in Justin's voice when he mentioned his daughter, and was warmed by it. Katie was lucky to have both a father and grandfather who cared so much. She listened to Justin go on about Katie's batting average and her ability to play several positions. She knew what he was doing, the same as he'd done all the way to the ball field. Chattering about Katie, the one subject he was certain would distract her from the upsetting scene back at the *Gazette*. For now, needing the distraction, she would allow it. There'd be plenty of time later to remember and relive.

Rachel shifted her gaze to Katie, who was moving up to bat. Pop's arm slid around the child's shoulders, and he turned her so she could see Justin and Rachel watching her. Trying to look confident, Katie waved and even smiled when they waved back. As the kids settled down, Pop went into a huddle with Katie, speaking solemnly. Equally as solemn, she nodded at him, her long braid bouncing along her back.

"What's he saying?" Rachel asked.

"Oh, that's Pop's keep-your-eye-on-the-ball speech." Dangling his arms on his bent knees, he smiled. "Pop has this theory that the game of baseball is like the game of life. You have to keep your eye on the ball at all times, the word *ball* being his euphemism for goal or target. He believes that in coaching baseball, we teach the kids more than how to play a simple game. We teach fairness and team spirit and to not let other people or things distract you from your goal."

"That's a lot for eight-year-olds to digest."

"Maybe, but Pop somehow gets his message across."

She nodded as she leaned forward. "Sure, because he cares about them, and they can feel it. They want to please him so they pay attention."

"You think that's the secret in teaching kids?"

"Absolutely. At this age, most children haven't put up barriers yet. They go by their senses still, and they can *feel* when someone cares for them. They respond instinctively to that sense of caring."

He angled his body so he was facing her more completely, absorbed in the conversation. "I never was totally convinced Pop's theory worked until I watched him with you. He cares about you, and you're different with him. You respond warmly to him.''

Rachel ran a hand through her hair being deftly rearranged by the afternoon breezes. ''I suppose I do. From the day I started at the *Gazette*, I sensed his feelings toward me.''

''But with me, you've put up the barriers.''

She thought of the kisses they'd shared, of how naturally she'd gone into his arms back at the office when she'd been frightened and upset, and sent him a rueful glance. ''You're doing a pretty good job of knocking them down. More than anyone else ever has.''

He took a chance, took her hand. ''That's because I care about you, too.'' Justin found he meant every word, far more than he'd planned to.

Rachel had no answer to that, had in fact never had a man say those words to her quite that way. The conversation was getting too serious, which was making her uneasy. She'd had so little experience with intimacy, physical or verbal. At that precise moment, she heard the crack of a bat hitting a ball just right. With a sigh of relief, she turned toward the ball field.

Katie hit a home run.

Amid affectionate hugs and cheers, Katie accepted her due, then ran over to her father and all but fell into his arms. ''Did you see that, Daddy?''

''You bet I did. Congratulations, babe.''

Grinning, she turned toward Rachel. With the spontaneity of a child, she reached out.

Rachel hugged the child close, swallowing around a sudden lump of emotion before praising Katie's ball playing.

Justin saw the split second of heartfelt feelings register on Rachel's face before she ducked her head and recognized it for what it was. Joy, gratitude, love. So easy to let yourself love a child. Why wasn't it just as easy to let down the barriers and allow yourself to love an adult? he wondered.

Scrambling to her feet, Katie grabbed her mitt from the grass where she'd tossed it. "Gotta go. I'm playing second base today, Daddy. Watch me."

"Go get 'em, babe," he called after her, as she ran out to join her teammates.

"She's such a terrific kid," Rachel said softly. "You and Pop have done a wonderful job with her."

"Thanks." Justin rather thought they had, too. But right now, he wanted to involve Rachel in a plan he had. "About that conversation we were having earlier."

Hadn't she known he wouldn't just let it go? She scooted a bit back from him, seemingly intent on the game. "Were we having a conversation?"

"I have a proposition for you," Justin said.

Well, that was putting it on the line. Did he think that intimate conversation naturally led to intimacy? Disappointment raced through her system, chilling her eyes as she swung to him. "And what might that be?" Let him say it, say it out loud.

After a moment Justin shook his head. "I wonder why it is you always think the worst first. What I meant was I need your help at the wildlife refuge tonight."

Taken aback, Rachel's face flushed. "I'm sorry." She was doing it again. "What about the wildlife refuge?"

He'd known exactly what she'd been thinking and feeling with that frosty look. When would she learn not every man thought a smile from a woman meant an invitation to a romp in the hay? "It's the one on the outskirts of town. Do you know where it is?"

"Uhhh, I think so. Near the Quincy ranch, I seem to remember."

"The property abuts their land, yes, and goes on for over a hundred thousand acres. All kinds of wild animals live there, under the protection of the U.S. Fish and Wildlife Service. But the section nearest the Quincys is occupied by a purebred herd of Spanish mustangs that have occupied that area for over a hundred years. Beautiful animals."

Still uncertain where this was leading, she nodded. "I've seen them from the road. What's your interest in all this?"

"The government funds to maintain the sanctuary were cut, so certain sections have been put up for sale in order to raise money. But, according to the will of the wealthy Texan who deeded the land, the area where the mustangs roam can't be sold as long as the rare breed of horse exists."

"I think that's as it should be."

Justin nodded. "I do, too. However, I heard recently that several horses have been found shot. I got to wondering who would want those beautiful animals dead. I figured it had to be someone with something to gain. Can you guess who that might be?"

Her eyes widened. "The Quincys?"

"You got it. This morning, I rummaged around in the records at the county building and found that Theo Quincy had petitioned the government to sell that parcel to him. They turned him down, citing the endangered-species ordinance. But, if he can get rid of those horses, anything's possible."

"Surely he's not going to methodically shoot every last one. There has to be about a hundred there, as I remember."

"A hundred and eight. I rounded up a committee and secured a head count as of last Monday. But I have a sneaky suspicion that the herd will be thinning out regularly."

Despite her earlier hesitancy, Rachel found her interest growing, especially since she realized she'd been wrong again about Justin. "You said you needed me there to-night. To do what?"

"I've studied the dates the dead horses have been dis-covered, and there's a pattern. Most ranches are lightly staffed on weekends, beginning Friday night when the hands are given time off for personal pursuits. That means fewer people around, fewer witnesses. Each time, the horses were found on Saturday mornings, probably shot the night before. I mean to go there tonight, lay low and watch. And I'd like a backup witness, in case I see some-thing worthwhile. I thought, since you're probably inter-ested in catching Theo red-handed, that you'd be the logical choice to go with me."

Rachel gazed out at the youngsters on the ball field and heard an eruption of laughter as one young girl slid onto a base, causing her shoe to fly off and whirl up into the air. Good, clean fun and the innocent laughter of children. The way life *should* be. The way it could be if it weren't for the Theo Quincys of the world with their browbeating ways making people afraid and desperate.

"You're right," she said finally. "I do want to catch him at something. I know he bullies people and now he's kill-ing animals. All in a day's work for Theo, because he thinks he's invincible. I'd like to show him he's not. I'll go with you."

"Good." Justin looked up at the sky. "A lot of cloud cover. Should be good and dark tonight, with only a sliver of a moon. I'll be by for you about nine. We should prob-ably do this right and wear black slacks and shirts."

Rachel smiled. "Sounds like James Bond and friend."

The game ended with much whooping and hollering. Justin stood and helped Rachel up. "I appreciate your helping me out."

"If you can get something on Theo, that's all the thanks I need."

"I hope you're not afraid of the dark."

She remembered that fateful walk through the woods she'd taken ten years ago. Although shady from the many trees, it had been in broad daylight. "It's been my experience that evil doesn't show up only at night. I'm not the bravest person you'll ever meet, but I'll be ready."

Rachel had had no idea how dark a moonless night could be. Holding Justin's hand, she crept along the grassy area bordering the low valley where the mustangs usually clustered for the night. Justin used his flashlight sparingly to keep them from running into unexpected trees or ravines, but otherwise they moved slowly and carefully, mostly by feel.

They'd sat until some minutes after midnight in Justin's van parked well off the road, waiting for the guards to clear out. Then they'd climbed the fence and made their way through a wooded area. Rachel had reason to be glad she was in good shape as they cautiously scaled a rocky slope.

She picked up the scent of the horses before she heard the occasional whinnying sounds in the distance. Finally they came to a grassy mound directly ahead.

"I scouted out this area when we came for a head count," Justin told her. "They're just on the other side of this hill. Let's crawl up to the top. I think we'll be able to make them out from up there." Taking a firmer hold of her hand, he urged her along.

Reaching the top, Justin lay on his stomach and waited for Rachel to join him. Carefully he set aside the camera he'd brought along, his Nikon loaded with night-sensitive infrared film. "I'm fairly certain that if someone is going to show up tonight to harm these horses, they're going to wait until later to make certain no guards lingered behind." Carefully he scanned the area with the beam of his powerful light.

Rachel saw them then, beautiful animals mostly huddled in a pack, making snuffling noises as the light passed by. An occasional one broke free and galloped off toward the bordering trees, while others stared back, shuffling their feet restively. She noticed two foals being guarded by the mares while the majority of the stallions pranced nervously nearby. "They're breathtaking," she whispered.

Justin snapped off his light and settled himself more comfortably. "This particular breed dates back to the Spanish conquistadors, the same as the horses you see in 14th- and 15th-century Spanish paintings."

"They look a little like pintos."

"I read that the original herd was brought up from Mission Dolores in Mexico sometime in the late 1800s. These have been somewhat domesticated, though. Through the years, various ranchers have stolen some and eventually crossbred them with other mustang lines."

"That's a shame." Rachel's head jerked up as she heard a night bird call to its mate in the treetops. "I hate to see anyone messing with wildlife. Pretty soon there'll be no purebreds left in the world."

Justin's eyes were adjusting to the darkness, though he could still only make out her outline. When he'd picked her up, he'd had all he could do to drag his eyes from her. If there was anything more beautiful than Rachel Hathaway, with her satiny tanned skin and natural blond hair wearing a black cotton turtleneck and jeans, he had yet to see it. He shifted so he was facing her, keeping his voice low so as not to frighten the animals nor allow the night breezes to carry the sound across the valley. "So you're an environmentalist, eh?"

Rachel flopped onto her back. "Basically, I guess I am. I like nature, the ocean untouched like it is at the north end of Padre Island, the trees left to grow wild in Kemper Woods."

The woods where Tyrone Quincy had died. Inadvertently she'd introduced a topic he'd been wanting to explore, Justin realized, as he wondered how best to approach her. Careful, he warned himself. "I'm curious about something Theo said this afternoon, that you used to cut through those woods and throw rocks at cats. Where would he have gotten that notion?"

Rachel sighed audibly. She hated remembering, hated having to defend herself. Yet she badly wanted this man to believe her. Maybe the place to start was to tell him the truth and see how he handled it. "I'm very allergic to cats. We found out when I was fairly young. If I were to pick one up, not only would I break out in a rash, but in minutes, I would have difficulty breathing. My nose closes up and my chest hurts—it's awful.

"So I tried to stay away from them. But I used to take this shortcut through Kemper Woods on my way home from school. And there was this one cat—kind of a scruffy, gray thing—he seemed to sense I didn't want him near me. He wouldn't leave me alone, always coming up and rubbing up against me."

"I've heard that cats sense fear in humans and like to taunt them."

"They sure do. Anyhow, I hated those attacks I got whenever I was exposed to a cat. Whenever I saw this gray cat, I'd pick up a rock and throw it against a tree, trying to scare him off. But I *never* aimed for him, nor did I ever even hit him accidentally. I have nothing against cats. It's just that they make me ill. Still, I wouldn't deliberately hurt one."

"How did Theo know about this?"

"Everyone knew. There was a beaten path through Kemper, and a lot of us kids took shortcuts through there. Otherwise you had to walk all the way around the Miller farm, about half a mile longer."

It wasn't really the cat story he was interested in. The sliver of moon lent just enough light so that he could make out the blond spill of her hair spread around her face as she lay in the grass, but he couldn't read her expression. Justin decided to plunge right in, to see if she'd trust him with her story. "Rachel, will you tell me what happened the afternoon that Tyrone died, as you remember it?"

She hesitated only a moment, having somehow known that one day he'd ask. "If you'll tell me why you're asking."

"This thing that happened deeply affected your life. It's only natural to want to know something like that about someone you care for." He reached to touch her, to trail his fingers along her cheek. "And I'm beginning to care for you far more than I'd planned."

It was the right answer. She, too, had found herself wanting to know more and more about Justin's past, how he felt about things. It would seem that learning to care brought about the need to know. She took his hand, lacing her fingers through his. Perhaps it was time for utter honesty. "I'm beginning to care for you, too. And it scares me."

"That makes two of us. I'd about decided that Katie was the only female I'd ever need in my life."

Maybe after he heard everything, he'd still think that was best. Rachel searched for the right words. "I'd graduated from high school in June and I'd planned to go to college in the fall. I wanted to teach, probably because of this teacher I'd had in my senior year who'd encouraged me. I got a job for the summer as a teaching assistant at the community college. The class let out around four and I was on my way home, shortcutting through Kemper Woods.''

She stared up at the cloudy night sky, but in her mind's eyes she'd traveled back to that dreadful day. ''When I got to the stream, Tyrone Quincy stepped out from behind this big tree and blocked my path. He was three years older and already a big man, just like Theo is now, only not quite as fat. He'd been after me for years and, like with the cats, I thought the best way to handle it was just to avoid him. Only this time, I couldn't.''

''He'd never caught you alone before this?''

''No. I was usually very careful and often one or both of my brothers would walk with me. Theo used to yell insulting remarks my way, but Tyrone was more persistent. He told me that day that he meant to have me and that was that. He opened his pants and lunged at me.''

Rachel took a deep breath, steadying herself. She was grateful that Justin was simply listening without interrupting. Yet his hand held hers tightly. ''I fought him. I remember I was carrying some books and I tried to hit him with those, but he threw them aside easily. He was so strong. I tried to kick, but he was surprisingly quick for a big guy. I finally managed to bite his hand. That's when he really got furious. He gave me a backhanded slap and everything went black. The last thing I remember is hitting the ground hard.''

She felt a shiver take her, fighting the reaction. Gently Justin's arm slid under her shoulders and he cradled her against his chest. She rushed on, needing to get it all out. ''When I came to, Tyrone was lying on the ground, facedown, not far from me. His pants were half off and half on, and the back of his head was bloody. Still woozy, I got up and that's when I heard footsteps coming toward us. It was

Theo. He'd seen his brother's car parked at the edge of the woods and come looking.''

"Did you touch Tyrone, try to get a pulse?"

She shook her head. "I guess I was too frightened. But Theo did, and then he started screaming. I don't know where he came from, but suddenly a sheriff's deputy came running into the woods—fortunately for me, because Theo was coming at me with his fists. He got off one solid punch to the side of my head before the deputy grabbed him. He radioed for an ambulance, but it was too late. Tyrone was dead, and Theo was shouting that I'd killed him."

His hands caressed her arms, his touch comforting. "I read about the trial, in the back issues of the *Gazette*. You went through hell, didn't you?"

"As close as I care to get. My lawyer found three other teenage girls who testified that Tyrone had forced himself on them, and still this town acted as if Tyrone had been the victim, and I'd been the terrible woman who'd done him in."

"You must have some theories after all this time. Who do you think made that fourth set of footprints, the ones with tire-tread shoes?"

"You *have* been reading about this. I wish I knew. To be honest, Tyrone wasn't very well liked, so it could have been any number of people. He was overindulged, spoiled and wild. Even worse than his brother, if that was possible. But his father signed a lot of paychecks in this town, and that buys a great deal of support."

"One day, Rachel, you'll be able to prove your innocence," Justin said, badly wanting his words to be true.

She gave a sad chuckle. "Do you believe in the tooth fairy, too?"

He shifted her in his arms so that his face was inches from hers. Her eyes were dark in the splotchy moonlight, her skin pale. "I believe in you," he said softly.

Rachel felt her eyes fill. "Oh, Justin," she whispered, and reached to stroke his cheek. When he lowered his head, it was the most natural thing in the world to open her mouth for his kiss.

The heart-flipping jolt was there again, just as it was every time he kissed her. And something else. He tasted familiar and wonderful and so very welcome. She returned the pressure of his lips, responding eagerly to the sensations he could so quickly arouse in her.

Shifting, Justin eased her closer, aligning their bodies. She fit perfectly in his arms, if not yet in his life. He was beginning to believe he had to make that happen. *Had to.* Because no one made him feel as much as Rachel did. No one could make him burn for her the way Rachel did. No one.

His hands thrust into her hair, holding her head steady for the onslaught of his mouth as he skimmed every inch of her face. The turtleneck frustrated him, keeping him from kissing the sweet line of her throat. He shifted and touched his mouth to the tip of one breast through her cotton shirt.

Rachel arched, then moaned softly, her hands in his hair now. Instinctively she pressed him nearer as the blood thundered through her veins and her legs beneath his moved restlessly. She became aware of his arousal pressing against her, the earthy feel exciting her beyond belief.

How could she walk away from this? Rachel asked herself, as he moved to make love to her other breast. How could she not reach out with both hands to capture this while she could? Closing her eyes, she almost said it aloud. *Please, please, don't let this feeling end.*

Justin returned to take her mouth, painfully aware they were moving rapidly toward desperate. He wanted her badly, but not this way. Not grappling on a grassy hillside. She deserved better. She, who had never known it, deserved romance, hearts and flowers, the whole package.

So he would stop, for both their sakes. In one more moment. As soon as he'd kissed her eyes closed, those incredible green eyes. As soon as he'd tasted her wondrous mouth one more time. As soon as—

Two sharp gunshots crackled and split the silence of the night. A third followed.

Chapter Seven

Justin jolted, scrambling onto his stomach, his arm circling Rachel to shelter her. "Stay down," he whispered, as his free hand groped for his camera. Finding it, he flipped open the cover, removed the lens cap and scrunched forward, propping his elbows on the hard ground.

"Can you see anything?" Rachel asked.

"Not really," Justin answered, as he focused in the general area where he thought the gunshots had originated. He shot several frames, moving sequentially in a half circle. The mustangs were shuffling around, skittish and nervous. Several reared up and whinnied at the intrusion of humans on their peaceful scene. Justin couldn't blame them.

Then he heard the sound of horse's hooves running hard, the sound diminishing gradually. It was a heavy thudding, made by a horse much larger than any of the mustangs. Someone on horseback running away? Justin kept on snapping pictures, aiming in the general direction of the receding sound, hoping his zoom lens would capture enough for identification.

Wishing now for a brighter moon, he stood. "I think the person with the gun is gone," he told Rachel, offering her a hand. "Come on. Let's go check it out."

It took but a few minutes to make their way down the other side of the embankment, sidestepping the rocks that delayed their descent. "Don't be afraid," Justin said, as they started into the pack of horses seemingly huddled together protectively. "They won't hurt us."

Though her heart was pounding, she wasn't afraid, Rachel decided. She was anxious to find some evidence that Theo had been the man with the gun.

They nearly stumbled onto the fallen mustangs, two females lying several feet apart on the outer edge of the circle of horses. Justin had been beaming his light to the left when suddenly a horse scurried aside and he saw the slain animals. As he bent to check them, he heard Rachel's sharp intake of breath.

"Both dead," he said, straightening. "It looks as if this one's got two shots in her." He felt the rush of anger that someone could do this so viciously. Needing the documentation, he snapped several more pictures.

A stallion near Justin reared as if protesting, or perhaps mourning a mate. He reached up a hand, wanting to comfort him. "Whoa, boy," he murmured, but the wild horse angled out of reach.

Rachel squinted into the darkness. "Justin, swing your light around, and let's see if we can pick out the direction the rider's horse ran off in."

He did, and in a few minutes they found the prints of the shoed horse. Bending low, they examined the trail. "He rode that way, toward the Quincy ranch."

"Do you think these prints can identify the horse that made them?" Rachel asked.

"No. There's nothing unique about them." He beamed the light on the tracks as they climbed the hill. "Let's follow them for a ways."

They kept their eyes on the ground, searching for something, anything. In some sections, the prints disappeared in the dust while in other stretches, they were plainly visible. When they got to the sparsely treed area, Rachel touched his arm.

"Wait. Look at this." She bent to retrieve the item and held it up for Justin to see. "A cigarette butt, gold-tipped and imported. Feel it. It's still warm. Now, who do we know who smokes this kind of cigarette?"

"Only one man I know of." Justin glanced around. "Theo probably sat on his horse right here by this tree, smoking and waiting for the best time to run down there and do his dirty work."

"We've got him now, haven't we? We found his cigarette butt, and I'm *sure* those horse prints lead to the Quincy ranch." In her excitement, her voice had risen.

Justin's arm slid around her. "It's not that easy, honey. Theo could claim that butt had been here for days. As for the tracks, he could say he came over to check on the mustangs himself, like we did. No law against that."

She sagged against him in disappointment. "We've just got to find a way to prove it was him." Finding a tissue in her pocket, she placed the butt inside and pocketed it anyway.

"We still have a chance." He held up his camera. "Maybe one of the pictures will reveal something concrete."

Rachel brightened immediately. "That's it, the pictures. I wish we could develop them right now. You should add a darkroom to the *Gazette*'s offices."

"I don't need to. I've turned a pantry off my kitchen into a darkroom. I do all my own developing. You want to come help me with these?"

She didn't hesitate. "Let's go."

His house was comfortable, like the man himself, Rachel thought as she followed him inside. Big, airy rooms, plenty of windows, lots of plants. Justin left her in his den while he went to get them a cold drink. It was a cluttered room done in browns and golds with a deep leather couch and framed memorabilia behind a rolltop desk. It was the glassed-in display case at that far end of a wall of bookcases that surprised her.

"You collect baseball cards," she commented, as Justin returned to hand her a frosty glass of root beer.

"Yeah, for years." He pointed out some of the older ones on the top row. "Babe Ruth, Mickey Mantle, DiMaggio. I go back a long way with some of these."

She should have guessed, with his love of baseball. "I imagine they're worth a great deal."

"Some of them. I used to do a lot of trading when I was young. Now they have stores that buy and sell them. Katie gets a kick out of showing off my collection to her friends." He sipped his drink as he turned to look at her.

It was late, and they'd been crawling around on the rocks and grass, yet she looked fresh and rested, her long hair hanging down her back. His eyes drifted lower to her sweater where his mouth had sought her. Remembering the feel of her, he felt the shock of awareness as she lifted her eyes to meet his gaze.

Rachel read the look and knew what he was thinking. Her face flushing, she crossed her arms over her chest and turned away. "I like this room," she said, her voice surprisingly steady considering her erratic heartbeat. Had it been a mistake, coming here, being alone with Justin and his incredibly sensual hold over her?

"I like it, too." He watched her turn toward his desk and pick up the baseball Ted Williams had autographed ages ago. "Everyone needs a sanctuary. This is mine."

Rachel gazed at the wall of photographs, several of Katie and Pop, another of a mustached man with a pipe. His father, perhaps, but she didn't ask. She wasn't surprised after the story he'd told her, that there were none of Katie's mother. Leaning closer, she studied a framed snapshot of a younger Justin standing near a twin-engine plane, two cameras dangling from around his neck as he squinted into the sun. "Were you a photojournalist? Is that why you have a darkroom?"

"Yes. In those days and maybe even now, you could pick up better assignments if you took the pictures as well as wrote the copy."

Just the other evening, sitting in his armchair, he'd pictured her here, in his home, among his things. Yet, now that she was here, her presence unnerved him somewhat. He drained his root beer. "Come on. Let's go develop the film."

Rachel was ready for some activity that would keep their hands busy and their minds on something other than each other. Following him, she wondered at this ambivalence that had her emotions churning. She wanted him, of that she was certain. Yet she was afraid of that wanting, of that need that had her so unsettled.

Justin's darkroom was small, but efficiently arranged. Though he'd closed the door and turned on the red working light, Rachel was soon too fascinated with what he was doing to dwell on the uneasiness of being with him in such close quarters. She watched his hands—strong, lean fingers removing the film and placing it into a coffee-can-shaped metal spool. "What's that?"

"It's for developing the negatives." While he spoke, he ran water into long trays and then reached for one of the bottles of chemicals. "The negatives go first into the developer for a couple of minutes, then we hang the strip up to dry."

After a bit, he removed the negatives and attached them to an overhead line. Rachel saw him squinting at the tiny frames as they dried and wondered if he could make out anything yet. Finally he placed them into something that looked like a projector. Interested, she leaned closer. "Now what's that machine?"

"The enlarger." He reached for the paper and slipped it into place, then flipped a button. "The light transforms the image to the chemically coated paper. Then they go into a three-part immersion operation. A chemical bath, the stop bath that halts the action, and finally into the fix tray where the picture forms. Then we'll be able to see what we've got."

Rachel leaned back against the edge of the counter. "Did you do your own processing when you were in London?"

"Not usually. Once in a while I borrowed a friend's darkroom, but mostly I mailed the film straight to my paper."

"Then they'd get to choose what prints to run?"

"Yeah, that was the drawback." He worked quickly, removing prints and dipping them into the baths. One by one, he removed them and hung them on the line, studying them as he worked. "That one's a bit blurred. I hope the rest are better."

They were. Justin switched on the light and narrowed the assortment down to the best three. He lay the still-damp prints on the counter to show her. "In this one, you can definitely see a figure on a horse with a rifle in his grip at the edge of the clearing, but it's pretty shadowy. He's farther away in this one and turning, but the picture's clearer." In the third one, the rider was scrambling up the hill on horseback. "I think I'll try a blowup."

While he did that, Rachel leaned down to study the photos. "You can't make out his features enough to recognize him, but it definitely is a man. I was worried that Theo might be setting me up to be blamed for those mustangs' deaths."

"There's not much I'd put past him, but he'd have a hard time proving that one since you have me as your alibi."

Rachel sighed. "An alibi. He commits a crime, and I need an alibi. What's wrong with that picture?"

He shot her a quick look as he turned off the overhead and snapped on the red light. "We're going to change all that, Rachel."

"I wish I felt as certain about that as you do. After accusing me of blackmail and killing cats, I'm just wondering what Theo has in mind next to try to drive me out of Schyler."

"Maybe he wouldn't be as determined to get you to leave if we found out who *really* killed Tyrone." Justin hung the three blowups on the line to dry, then reached for a rag to wipe his hands.

The red light was behind her head, haloing her hair, casting a blush on her face. Her eyes were huge, and he could see that her nerves were on edge. He moved closer, running his hands along her arms. "We'll find him, Rachel. And when we do, you'll be free."

She managed a smile she didn't quite feel. He'd been wrestling with her problem for a few weeks while she'd been dealing with it for over ten years. He had no idea of the uphill course he was in for. But she wouldn't shoot him down for trying. Still, he would have to forgive her if she wasn't wildly enthusiastic, either. "Sounds like the impossible dream."

He cupped her chin lightly. "*Nothing* is impossible."

"Still, I'm frightened," she confessed hesitantly. "The Quincys are powerful. They've made it impossible for me to stay before. It sounds well and good to track Theo, but it's risky. Maybe too risky."

"If you hope to make a gain, you have to take a risk. Pop always tells the girls that when he's coaching baseball. It's the same in life. The old adage—no pain, no gain—is true." He brushed his lips across hers briefly, then turned to the prints. "Let's take a look at these."

They hit pay dirt on the third enlargement.

"The man's dressed in white," Rachel exclaimed. "Even his horse is white." Though it was a black-and-white print, the pale clothing and horse stood out starkly.

"It looks like Theo, all right. So, let's say we can place him at the scene. Proving his reason for being there is another story."

"What do you mean?" She was indignant. "Look at these! A big man, all in white. Everyone in Schyler knows Theo wears white most of the time. Then there's the cigarette we found. And surely, we can go to the Quincy ranch and find that white horse as well. What more do we need?"

Justin laid his hand on her shoulder, sharing her concern. "Calm down. We have to go at this the right way, or we'll blow it. As I said earlier, Theo could very well agree that he's the man on horseback. But proving that he shot the mustangs is another matter."

Disappointed, Rachel brushed back her hair with an angry hand. "Then all this was for nothing?"

"No. I have a plan. Tell me what you think." Snapping off the light, he opened the door and led them into the kitchen. "Suppose we print a couple of these photos on the front page of our next issue—one of the dead mustangs on the ground and the other of the man in white, hurrying away with a rifle tucked under his arm. And I'll write an accompanying article saying that I staked out the wildlife refuge, heard the shots and took the pictures. Then we'll ask our readers if they can identify the man on horseback."

At the kitchen counter, she leaned back, impressed. "You mean let the townspeople be the judge instead of making outright accusations?"

"Right. And I don't want to mention that you were there, or Theo will say you're making things up to get even."

She thought that over and nodded. "That makes sense." But the doubts resurfaced. "Do you think it'll work?"

Justin shrugged. "It's worth a try, and it's the best thing we've got going for us at the present time. After all, Theo's running for sheriff, remember. There are some good people living here, and if we can cast some reasonable doubt on his honesty, they might start to question other things. And they might realize that he's one of the few who'd benefit from having that land available to purchase."

"Why do you suppose Theo risked being seen by doing the shooting himself, when he's got all those hired hands?"

"He's got his enemies, too. Sometimes having even one person know you're doing something illegal is enough to get you caught. He probably figured that going himself was the lesser risk."

"The Quincys must want that property badly."

"I'm going to check something else in the morning. The herd looked light to me, though I couldn't see too well. I wonder if there aren't more missing."

"You mean he may have shot others and hauled them away or buried them?"

"Or sold them. There are plenty of Texas ranchers up north who'd buy those mustangs, no questions asked. I'm going to organize another head count."

Encouraged, Rachel allowed herself to relax a bit as Justin came to her. "I'd give a lot to watch Theo's face when he sees the next edition of the *Gazette.*"

Justin smiled down at her. "I'm glad you came with me. We make a pretty good team, don't we?"

How was she supposed to answer that? Rachel wondered. "I'm not sure. I've never been half of a two-part team, so it's hard to judge."

He slid his hands around her slim waist. "Never?"

She shook her head as she watched his gray eyes darken while he studied her. The seconds slid by, and she felt her mouth go dry. "When you look at me like that, I can't help but wonder what you're thinking."

"Can't you guess?"

She swallowed nervously, her hands settling on the buttons of his shirt. "That you want to take me to bed?"

"That I want to make love with you," he corrected. "In bed, on the floor, out in the grass. Anywhere. Everywhere."

She heard the grandfather's clock in the living room strike three, startled to realize how late it was. She should go. But his words held her rooted to the floor. "I wonder why. Is it because I'm a challenge, *that Hathaway woman* that everyone whispers about? Or is it because . . ."

He framed her face with his hands. "Because for weeks now, you're the first thing I think of each morning, and the last thing I think of at night."

She gave him a trembling smile. "Words, beautiful words. I've heard a ton of them before, in an effort at *friendly persuasion.*"

Justin frowned in annoyance. "Is that what you think I'm doing, trying to flatter you, to sweet-talk you into my bed?" He shook his head as his thumbs slowly caressed the silk of her cheeks. "No, Rachel. It's not because you're a challenge or because of this reputation you seem to think you have. It's for an altogether different reason."

She felt her heart thud against her rib cage. "What's that?"

"For a long time now, I've been looking for something, not even certain what I was searching for." His hands lowered to draw her into the circle of his arms. "When I met you, I felt as if I'd found that something."

"I've been looking, too," she said, suddenly aware that she spoke the truth. Slowly she slid her hands up to rest on his shoulders. "Perhaps it's time to see if we've found what we're looking for."

He wanted it this way, in the still of the night, both of them aware of the step they were taking, not falling into bed simply because they'd worked themselves into a passionate frenzy. There would be passion, of that he was certain, but he wanted each of them to realize the consequences of their decision. "This could change our lives."

Rachel had no doubt it would change hers, more than he knew. "My life could use a little changing."

He led her to his bedroom and left her in the doorway while he turned on a low lamp in the far corner. A window was open and a soft breeze drifted inside, heavy with the scent of honeysuckle growing alongside the house. Shadows played across her features as he took her hand.

She was small and delicate alongside him, and he suddenly felt hesitant. Her beauty took his breath away, yet in her eyes was a vulnerability he couldn't ignore. And there was something else, a kind of plea for understanding, that turned his heart right over. His whole body was tight with hunger too long denied, yet he didn't move. There was an untouched quality about Rachel that had him wondering if they'd be this far along if circumstances hadn't thrust them together alone in the quiet night.

Rachel saw a hint of nerves skitter across his expression, and the knowledge oddly relaxed her. She hadn't considered the fact that Justin might also have his uncertainties. She sought to ease his mind by rising on tiptoe and touching her lips to his.

Justin felt her open to him like the night-blooming flower in his backyard. At first taste, a fierce need for her caused his body to react swiftly. He must not rush her, he reminded himself, as he gently gathered her closer. Her hair cascaded over his arms like silken ribbons unfurling. He shifted, pressing closer, and he knew he was lost.

There was no hesitancy in her kiss now. It was as if, having made the decision, she committed herself to being an eager partner. When Justin's tongue entered her mouth, she met it boldly, joyously fencing with him. He felt her hands move between them and fumble with the buttons of his shirt, pulling the cloth aside. Easing back, he looked into her face and found her eyes closed.

"I . . . let me learn you," she whispered, her head tilting back as her hands shoved the shirt from his shoulders. Slowly, as if by braille, her fingers wandered his chest, threading through the thick mat of hair there, tracing the outline of his muscles, trailing down the hard line of his stomach. She couldn't see, could only feel—and she felt so much. Strength and gentleness, smooth skin and rough textures, rigid control and quivering need.

Opening her eyes finally, she wanted to say that she'd never known how glorious it would feel to touch a man so freely, but she was afraid he would think her foolish.

"My turn," Justin said, and reached for the hem of her shirt, pulling it off over her head. He watched her shake back her hair, then slid his fingers into its thickness. His mouth returned to hers, unable to get enough of kissing her. His arousal strained against his zipper as his desire grew. When he pressed against her intimately, he heard her low moan.

His fingers fumbled with the catch of her bra, and he silently cursed the minute it took to free her. Then his hands were holding the weight of her breasts, and he saw her eyes close as a shudder raced through her. Her head fell back and he kissed the vulnerable length of her throat as his hands massaged and caressed.

Rachel wasn't certain how much longer she would be able to stand, as her knees threatened to buckle. When he dipped his head and put his mouth to her breast, she whispered his name as she let out a gasp of surprised delight. She felt the heat spread, quickly moving lower, causing her to throb with need. By the time he eased her backward onto the bed and followed her down, she was trembling.

On his side, Justin pulled her to him, brushing her breasts against his chest, watching the flush of passion appear on her cheeks. Tenderly he stroked the soft skin of her back, savoring the freedom to explore her. When those incredible green eyes opened, the message she unwittingly sent was impossible to misinterpret.

She wanted him. Her face was shadowed, her hair fanned out around her. Her breathing was as labored as his, the needs that pounded at her as fierce as his, evidenced by the way her small hands moved restlessly on his bare back. Her scent as he inhaled was sweeter than the sweetest rose, and utterly feminine.

He would give her one last chance. "Are you sure?" Justin asked.

"Very sure." Her voice was steady, unwavering.

He had his answer and quickly tugged off her shoes, then her jeans, leaving her one last silken barrier while he hastily removed the rest of his clothes. Her eyes followed his every move, widening briefly when he paused for a moment, fully naked in front of her. Her gaze shifted to his face, and she smiled almost shyly before she opened her arms to invite him back.

The kiss was hungry, sweetly demanding, wildly sensual as Justin's tongue thrust once, withdrew, then plunged again. He rolled onto his back, taking her with him. Pressed tightly together, flesh to flesh, he let her passion build, hoping he could keep control of his own.

Sensations piled atop one another for Rachel as she struggled to keep up. She felt his knee slide between hers and instinctively locked her legs. After a frozen moment, she relaxed and let his leg ease between her thighs. Distracting her with openmouthed kisses, he trailed along her arched throat, then returning to sample again each breast.

How could she have known she could feel so much, need so desperately, want so completely? This was his first time with her, and he seemed to know just where she longed for his kiss, the exact spot she craved to be touched. His lips raced over her sensitive skin, distracting her as his fingers moved lower, then slipped off her panties and found her moist heat.

Rachel arched, not in protest but rather in startled pleasure. Aroused beyond belief, she shifted, needing to touch him. When her fingers closed around him, she felt the quick shudder that went through his body as if it were her own.

Justin realized that she was swiftly becoming as impatient as he. But one of them had to be sensible. "Do I need to get protection?" When she didn't answer, he became more specific. "Are you on the pill?"

Hazy with passion, she shook her head as she brushed back her hair. Seeing the surprise on his face, she decided to explain. "There's never been a need."

He noticed that she wouldn't look at him. "Never?" As she again shook her head, he found himself shocked at the implication. Surely this beautiful woman, at twenty-seven, had had lovers. He leaned down to her, not wanting to spoil the moment but needing to know. "Rachel, have you... ever done this before?"

Her hand on his shoulder traced an imaginary pattern. "Will you stop if I say no?"

"The only way I'll stop is if you tell me you don't want me."

Finally she looked at him. "I've never wanted a man the way I want you. That's why there hasn't been one, until now."

Her confession changed things for Justin. Humbled, he reached into his nightstand for protection. Reining in his own need, he turned back to kiss her gently, wanting to make it perfect for her, hoping he could hold off long enough.

But Rachel was afraid she'd ruined everything. Pulling back, she touched his face. "I'm sorry. If this is a problem..."

He brushed her cheek with infinite tenderness. "A woman never needs to apologize to a man for offering herself for the first time. I'm just glad you told me now, so I can try to go slowly.'' Lightly he touched his lips to hers while they kept their eyes on each other. "I don't want to hurt you.''

Humor came into her eyes as she squirmed slightly against the weight of his body half-draped over hers. "It doesn't feel anything like pain so far.''

But Justin wasn't in the mood to smile. With great care, he kissed her, intent on taking her back up again. He moved with certainty now, tasting her sweetness, touching her softness, driving them both. His hands tangled in her hair as he rolled them over and pinned her beneath him.

He wanted her dizzy with wanting, reaching for more, as desperate as he. He wanted to show her all that could be— the intoxicating climb, the delirium, the madness.

Rachel forgot her earlier hesitancy, set aside her fears, lost all sense of self-consciousness. There was only pleasure now, a humming pleasure that rippled along her skin and had her blood racing. His hands touched everywhere, followed by his seeking mouth. She writhed in astonishment, releasing a sigh of satisfaction such as she'd never known.

He waited but a minute, scarcely letting her recover. Bracing his weight on his elbows, he pulled himself over her and entered her welcoming warmth with more gentleness than he'd thought himself capable of. He stilled a moment, allowing her to adjust to his presence inside her. When her hips began to move involuntarily and her hands on his back urged him closer, he began to move.

Slowly at first, watching her face, waiting until she picked up the answering rhythm. He saw a rising blush stain her cheeks as he picked up the pace. She whispered his name, then her eyes drifted closed.

Rachel no longer could hear the warm evening breezes rustling the curtains at the open window. She couldn't feel the nubby bedspread beneath her nor smell the hint of jasmine she'd noticed upon entering the room. For her, there was only damp skin sliding over smooth, an earthy male scent filling her nostrils, and a pounding heartbeat that echoed her own. Closing her eyes, she let the sweet friction seduce her.

Still, when the explosion came, she was unprepared for the impact on her senses. Feeling as if she were splintering, she gave in to the myriad sensations. A moment later, she felt Justin shudder and bury his face in her hair.

She lay like that, cradling his weight, enjoying the feel of so much strength that moments ago had been made weak by her touch. The slide back to herself came slowly, her heartbeat leveling finally. Her breathing was still shallow when she opened her eyes.

His head lay against her breast and she gently stroked his damp hair. Did every woman feel this way afterward, this rush of tenderness replacing the edgy passion that had plagued her for weeks? She examined the other feelings creeping into her consciousness. She felt uncharacteristically cherished, cared for, loved.

Love had been in short supply in her life, yet she recognized the symptoms. Or was she so longing to be loved that she was misreading the signs? Men, she was well aware, took physical intimacy far more lightly than women. Was she foolishly putting more value on what had just happened than she should? Was that another mistake women made too readily, expecting promises after the passion?

She'd waited a long time by today's standards to offer herself to a man, though many had wanted a place in her bed. She wasn't sorry she'd waited. Yet now, with desire satisfied, she wondered about the aftermath etiquette.

Justin lifted his head, then shifted his weight, thinking he was crushing her. When she made a small sound of protest, he brought her to him. Their faces close, he brushed a strand of hair from her face and kissed her lightly. "Are you all right?"

Rachel wasn't quite sure what he meant. "If you mean, did you hurt me, the answer is no." She saw by his unchanging expression that that wasn't what he'd wanted to know. She snuggled closer, trying to give him her answer in body language as well. "If you mean...something else, then I'm more than all right. I feel wonderful."

He smiled then, just a slow smile, drowning in the green of her eyes. There had been women in his life, but here in his arms was a woman like no other he'd known. She made colors appear brighter, the scents smell richer, the day stretch more sweetly because she was in it. Yet he dare not tell her all of it.

Justin wasn't a man who often kidded himself. He doubted if making love with him had changed her mind about leaving. She was capable of sacrificing her own happiness—even leaving everyone she knew and loved—and starting over rather than remaining in an uncomfortable situation. She'd done it before. How could he be certain she wouldn't again?

Could he ever clear up her past enough to make Rachel want to remain in Schyler with him?

She'd seen his eyes turn troubled. "Is something wrong?"

He forced a smile. "Only that I'm trying to figure out how I can keep you here until we're both too weak to walk."

That wasn't it, Rachel was certain, but she'd let the explanation stand for now. She returned his smile. "That depends on just how many of those foil packets you have in your nightstand drawer."

He caught the odd note in her voice and guessed what she'd been thinking. "You're wrong, Rachel. No woman's been in this bed with me except you. Katie sleeps on the other side of the wall. I wouldn't take that chance. She's at Pop's tonight, but it's very rare that I'm out covering a story this late."

She hadn't wanted to be jealous yet knew that that was exactly what she'd been feeling. "You don't owe me explanations."

"All the same, it's the truth." He nuzzled her neck. "Don't you know how special you are to me?"

She wanted to believe him and did. A little. But believing men was a dangerous and disappointing pastime. They needed more time together, she and Justin, for her to form a lasting opinion. And she didn't have a lot of time left. Still, there was no denying that she cared for him. "You're special, too, or I wouldn't be here."

He eased back and met her eyes. "I'm very glad you're here," Justin said softly.

"So am I." She heard the clock in the living room strike four. "I should go. It'll be light soon, and—"

He cut her off with a kiss that was long and lingering and most thorough. "Stay. There's so much more."

Her pulse quickened as her imagination took flight. His hand slid down to cup her breast and she almost lost her voice. How could she want more, when minutes ago she'd felt so sated? "Shouldn't you be thinking about how being seen with me—especially in the wee, small hours of the morning—is going to affect your reputation in this town?"

Justin moved his other hand between her slender thighs and watched her reaction to his intimate caress. "What I'm thinking about is how many more ways we can make love before the first light of dawn." His fingers eased inside her. Involuntarily she moved closer to his touch. "Stay with me,

Rachel.'' His lips brushed along hers, waiting for her answer.

Senses whirling, Rachel sighed. ''Well, maybe another minute longer.'' And she reached for his kiss.

Chapter Eight

On Wednesday afternoon, Justin left Edna's Diner extremely pleased about the hour he'd spent at lunch. The *Gazette* had been on the newsstands since early morning. The pictures and article on the front page were very much on the minds of everyone he'd run into so far. Actually, he thought, as he headed for his office, most of the townspeople were abuzz with the shocking death of the mustangs at the wildlife refuge. They'd known of the previous killings, but the pictures brought the slaughter more clearly into focus. Which was exactly as he'd hoped.

He'd strolled along Main Street much of the morning, finding excuses to go into the bank, the post office, and other businesses, giving people an opportunity to question him. And they had. From Hal Fisher, the president of Schyler Bank and Trust, to clerks in the drugstore—all were curious, speculative, and some even outraged. Justin had casually asked several who they thought the man on horseback might be. A few openly mentioned Theo Quincy's name while the majority looked nervously about, then dropped their eyes as if unwilling to hazard a guess, especially to a newspaperman.

Justin understood. There were jobs to be protected. Men who had to put food on their tables weren't about to risk being fired over something that didn't personally affect them. However, others were fortunately beyond those fears and spoke more freely.

He'd heard from Edna, of course, and Ray Brewster, an attorney of some reputation in Schyler. Even Hal Fisher had agreed, despite the fact that Roy Quincy was a member of the bank's board of directors. Others, he knew, would be talking quietly among themselves. At the very least, he'd stirred things up and had people thinking about Theo's qualifications for public office. At the most, he'd started a groundswell of opinion that would eventually force Theo to withdraw his name.

But, Justin realized, proving Theo Quincy guilty of wildlife endangerment wasn't his real goal. Far more important was his need to find the person who killed Tyrone so that his brother would back off from harassing Rachel.

Rachel. Walking along in the afternoon sun, Justin found himself smiling at the mere thought of her name. They hadn't been alone together much since the night she'd spent in his bed, but that didn't matter. Just seeing her across the room at the *Gazette* brightened his day. Working alongside her, then walking her home occasionally, gave meaning to hours that had just been time spans before. Watching her with Katie, who no longer bothered to hide her feelings for Rachel, warmed him. And worried him.

Rachel refused to discuss whether she would go or stay after her brother returned to Schyler. Gloria's condition hadn't improved. According to Rachel, her mother had to rest several times on the climb up the wooden steps to her apartment, her shortness of breath a real problem. The Texas humidity didn't help, but Gloria still stubbornly refused to consider moving—or to stop smoking. Justin felt torn between wanting Gloria to seek a better climate for her health and wanting Rachel to remain.

So he'd decided to take it one day at a time, quietly working behind the scenes to dredge up interest in the old case of Tyrone Quincy's death. He'd pulled a few strings and, with the help of Ray Brewster, who'd defended Rachel ten years ago, gotten a transcript of the trial and copies of various pertinent reports. At night, he'd pore through them, hoping to find that elusive *something* that would set off a bell in his head and set his investigative juices flowing.

It was slow going, but worth the effort. Because Rachel was worth the effort. She was...

In mid-thought and mid-stride, Justin stopped as he reached the front of the *Gazette* office. Across the street and down two doors was the late-model silver BMW he'd first noticed at Orrin Hathaway's funeral. Standing next to it, partly hidden from view by a large crepe myrtle bush, was the tall, bearded man talking with a slender woman. Rachel.

He didn't want to stare, yet he couldn't seem to move. Her back was to him and she was looking up at the man, evidently absorbed in their conversation. Why did this someone she once knew keep popping up? He wasn't from around here or Justin would have recognized him. What was his connection to Rachel?

As he watched, Rachel reached up to hug the man. Justin found himself fighting a rush of jealousy at the sight. Annoyed—with himself and Rachel—he hurried inside the office.

It took him a moment to calm down and another to locate Pop in the rear of the building. "Pop, could you come up front a minute? I want you to take a look at this man outside and tell me if you recognize him."

Pop set aside the file he'd been thumbing through. "Sure." He followed Justin to the door, which opened as they arrived.

"Hi," Rachel said, entering and walking to her desk.

Justin glanced out in time to see the BMW drive past. "Never mind," he muttered to Pop.

"Anything wrong?" Pop asked, looking at his grandson curiously.

"Not a thing." Still struggling with his irritation, Justin sat in his swivel chair. He stole a quick look at Rachel and saw she was preparing to do some typing, seemingly oblivious to his aggravated state.

"Well, maybe I can cheer you with some good news," Pop went on. "The *Times* has picked up your story on the mustangs. The editor who called says he thinks it's worth launching an investigation."

Overhearing, Rachel rose to join them. "No kidding?"

"Well, I'll be damned," Justin said. "That's just the kind of publicity we need. With the Associated Press behind us, possibly we can get more money for guards around the clock out there. Maybe with enough attention, we can get the sale of that land more securely protected."

Pop nodded in agreement. "They're going a step further. There's to be a meeting on Thursday and Friday in Dallas on wildlife preservation, grants to refuges like ours, and legislation governing endangered species. They've invited one or both of us to attend."

Justin's good humor was restored. "That's great. Why don't you go, Pop?"

Pop adjusted his glasses more comfortably on his thin nose. "Can't. Ben and I are going fishing up to Fayette Lake, don't you remember? We've had the cabin rented for months." He turned to Rachel. "Great bass around there. Fellow I know caught a striped bass that weighed over thirty pounds just last year."

"Really?" She smiled at Pop, but she was far more interested in what was happening right here in Schyler. She looked at Justin, who seemed lost in thought. "I'm concerned about the mustangs, as you know. But what about the man on horseback? Have you heard any speculations around town?" She'd had the morning off, as she usually did on the day the paper came out, and had spent it giving her mother a permanent.

"I'll say we have." Justin told her what he'd heard, and Pop joined in with several comments from folks he'd run into. "More than one person came right out and said they felt it was Theo."

Rachel felt a flicker of hope come to life. "And is the Associated Press going to run the pictures *and* the story?"

"So they say," Pop answered. "It's important that you attend Friday's meeting, Justin, don't you think?"

"Yeah." He rubbed his forehead, thinking. "But I don't know if Emily can take Katie in for me. She's not crazy about having kids stay overnight. I can't blame her after having a houseful all day."

"She can stay with me," Rachel offered instantly. But Justin's expression when he shifted his gaze to her was unreadable. She hurried to amend her offer. "Unless, of course, you feel that wouldn't work out."

Pop touched her shoulder. "Nonsense, Rachel. Katie's crazy about you. Right, Justin?"

"Yes, she is. Are you sure you don't have any other commitment?" He was being stubborn and spiteful, Justin realized, still struggling with his jealousy at seeing her in the arms of another man just a short time ago. Another man that he'd once mentioned to her, and she'd all but told him to mind his own business. But hadn't Rachel become his business?

The phone rang, and Pop walked across the room to answer it. Justin kept his eyes on Rachel, wondering what she was thinking.

He didn't trust her, Rachel thought immediately. There was something in his gray eyes, something she couldn't make out. A hesitancy, a question. Yet she had a feeling that it had nothing to do with Katie. "I have no other commitment," she said quietly. "However, if you feel you don't want to leave her with me, I'll understand."

Justin had seen the quick flash of hurt flicker across her features before she'd averted her eyes. This business of caring so much so quickly had its drawbacks, like making him act stupid occasionally. Standing, he reached for her hand. "I think Katie would love staying with you, and I thank you for offering."

Rachel blinked back a rush of emotion, wondering why her feelings were so close to the surface lately. "Are you sure?"

Gently he trailed two fingers along her cheek. "Positive."

She found a smile as she thought of something else. "Having her at the apartment will be like a tonic for Gloria. She's been a bit down lately."

"Then it's settled." Perhaps this was what they'd needed, Justin thought, something to prove to Rachel that he trusted her. Maybe then, she'd allow herself to trust him, at least enough to explain the bearded man.

Black Beauty was one of Katie's favorite books. Justin had told Rachel that Katie loved reading aloud, so the two of them had decided to read the book together, alternating pages. They sat on the couch with the child snuggled close to Rachel, and both read loudly, so that Gloria, listening across the room in her rocker, could also hear.

Rachel's arm was around the warm little body, her face inches from Katie's freshly washed dark hair. She smelled of the bath powder Rachel had given her when she'd sent her in to bathe. Shyly Katie had admitted she'd never had any of her own. Rachel hadn't been surprised, since the little girl had been raised mostly by men. That missing woman's touch. Perhaps her life had had something missing, too, Rachel thought. The presence of a child.

Listening to the familiar tale, Rachel let her mind drift. She'd been drawn to children early, having cared for her two brothers regularly and often. And there were her students, many of whom she'd become very fond of. But there was something about Katie Wheeler that had captured her heart from the beginning.

"Your turn, Rachel," Katie reminded her.

Semidozing in her rocker, Gloria roused herself. "Are you daydreaming again, Rachel? Don't mind her none, Katie. She's been doing that since she was your age."

"Guilty as charged," Rachel answered.

Katie looked up with her huge blue eyes. "Daddy says all writers are dreamers. You write, too, don't you, Rachel?"

"Not like your dad does. Is he a dreamer?"

"I think so. He makes up these stories he tells me. My favorite one's about the elephant that loses his memory and wanders all over the jungle looking for it. It's real funny."

"Maybe I can get him to tell it to me sometime," Rachel said, as she squeezed Katie's arm and turned to the next page.

Gloria coughed several times, then sat up straighter as she searched in her pocket for her cigarettes. "I suspect you could get that man to tell you anything you wanted to hear.'' Flicking on her lighter, she inhaled deeply.

Rachel sent her mother a warning glance that Gloria chose to ignore. Ever since the night she'd not come home until just before daybreak, her mother had been eyeing her curiously and tossing out leading remarks, obviously hinting for Rachel to confide in her. But Rachel had left home too young and had never formed the habit of confiding the personal details of her life to anyone. Besides, what she'd shared with Justin was too private to discuss even with her mother, most especially in front of his daughter.

Rachel began reading the next page before Katie became restless, but her mind was elsewhere. As usual these days, it was with Justin.

He'd driven to Corpus Christi early this morning and flown on to Dallas. He'd called after dinner to check on Katie, who'd told him that Rachel had walked to the school to meet her, then they'd stopped for a soda at Edna's before coming to the apartment. Katie had sounded pleased that Rachel hadn't returned to the *Gazette* but had stayed to play cards with her. Afterward they'd stuffed themselves on Gloria's wonderful fried chicken and were about to start a game of checkers.

Then he'd wanted to talk with Rachel. Anxiously she'd asked how the meetings were going. Justin had said he felt they were making progress, that his article and pictures had raised the sensibilities of people who were horrified at losing the purebred mustangs and other endangered species. And then he'd lowered his voice to that intimate level that quickened her heartbeat, and said he missed her. Missed her badly.

In the close confines of the small apartment, she'd been unable to respond beyond a simple "Me, too." It had been enough. Justin had asked if she'd keep tomorrow evening free for him. She'd agreed without hesitation.

Rachel finished the page and slid the book closer to Katie. Listening to her pick up the story, she absently stroked the child's hair, rich and thick like her father's and even her grandfather's. They'd snared her in, the Wheelers. She loved them, all three. The realization no longer surprised her.

Love was such a sneaky thing. If it had been offered to her before, outside her own family, she hadn't liked the package it had been wrapped in nor the strings that had been attached to it. First, she'd been drawn to Pop with his acceptance and unconditional caring. Then Katie had literally charged on the scene, her need for love as great as Rachel's own. Only Katie wasn't afraid to lead with her heart, to let her feelings show, to risk rejection.

Then there was Justin, who'd also been wounded and made wary. His solid presence had allowed her to let down the barriers gradually. He hadn't pressed, hadn't rushed. He'd waited for her to come to him and she had. The male-female awareness she'd turned away from for years had come roaring to life at his touch. He'd awakened a dormant sensuality in her that had led to the ultimate intimacy. Overwhelming as that had been, it was the love that she felt for the man himself that filled her with wonder. Though she'd been subconsciously seeking that bonding with another that would make her feel half of a whole, she'd not had serious hopes of finding such a man, especially not in Schyler.

Yes, the Wheelers packed a powerful punch in the emotion department. How on earth was she going to leave them?

With no small effort, Rachel dragged her attention back to the story of the marvelous black horse. Katie had just about finished her page when they heard footsteps trudging up the stairs to the apartment. In a moment, a man stepped onto the landing, impossible to recognize in the night shadows through the screen, and knocked heavily on the door.

"Who on earth?" Gloria asked, frowning.

"I'll get it." Rachel rose and snapped on the porch light. She tried to keep the surprise from showing on her face as she looked into the pale blue eyes of Sheriff Duncan. "Yes?"

"Evening, Rachel." Duncan removed his hat, seemingly to be polite but more likely because it was a hot and humid evening.

Rachel stood her ground on the inside of the screen door. "What can we do for you, Sheriff?"

"There's been a fire over at the Quincy ranch. Started in a shed and spread on to the garage. Fire department got to it just before it got the horse barn and maybe even the ranch house." He twirled his hat between his thick fingers as he shook his head. "Nasty business, fires."

The moment she heard the name Quincy, Rachel's heart jumped to her throat. She'd heard the sirens some hours ago, but hadn't given them further thought. Her hand on the door frame tightened, but she remained otherwise composed. "I'm sorry to hear that," she said, her mind racing. "What has that to do with us?"

Duncan shifted his feet, looking oddly uncomfortable. "We have reason to believe you were involved, Rachel. You'd best open up and let me in."

Justin decided to take an earlier flight. He'd gotten all he needed from the Friday-morning meeting, changed his reservations, and landed in Corpus Christi just before noon.

There was one reason and only one for his burning need to be back in Schyler.

He'd come to realize he loved Rachel and couldn't wait to hold her in his arms and tell her.

A man in a hurry, he rushed to phone the newspaper office. But Matt said Rachel wasn't in yet. When he called the apartment, it was Gloria who answered and told him that her daughter wasn't there, she'd gone walking.

Walking? Surprised at that, he'd wanted to question her further, but Gloria's voice had sounded tired and he'd apologized for bothering her before requesting that she ask Rachel to meet him at his house in an hour. Wearily Gloria had agreed and Justin had hurried to his car.

Driving south on Highway 77, Justin kept his cruise control on the speed limit. He wanted no tickets now, no delays. A man in love couldn't afford to waste time.

In Dallas all alone last night, he'd lain in bed in his hotel room after talking all too briefly with Rachel, missing her like hell. It was a small sample of what life for him would be like if she moved away, if he lost her. The thought was inconceivable.

There had to be a way they could work things out. Somewhere in the middle of the night, after he'd wrestled amid the sheets for hours, he'd reached a conclusion of sorts. One of them would have to compromise. He still wasn't sure which one.

If he could find Tyrone's killer, clear Rachel's name and convince the Quincys she'd never been at fault, perhaps she'd agree to give Schyler another chance. He also knew how deeply her mother's potentially fatal illness was affecting her. Even after Curt got out of the service, Gloria might still refuse to leave.

Knowing how Rachel felt about her mother, she would likely stay to see Gloria through this time of need. Later, if

Rachel insisted, he and Katie could move with her somewhere.

Justin pulled out to pass a slow-moving truck, then dropped back into the right lane. He hadn't planned on moving away from Schyler, thinking that he'd finally found a place where he belonged after too many years of roaming around. And he wasn't crazy about taking his daughter away from the solid anchor of her home base and her loving grandfather.

However, he firmly believed that it was people who were important, not places. With Katie and Rachel, he could be happy anywhere. He could start another newspaper somewhere, or work for one. It wasn't where he was that counted, but rather if the people he loved were with him.

They could be a family, such as he'd never known. He'd never thought he'd consider marriage again, but for the last little while, it was all he'd thought of. To have Rachel as his wife would make him complete. He'd even wandered afield to the thought that they could have other children. Katie had often asked him for a brother or sister. He wanted that for her rather than the lonely life of an only child such as he'd had.

The unknown factor here was Rachel. He knew she cared for him, responded to him, enjoyed being with him. And he knew Katie loved her. But he'd never mentioned marriage to Rachel and had no idea how she felt about the possibility. Or of having babies, though she seemed to like children.

So many questions with missing answers. Justin checked his watch. Twenty minutes and he'd be home. He hoped Rachel had gotten his message by now and would be waiting at his house. They'd have a couple of hours of privacy before Katie came home from school. How his arms ached to hold her.

His eyes on his rearview mirror, Justin stepped down on the gas.

Rachel had never been a pacer. She'd always released her tensions by running. And she'd done that for over an hour this morning, only to return to the apartment unable to sit still. She'd showered and dressed for work but hadn't been able to face going in. So she'd called Matt and told him she'd be by later. Then she'd gone for a walk.

That hadn't helped, either. Her mind was churning—with memories, with frightening scenarios, with raw fear. She couldn't handle what was happening, not again. Which was why she'd come to a decision: she had to leave. But she couldn't until she said goodbye to Justin. Perhaps he wouldn't understand, but she had to try to explain.

When she'd returned and Gloria had told her of Justin's call asking her to meet him at his house at one, she'd almost sagged in relief to know he was coming home earlier. She'd arrived at his house half an hour early and now found herself restlessly pacing, listening for his car, waiting for his arrival.

She was sitting in an old tire rigged up as a swing to an old tree in Justin's front yard when he finally drove up. Struggling with her jumpy nerves, she rose and walked toward his car.

Her pulse leaped as she saw him get out, slam the door shut and start toward her wearing that heart-stopping smile that she loved. Choking back a sob, Rachel ran the last few feet and let him catch her in his arms and swing her around right there on his front lawn. She closed her eyes as his mouth claimed hers.

Her kiss had a desperate edge that Justin recognized immediately. He'd been feeling a little desperate himself, but there was more. She was clutching him, wound so tightly about him that her heavy breasts were crushed against his chest. Rachel was too private a person to be acting this way in broad daylight in clear view of half a dozen nearby houses. Something was very wrong.

He pulled back, though her hands bunched in his shirt held him bound to her. "What is it? What's happened?" His heart was pounding with sudden possibilities. "Is it Katie?"

Rachel shook her head. "Katie's fine. She's in school."

"Then what?"

It felt so good to hold him again. How could she walk away from this? But she must. "Hold me. Please hold me, Justin."

He did and found she was trembling as she rose on tip-toe for his kiss. In the distance he heard a car approaching and broke away again. "Inside. Let's go inside."

Rachel wouldn't let go of him, but held on to his arm while he unlocked the front door. In the living room, she grasped him to her, her eyes huge and dark green in the shadowed room as she looked up at him.

She wanted him with a desperation she'd never known, and she knew why. Because it would be the last time. "Make love to me, Justin," she said, her voice a ragged whisper.

Questions raced through his mind, followed by a litany of unreasonable fears. Rachel was usually so calm. Something had to have happened. Or had she somehow reached the same conclusions he had while he'd been gone—that she loved him—and it scared the hell out of her?

With a hopeful heart, he framed her face with his hands, trying to ease her anxiety with gentleness. "I've thought of nothing else but making love with you since I left."

Rachel scarcely heard the words, caught up in an emotional roller coaster that had her hands yanking off the tie that had been hanging loose around his neck, then moving to unbutton his shirt. "I didn't want to need you. Damn, but I *hate* needing you." She shoved his shirt off, then moved to fumble with his belt buckle.

"It's all right," Justin murmured. "I need you, too."

Rachel slipped out of her sandals, then pulled her shirt off over her head and tossed it aside. "Let's not talk. I don't want to talk now." Again, she wound her arms around him, pressing her heated body to his. "Kiss me."

He did, tasting her uneasiness, absorbing her tension. Justin tried to walk her toward his bedroom, but she would have none of it. Dropping to the carpeted floor in front of the fireplace, she pulled him down and hurried to tug off the rest of their clothes.

Flesh to flesh on the floor, Justin let her take over, knowing she needed to prove something, if only to herself. Hot and throbbing, she lay over him and placed wild, frenzied kisses all over his face. The onslaught on his senses almost sent him reeling as her hands raced over him like a whirlwind, followed by the mad delight of her roaming mouth.

It was going too quickly, Justin thought with the small portion of his brain still functioning. The pressure was building too fast, fueled by their week's abstinence and the emotional turmoil driving Rachel. He needed to take control. Rolling with her, he stopped as she lay on her back and waited until she opened her eyes to look at him.

There was something in the way he looked at her that spoke of his need to take the lead. She'd already sampled a whole night of him. She knew how thoroughly he could make her forget even her own name. And she badly wanted to forget everything but the here and now.

Justin fought back the urge to rush, to hurry them both to the finish line so he could find out what was driving her.

There would be time for that later. For now, she needed him and wasn't even aware that he needed her no less.

He bent to taste her honeyed skin, his tongue skimming over her rigid nipples, pleased when she shuddered deeply. Taking her in his mouth, he drew on her flesh and heard her groan out his name. He shifted his attention to the other breast and in moments she was arching restlessly, her hands buried in his hair.

Rachel felt a clenching inside, then a rhythmic unclenching as the pressure built moment by moment until she thought she'd cry out with the startling mixture of pain and pleasure. She wanted it to end; she wanted it to go on forever. And then his mouth trailed downward.

Sensations ricocheted through her body as he made love to every inch of her flesh, finding pulse points she hadn't been aware she had. He left her with no choice but to react to the touch of his hands, his lips, his tongue, as he sent her on a sensual journey such as she'd never before even imagined.

Justin had never known such a responsive woman, one so new in loving yet so attuned to each nuance. He had no doubt that the distraction he was offering her was temporary. Yet for now, her mind was his, her body was his. She was his.

Her hands were urging him on now, wanting the completion that would release them both. He would draw out the pleasure a moment longer, testing his own limits, knowing the summit would be all the sweeter for the wait. He moved back to her and stroked her damp face. "What are you thinking, Rachel?"

Her head moved restlessly as her heavy lids rose to reveal eyes smoky with passion. "I can't think at all."

"Good. Don't think. Just feel. Let yourself feel."

"I feel so much." Her eyes drifted closed.

Finally he moved over her, slipping inside to a warm welcome. Slowly he took them both up the long climb as her arms tightened around him. They flowed together like longtime lovers, perfectly meshing and seeking the same goal. His breathing was labored now, his control being ripped away by her answering thrusts. Running out of patience, Justin escalated the pace.

Steeped in pleasure, he brought his face close to hers and saw she was watching him, her green eyes open and aware. Her skin was damp and slick and shimmering in the afternoon shadows. "I love you, Rachel," he said, and saw the shocked surprise register on her face.

Then he lowered his mouth to hers a moment before they were both engulfed in a shattering climax that left them both stunned.

She wasn't aware she was crying. Rachel lay on the soft rug in the sheltering cocoon of Justin's arms, wishing this afterglow could be like the others she'd known the first night she'd spent with him. But as her body came down from the incredible high, her fearful thoughts came flooding back.

It was over, all over. How ironic that just when she'd found Justin and Katie and the love she'd been searching for all her life, she had to leave them. And her mother. Gloria would understand, as she had before. But Justin was another story.

She felt him lift his weight from her and ease onto his side. His eyes, when they met hers, were filled with concern. It was almost her undoing.

"You're crying," he said, brushing the tears from her cheeks.

She never cried, not anymore. She'd put all that behind her when she'd left Schyler and left her teens, schooling herself into rigid control. To realize she was again vulnerable to that particular weakness frightened her almost as much as the situation she was facing. "I'm sorry, Justin." Sorry to have involved him in the mess that was her life.

"What's happened, Rachel? Tell me. We can take care of anything together."

"No, we can't. Not this time." Feeling exposed emotionally and physically, she shifted and sat up, looking around for her clothes.

Justin touched her arm. "Didn't you hear me? I love you. I want to marry you."

Wearily she turned to face him. "You won't when you hear what's happened. I only came to explain. And to say goodbye. I'm leaving in the morning."

Chapter Nine

The words Justin had been dreading echoed through the quiet living room. "Leaving? What are you talking about?"

Hastily Rachel pulled on her clothes, suddenly in need of all the protection she could find. "Just what I said. I'm going back to California." But would she be safe even there?

Justin stepped into his pants and yanked the zipper up before grabbing her arm and pulling her around to face him. "Damn it, talk to me. What's this all about?"

Running out of steam, Rachel shook off his hands and sank into the couch, releasing a trembling sigh. There was no question that she owed him an explanation. As he sat beside her, she thought how best to tell him. "Last night Sheriff Duncan came to the apartment. He told us that there'd been a fire at the Quincy ranch. Theo told him I set it."

"What?" Justin's exclamation exploded from him. "That's the craziest thing I ever heard."

His angry reaction warmed her. Again, he seemed to believe her before she'd explained it all. Rachel felt fresh tears blur her vision and quickly brushed them away. "I was with Katie from the time I picked her up from school until the sheriff arrived. Mom was with us in the apartment from about five on."

He took hold of her hands, banking his fury, knowing how badly she needed his support. "You don't have to convince me. I believe you."

Her eyes were huge in her small face. "The sheriff didn't. He said that mothers often lie to protect their children, and someone Katie's age is unreliable as an alibi."

Fleetingly he wondered if Duncan had moved to being directly on the Quincy payroll. "But why you? I don't understand. What kind of proof did they come up with to indicate you were anywhere near the Quincy ranch?"

She shrugged wearily. "My word against Theo's—and you know who the sheriff's likely to believe."

"And what is Theo's story?"

"That except for his mother sleeping off a sick headache, he was alone in the ranch house when along about seven, he smelled smoke. He ran outside and found the shed in flames and the fire already spreading to the garage. On his way to the bunkhouse to get some of the hands to help him, he saw my Toyota racing down their drive." Finding a tissue in her pocket, Rachel wiped her face.

"That's ridiculous. If that's all they've got, we can find someone who saw your car parked alongside the apartment about that time."

"There's more. A note was found tacked to the big tree near their back door. It read: 'First Tyrone, now you.'"

Justin reached inside himself for the dispassionate reporter instead of the emotional lover. "We'll get a handwriting expert, we'll find witnesses."

Rachel shook her head, feeling hopeless. "It doesn't matter. I'm leaving."

Leaving. Hadn't he told himself she'd surely leave one day? "Have they formally charged you with anything, Rachel?"

"No, but they'll find a way. The sheriff warned me not to leave town." She made a muffled sound. "Just like last time."

Fiercely he gathered her close to him. "No, it's not like last time. *I'm* here this time, and I'm not letting anything happen to you." As if to prove his point, he lowered his head and kissed her long and lingeringly. "I love you, Rachel. Do you believe that?"

There was a knot in her stomach larger than her fist. So long she'd waited to love and be loved, and now the Quincys were again robbing her of her future. "It's too late."

"No!" His hands settled on her upper arms, forcing her to look at him. "How do you feel about me?"

The knot was growing, burning. It wouldn't work. Didn't he see? "It doesn't matter."

"It does to me. Tell me."

"All right, yes."

"Yes, what?"

He needed the words. Perhaps she needed to say them, for all the good it would do. She felt her lips tremble. "I love you, Justin."

He pulled her into a bone-crushing kiss that took her breath away. His eyes were brighter when she pulled back. She badly wished she could feel some measure of joy, of hope. "It doesn't change anything." She leaned forward to hunt for her shoes. "I'm still leaving."

Justin had thought he couldn't get angrier than when she'd told him of Theo's accusations. However, faced now with her stubbornness, he realized he'd been wrong. But to show her that anger would only speed her on her way. He switched tactics, hoping he was making the right decision. "I guess it is easier to run away." Calmly he reached for his shirt and shrugged into it, busying himself with the buttons.

Slipping her feet into her sandals, Rachel grew incensed. Tossing back her hair, she glared at him. "Easy? What the hell do you know about easy? You think it's easy for me to walk away from you and Katie, from my mother who's desperately ill? But I've been through this before, and they almost destroyed me. If I stay now, they'll finish the job."

Finished dressing, Justin folded his arms across his chest and regarded her. "It won't work. It never does."

She let the anger build. It was so much easier to deal with anger than hurt. "*What* won't work?"

"Running. I ran once, too. Remember, I told you?" He took a step nearer, close enough to touch her, but he didn't. "When push came to shove, I always took the easy way out. In my work, in my marriage. Until I was faced with the loss of someone I loved more than life itself. Katie." His hand lifted to caress her cheek. "How much do you love us, Rachel?"

Her eyes widened as she struggled with that. "You don't play fair."

"How much, Rachel?"

But the door burst open before she could answer, and a breathless Katie came inside. Her small, freckled face was streaked with tears, and her entire body was shaking as she stared at both of them with her huge blue eyes.

Justin whirled toward his daughter. "What is it, Katie?"

But Katie focused on Rachel as she tossed down her book bag and ran to her, burying her face against the front of her in an intense hug. "I don't believe them. I don't," she wailed.

Startled, Rachel's arms went around the child and she lowered her cheek to rest on Katie's dark head. "Don't believe who, honey?" she asked.

Katie hiccuped out a half sob. "My friends at school. They're saying bad things about you, and I don't believe them." Clinging to Rachel, Katie's tears reappeared.

Feeling her heart twist, Rachel glanced toward Justin. Silently he stood watching the two of them, leaving it all up to her. She stroked the child's hair. "It's all right, honey," she whispered.

Still snuffling, Katie looked up at Rachel. "Daddy always says you have to believe in the people you love. I love you, Rachel, and I know you couldn't do a bad thing like start a fire where someone could get hurt."

Rachel blinked back the tears that wanted desperately to join Katie's. In the final analysis, it came down to this: a child taking the decision out of her hands, making her vindicate herself so that Katie's belief in her wouldn't be misplaced. Not her mother's silent plea nor even Justin's declaration of love. She looked down at Katie. "I didn't have anything to do with that fire, Katie, and I thank you for believing in me. I love you, too."

Katie brightened immediately. "I knew you did. I told Daddy last week that you loved us. You love Daddy, too, don't you, Rachel?"

Rachel's eyes locked with Justin's as he walked to them. "Yes, I love your Daddy, too." She felt Justin's arms enfold them both, and they stood like that, all struggling with their emotions, until Katie finally pulled free.

Frowning, she wiped her face with smudgy hands. "Why wouldn't the sheriff believe me last night, Daddy? Rachel was with me every minute from after school to bedtime, except when I was taking a bath."

"I don't know, honey," Justin said. "But we're going to find a way to prove to him and everyone else that Rachel didn't do anything bad. I don't want you worrying." He kissed the top of her head. "Now, in case you're interested, there's a brand new Houston Astros baseball cap in the side pocket of my case out in the van."

"You didn't forget!" Katie grinned at them both, then skipped outside.

Justin slipped his arms around Rachel and leaned back at the waist so he could study her face. "So, what's your decision?"

"I think you already know." Rachel sighed, a ragged sound in the still air. "I'll stay." But even as she said the words, she felt fear race along her spine.

"I'll be with you all the way, I promise." Pressing her cheek to his chest, he held her close to his heart.

Rachel wished she felt as confident as Justin sounded. He hadn't been here the last time, hadn't seen the pure hatred on the faces of Theo and Roy Quincy before and after the trial. But surely this time...

When the phone rang, she jumped back like a startled bird that had landed on an electrified fence.

"Easy," Justin said as he went to answer it. "Oh, hello, Gloria. Yes, she's here. What's that again?" He listened intently for a moment. "All right. We'll be right there." Slowly he set the phone down and turned to Rachel.

"Tell me," Rachel said, bracing herself.

He went to her, taking her chilled hands in his. "Sheriff Duncan's at the apartment. He claims to have found some evidence in Gloria's backyard that you set the fire at the Quincy ranch.''

"That's impossible.''

"I know that.''

Rachel swallowed hard. "You still think I can beat the Quincys?''

Justin's face took on a look of fierce determination. "Yes. We haven't even begun to fight. Come on.''

For the first time since he'd known the man, Justin thought Sheriff Duncan looked uneasy as he sat in one of Gloria's straight-back kitchen chairs that he'd carried into her small living room. Could it be that Duncan, close to retirement, was getting tired of having the Quincys rule his every move? Something to think about, he decided.

They'd dropped Katie off at Emily Porter's, then hurried to Gloria's, where they found her chain-smoking in her rocker, while Duncan sat twirling his sweat-stained hat between his thick fingers. Justin had guided Rachel to the couch, feeling the tension emanating from her as if it were his own.

"Aren't you supposed to have a search warrant in order to poke around people's yards, Sheriff?'' Justin began.

"Didn't need one,'' Duncan answered in his slow drawl. "Miz Hathaway here told me she don't have nothing to hide and to go take a look. So I did.''

"And I'm telling you I was in that shed yesterday,'' Gloria insisted in her raspy voice, "and none of those things you found were there then.''

"Can't help that, ma'am,'' Duncan said. "They was there just now.'' He pointed to the kitchen table. "There's a near-empty can of gasoline, some rags that smell like they been doused, a funnel of newspaper rolled up kind of odd-like. And this here.'' He reached under the chair and held out a writing tablet.

Leaning closer, Justin took it from him and examined it closely. ''Looks like an ordinary notepad you could buy in any drugstore.''

''Sure is,'' the sheriff agreed. ''But it's the same kind of paper like that note we found nailed to the Quincys' tree. See how it's got that jagged rip up at the top where someone tore off a sheet? The note's got the same kind of tear.''

''I've never seen that tablet before in my life,'' Rachel said at last, her voice tight with her effort to control it.

''We don't use gasoline around here,'' Gloria went on, ''so why would we keep a can in the shed?''

''Sheriff,'' Justin said, trying to be reasonable, ''did it occur to you that someone might have planted all those things in the Hathaway shed?''

Duncan cleared his throat noisily. ''Hard thing to prove, something like that. 'Less, of course, one of you folks saw someone on your property who didn't belong there.'' His pale blue eyes slid over each face in turn. ''Barring that, and with Theo Quincy swearing he saw that yellow Toyota you got parked downstairs leaving his driveway 'bout the time of the fire... well, it don't look good, Rachel.''

''Are you issuing a formal charge here, Sheriff?'' Justin asked, wanting to know just where they stood.

Duncan rose and placed his hat carefully on his head. ''I got a job to do, you know. Evidence adds up. I'm going to have to issue a summons charging you with arson, Rachel. I won't bring out an arrest warrant if I can have your word you won't leave the jurisdiction of the court.''

Pressing herself into the corner of the couch, Rachel looked at him with bleak eyes. ''I won't leave, Sheriff.''

Nodding, he gathered up the evidence and walked to the door. ''Folks, I'm sorry about all this.''

Justin pointed at the gasoline can that the sheriff had placed in a plastic bag. "Are you going to test that for fingerprints?"

"Yes, sir, but I wouldn't count on much help there. It looks like someone wiped it clean." Duncan opened the screen door.

"One more thing," Justin said, following him over. "What made you think to come here and search the Hathaways' shed?"

Duncan averted his gaze. "We got a tip, by phone." Turning, he started down the steps.

"I never should have asked you to come home for Orrin's funeral," Gloria said. Blinking, she struggled with her tears. "Rachel, honey, I'm so sorry."

Rachel moved to her mother's side, squatting in front of her and taking her hands in her own. "It's not your fault, Mom. It's the Quincys'."

"I just never dreamed they'd start up again." Gloria's cheeks were wet now.

Justin stepped closer. "We're going to stop them, Gloria. We'll hire an attorney and fight this."

Gloria coughed twice, her breathing labored. "I don't have much money. I could sell the tavern."

"No," Rachel said quickly. "That won't be necessary."

"Don't worry about the money," Justin added.

The older woman looked from Justin to Rachel, realizing the implications of what he'd said. She nodded with understanding, but the sheriff's visit had taken its toll on her emotions. She began coughing from deep in her chest. Soon she was struggling for each wheezing breath.

Rachel helped her up. "Come on, Mom. Let me set you up with your oxygen. You need to rest." She led Gloria into her bedroom.

Some minutes later, when Rachel came back out, she found Justin sitting on the porch swing. It was the dinner hour, and the streets below were nearly deserted, with only a couple of people milling around Herb's Gas Station across the way. The stifling humidity had her cotton shirt sticking to her back, and she rearranged it as she sat down. "I haven't had a chance to ask how everything worked out in your meetings in Dallas."

Justin slipped his arm around her. This need to touch, to have a woman close to him was new to Justin, yet already seemed as natural as breathing. "We managed to get approval for an increase in the grant so that the wildlife refuge will have guards patrolling around the clock. That's the good news. However, the bad news is that it won't go into effect for another couple of weeks while the paperwork clears."

"In the meantime?"

"In the meantime, I hope to initiate another head count and perhaps ask for volunteers who'll act as lookouts until the night guards arrive."

"What about the picture of the man on horseback?"

Justin shrugged. "Everyone agreed that positive identification was infeasible, and proving that Theo was the man who shot the horses even more impossible. Our best bet is still hoping that enough people in Schyler begin to suspect that Theo's behavior is self-serving, that he talks a good game in his desire to be sheriff but plays by a separate set of rules."

"I had a lot of time to think this morning, waiting for you to return. That's why Theo set me up, I believe, because we ran those pictures and started people talking. He's not stupid enough to go after you, but I've always been fair game."

"I've thought that, too. He's seen us together and knows there's something between us, so he went on the attack. He wants you out of town and me, too, probably." He squeezed her arm. "We aren't going to let him win."

Justin heard the sounds of coughing coming from the bedroom and waited until Gloria had stopped. "I didn't know she'd progressed to the point of needing oxygen."

Rachel leaned into him, needing his comfort. "I talked with Doc Tremayne a week or so ago and he prescribed an oxygen tank to keep at her bedside. If she'd just quit smoking, Doc says, she'd have a fighting chance. Naturally there's no cure, but she could stop further damage and stabilize her condition. I worry that an emotional upset may trigger an attack." She sighed wearily. "My mother probably would have been better off if I'd stayed away."

He pulled her closer. "I doubt that. She loves having you here, and she probably needs your nagging about her cigarettes."

"At least she can't smoke while the oxygen's going." Rachel sighed heavily. "I wish I could get her to quit smoking."

"Stubbornness seems to run in your family."

She leaned back to look at him. "It does. Are you still so certain you want to get entangled with the Hathaways?"

Justin brushed his mouth across her lightly. "Honey, I *am* entangled and I'm not one bit sorry." He angled his body toward her more comfortably. "When this is all over, I want you to marry me, Rachel."

She took his hand, her heart heavy in her chest. "Oh, Justin, a life with you and Katie seems like a dream I'm afraid to talk about. But right now, with everything in such a mess—this arson charge and my mother's health—I think we have to put off making plans for the future. I'm not even sure I'll be free or if I'll be..." She couldn't complete the thought.

"You will be free. We'll beat the Quincys. You've got to believe that."

"I want to...."

"I'm going to go see Ray Brewster. I've already talked to him, and I think he's a fine attorney. And he's familiar with you and your problems with the Quincys."

"When did you talk with him? This just happened."

"Last week I asked him to get me transcripts of your old trial. I've been going over them, trying to find something that might lead to the person who killed Tyrone."

Moved, Rachel reached to touch his face, rough with the day's growth of beard, loving the feel of him. She didn't—couldn't—say anything. He wanted to help her, and somehow she knew he would find a way. No one had come to her aid before, so she'd had no experience in accepting help. She could only stare at him and hope he understood how much his support meant to her.

Justin sensed her emotional confusion. He also knew she hadn't had many close relationships and wasn't used to putting her thoughts and feelings into words. Right now, she didn't need to. He could read it all in her eloquent eyes.

"I love you," he whispered, then bent to kiss her.

Ray Brewster had a full head of auburn hair that often made Justin wonder if he was related to Ted Koppel. He sat across from the young attorney in his small office on Barlow Road in the same building where Dr. Tremayne practiced medicine. In their brief conversation this morning, Ray not only had demonstrated a keen legal mind but a working knowledge of most of Schyler's residents and a phenomenal memory of detail.

"Getting the judge best suited for each individual case is often half the battle," Ray stated. "If we could get Ernest Powell, the judge who presided at Rachel's murder trial, we'd have a better chance."

Justin had heard the name but had never met Judge Powell. "What's so special about him?"

Ray leaned back in his red leather chair and anchored his thumbs under his plaid suspenders. "Small southern towns are unique, as you may have discovered by now, Justin. There are the haves and the have-nots as everywhere, but it's more than that. Edgewater Drive runs along past Lake Willow, and so do the railroad tracks. Folks around here are born literally on either the right side of those tracks, or the wrong. The Hathaways live on the wrong side. That's where Judge Powell was born and lived for a lot of years."

"Instant connection, you mean."

"Right. He's moved across now, physically, to a better section of town. But he relates and he remembers. Folks like the Quincys aren't his favorite kind of people."

Justin crossed his legs thoughtfully. "Are you saying that the judge is predisposed to being prejudicial?"

"Oh, I wouldn't go that far. But judges are human beings, and we all have our leanings." Ray straightened and picked up his pen. "I'll want to meet with Rachel as soon as possible, of course. The thing that's the most damaging as of this minute is Theo claiming he saw her car driving off his ranch. If we can discredit that, we'll be on our way."

"I want to help in the investigation. I used to free-lance as an investigative reporter, and I've done my share of snooping around."

Ray's serious brown eyes weighed his offer a moment. "I read some of your syndicated stuff years ago. Pop used to have copies in his office. I certainly wouldn't be one to turn down your assistance. But I would like to ask what your interest in this case is."

Pop had taught him a long while ago that it's stupid to lie to your doctor, your lawyer or your CPA. He told Ray the truth. "I love Rachel, and I want to marry her."

Ray paused. "An investigative newspaper reporter has to be detached and impartial, unemotional, as does an attorney. Can you do that, in this case?"

"If I find that's a problem, I'll back away before you have to ask. I don't want to do anything to hurt Rachel's case."

Apparently satisfied with that answer, Ray nodded. "We need to coordinate who we talk with and why, so we don't duplicate our efforts. After I talk with Rachel, I'll work up a list and we can go over it together."

Justin stood, shoving his hands in his pants pockets. "I know all this takes time and, ordinarily, I'm a fairly patient man. But I feel frustrated not being able to do something right away."

Ray also got up. "Maybe there is something you can do, something I couldn't do as well."

"Name it."

"From all you've told me and from my previous knowledge of Rachel Hathaway, she's being set up by Theo Quincy. He's spent ten years hating her and might not stop even if we could find who killed his brother. I've spent those same ten years living in this town with Theo, and I frankly think his erratic behavior is indicative of a very sick man."

Justin waited while Ray walked around his desk and leaned against the front corner. "We need to find ways to discredit him. You're known around here as someone always asking questions, so no one will think too much of it if you ask more. Nose around quietly. Let's see if he's been seen doing questionable things behind the scenes that haven't come to light. Maybe there's a Quincy ranch hand who saw something or heard something. Or someone in one of the stores along Main Street. Find out if he's running around on his wife, or if he's into drugs. Something, anything.''

''People are already talking about the picture in the *Gazette* of the man on horseback. I think quite a few think it's Theo, but they're afraid to step forward and say so.''

''We need to find the ones who aren't afraid. On the other hand, we need also to find people who'll testify as to Rachel's sterling character.''

Justin felt his spirits sag. ''That's not going to be easy. She's been back a little over a month, and, as I told you, the Quincys have been trying to hold her responsible for everything from a blackmailing letter to a kitten's death. And now, arson.''

Ray clapped Justin on the shoulder. ''I never said it would be easy.''

Justin shook hands with the attorney. ''Thanks, Ray. Stay in touch.'' He left the office and walked toward his van, wondering where to begin.

''I like hamburgers better than hot dogs, don't you, Rachel?'' Katie asked, as she set three plastic plates on the backyard picnic table.

''Mmm, I like hot dogs at the ballpark. Here, I like your dad's hamburgers better.'' She handed the napkins to Katie, then glanced over at Justin cooking on the grill. ''How's it coming, master chef?''

''Won't be long now.'' He took a long swallow of his cold beer. ''Did you two make potato salad?''

"Yup," Katie answered, walking to the grill to join him. "And Rachel taught me her recipe for baked beans. Wait'll you taste them, Daddy. They're made with bacon."

Justin smiled at Rachel over his daughter's head. "I can hardly wait."

Rachel strolled over. "You want to bring out the catsup and mustard for us, Katie, please?"

"Okay." She skipped off inside.

Watching her, Rachel slipped an arm around Justin's waist. "I'm glad you talked me into taking the afternoon off. Katie and I had a nice time."

Justin flipped the burgers carefully. They were short-handed at the *Gazette* with Matt asking for and receiving a week off to write a term paper, but he'd thought Rachel's peace of mind far more important. "You don't have to keep buying her presents, Rachel. You're spoiling her."

"I suppose you're right, but I'm enjoying myself too much to stop. Children should be spoiled a little now and then. The extra attention lets them know they're loved."

He heard the wistful note and knew there'd been precious little extra time or money in the Hathaway house for spoiling children when Rachel was growing up. Which was only one reason he let her indulge Katie. He edged them back from the smoke of the grill and studied her a moment. "Are you all right?"

"I guess so." Restlessly she kicked at a tuft of grass. "This whole thing's taking so long. I hate the waiting and wondering."

"We're not exactly standing still. Ray's discovered some important things for our side. Learning that Theo bought additional fire insurance for the ranch outbuildings just a week before the shed went up in flame is certainly going to count against him and help you."

"Yes, but what about the clerk at the drugstore?"

Both he and Ray had questioned the woman, and she'd stuck to her story that Rachel had made half a dozen purchases several days before the fire, including a home permanent and a tablet such as the one in question. Justin reached for the package of buns. "I can't figure out why she's lying, but we know she is. I'm going to visit her again. Something wrong there." He piled burgers and buns on a plate.

Katie came out with the condiments as Rachel went in for the potato salad and beans. Justin poured milk for his daughter and Rachel.

"You still drink milk, Rachel?" Katie asked. "Do you want to grow taller?"

Rachel laughed. "Not particularly. I just happen to like milk."

"We always have lots of milk at our house," Katie went on, her eyes shifting to her father. "Probably enough left over for a kitten, even. They don't drink much."

Justin spread catsup on his burger. "What's this about a kitten?"

Katie abandoned all pretense of eating, jumping into the subject that she'd obviously been dying to bring up. "I know where we can get this really cute kitten, Daddy. He's the last one left out of the litter, and Susie Blake says her dad's just going to put him out in the woods if someone doesn't adopt him. Please, Daddy, could we take him in?"

Justin glanced at Rachel, then his daughter. "We have a little problem with that, honey. See, Rachel's allergic to cats. She gets real sick around them, and if we want her to come live with us like we talked about..." He let the words hang, wondering at Katie's reaction.

"Oh. I didn't know." She turned to Rachel. "I'd rather have you here than a kitten."

But Rachel was uncomfortable with that, especially since her future was so uncertain. "Listen, Katie, I'm not here yet. If you want a kitten..."

"I have an idea," Justin interrupted. "What if we go looking for a puppy instead? You're not allergic to dogs, are you, Rachel?"

"Not that I know of. But I..."

"Wouldn't a puppy be more fun, Katie? You could teach him tricks and take him on walks."

She warmed to the idea immediately. "Could we get one soon?"

"I don't see why not." Justin bit into his burger, thinking he'd handled that rather well. "Of course, you'd have to help take care of him. Puppies require a lot of care."

Katie was suddenly enthusiastic. "I would, honest. I wouldn't be like Diane Quincy. I'd give him baths and feed him and even sleep with him."

The Quincy name set off an alarm with both Justin and Rachel. He lowered his voice in an aside. "Diane Quincy's Theo's daughter. She's Katie's age and in her class." He turned his attention back to his daughter. "What about Diane, honey?"

"She got punished and it was awful, Daddy." Katie put down her sandwich, her big eyes sad. "She asked for a kitten and she got one the next day. Only her daddy told her if she didn't take care of it, he'd get rid of the kitten. Diane sort of forgot to feed him and the next day, she came home from school and the kitten was hanging from her Grandma's tree."

"Oh, no." Rachel felt sick at the thought. Could Theo have done that to his own child?

"Are you sure, Katie?" Justin asked.

"Honest, that's what Diane told us. The next day, her daddy said he was sorry and they buried the kitten in a shoebox, but Diane cried and cried." Somewhat disinterestedly, she picked up her burger again. "I'd take care of my puppy. Really I would."

Justin touched his daughter's shoulder. "I want you to, but if you didn't, you have to know that I wouldn't hurt the puppy to punish you."

"I know. I told Diane you wouldn't. And I told Susie you wouldn't just leave a kitten out in the woods all alone, either."

"Maybe tomorrow we can see if we can find that kitten a home," Rachel suggested. "Want to help me ask around?"

Katie nodded. "Probably there's lots of people who aren't allergic, right?"

"I'm sure we'll find someone." Rachel shifted her gaze to Justin and found him looking grim. "I suppose we should have guessed. We certainly knew he was capable of such a thing."

"And a lot worse, I'm afraid. He used the incident to get at you. But we can't drag his daughter into court to prove it." Justin drained his beer, feeling his frustrations mount. "We need a break. One good break."

"I think we've got one," Ray Brewster said, as he stuck his head over the back fence. Unlatching the gate, he stepped into the yard. "I called earlier, but you were both out."

Justin rose. "Hi, Ray. Can I get you a beer?"

"That would be great." The lawyer set down his briefcase and approached the table.

"So what have you got, Ray?" Rachel asked as she slid over on the bench and made room for him.

Ray sat and leaned forward. "An eyewitness who can place Theo and his white Cadillac near the Hathaway apartment the night the so-called arson evidence had to have been planted in that backyard shed."

Chapter Ten

"No kidding! Who is it?" Justin returned to the table and handed Ray a frosty bottle.

"Matt Russell." Ray took a swallow of his beer. "I bumped into him at Edna's Diner earlier. He hadn't been at the *Gazette* all week, so I hadn't had a chance to interview him."

Rachel pushed back her plate, her mind no longer on food. "He had time off to write a term paper. So tell us, what did he see?"

Ray loosened his tie. "It seems that Matt and his girl were parked on the edge of the woods that evening, undoubtedly doing a bit of…ahem…research. Anyhow, Matt recognized Theo's white Cadillac sitting near the gate that leads into Gloria's backyard. He doesn't recall seeing it arrive, but he did see Theo come out of the yard, close the gate behind him, look all around, then get in his car and drive away kind of slow and easy with his lights off. He thought that was odd because everyone knows Theo races around town at high speeds."

"And Matt would be willing to testify to that?" Rachel asked.

"Oh, yes," Ray said. "He thinks the world of you, Rachel."

"But how good is that sort of testimony?" Justin asked. "I mean, it isn't as if he saw Theo enter the yard with the gas can and tablet in his hand *before* he planted the stuff."

Ray nodded. "That would have been better, of course. But Matt can testify as to what he saw, a man who had no business being in the Hathaway yard leaving furtively on the night in question. And let the suspicions build in the judge's mind. Remember, Theo had probable cause to set Rachel up. For weeks he's been telling everyone that he wants her out of Schyler."

Justin was still doubtful. "Maybe she should have opted for a jury trial. I hate having Rachel's fate be in the hands of one man—the judge. A bench trial is more risky."

"I disagree," Ray said firmly. "Rachel and I talked this over right before her arraignment. It would be damn difficult in this town to find twelve unbiased citizens to sit on a jury. And we still might get lucky and draw Judge Powell. He's very fair and can't be bought, that we know."

"Daddy, can I be excused?" Katie asked, indicating her empty plate. "I want to go in and watch TV."

"Sure, honey." He watched his daughter finish her milk and go inside, then turned back to Ray. "Have you had dinner, Ray? I could make you a burger."

"No, thanks. I ate at Edna's. She's going to make a great character witness for you, Rachel. She's pretty well-thought-of in this town."

Rachel smiled sadly. "Edna and my mother. Justin, Pop and Matt. That probably completes the list of people in my corner, right?"

Ray shook his head. "Don't be too sure. I've spent the last two days talking with folks. You know, dropping in at stores, visiting Edna's Diner, chatting with some of Gloria's regular customers. They're not drunks who hang around the tavern, you know. Just lonely people who have nowhere else to go. Many of these average citizens watched you grow up, and they believe you never should have been accused in that first trial."

Rachel found herself surprised. "You're kidding."

"Not at all," Ray went on. "Theo's not very likable. I think people are beginning to wake up around here. The tide could very well be turning in favor of the underdog."

She looked at Justin, wondering if Ray could be right. "Can you believe that?"

"Yes, and you should, too," Justin answered.

Ray swung his gaze to Justin. "Have you found out anything I should know?"

Justin told him the story of Theo's daughter's dead kitten. "Naturally we can't involve the child. And we can't prove Theo hung the kitten."

Ray removed his notepad from his shirt pocket and jotted down a couple of reminders. "I doubt if Theo's going to bring up that incident. But if he does, we'll find a way to make our point."

"The man's unbelievable," Rachel said, her voice heavy with disdain.

"You've got that right." Ray flipped through his note pages. "I've learned a few things that make his campaign platform to clean up Schyler laughable. Two years ago, Theo got a woman who lives down near Raymondville pregnant. His daddy paid for the abortion and gave her a job at Quincy Dry Goods. He's also been stopped more than once for speeding and for driving under the influence, this man who wants to close down the tavern because of the so-called undesirables who hang around there. But he's never been issued a ticket, probably because Sheriff Duncan's managed to intervene."

Justin had suspected as much. "I knew he was talking out of both sides of his mouth. The thing is, Theo's smart enough to do most of his running around outside of Schyler."

"Yes, but his activities aren't going to stay covered up much longer now that we're poking around. The word I hear around town is that Theo's nervous. I want you to stick close to Rachel, Justin. He's liable to try something before we go to trial."

Rachel's eyes grew wide. "What do you mean? What else could he do?"

Ray shrugged as he put his notepad away. "Hard to say. But you're too vulnerable, for instance, if you go running in the woods or even walking along the lake paths alone. A dangerous man who feels threatened is liable to do most anything."

Justin was quick to agree. "I think you should move in here with me."

Rachel shook her head. "I can't do that. There's Katie to consider, and I'm a teacher. My reputation in this town is suspect already. I'm not going to give them any more ammunition."

"I think she's right, Justin," Ray commented as he rose. "Just don't let her go anywhere alone." He ran a hand through his mop of thick hair. "I'm going up north tomorrow. My sources tell me that a particular ranch up around Stamford all of a sudden has some interesting additions—Spanish mustangs."

Justin stood. "The last head count at the wildlife refuge shows they're thirty head short, aside from the dead horses. But how can you tie the rancher up in Stamford to Theo?"

Ray grinned. "Turns out he went to college with Theo. Isn't that a coincidence? I'm going to want to see that bill of sale or get an explanation as to why he doesn't have one."

"Won't you need a court order to look at his books?"

"If he won't cooperate. Then again, perhaps I can persuade him to listen to reason. Purchasing stolen goods is no small offense, and he may well talk to save himself from prosecution."

Justin nodded. "Maybe we'll be able to solve two crimes."

Rachel walked to the gate with them, nerves causing a knot in her stomach. "I just wish it was all over. How long before we have a trial date, Ray?"

"We'll probably be assigned the judge next week, and I'll press for a speedy trial. Hopefully in a week or two. The circuit court dockets aren't too full right now." His hand on the gate latch, Ray turned to Rachel. "Try not to worry so much. We're building a strong case here."

"I'm not sure reasonable doubt's going to do it again, Ray," Rachel said with a frown. "Theo's a rich and powerful man in this state, even without Roy Quincy."

"Rich and powerful men have been known to fall from grace, too. Let's have a little confidence here." He gave her arm an affectionate pat. "We're going to win, Rachel."

Justin shook hands with the attorney and watched him walk to his car. Slipping his arm around Rachel's waist, he drew her close to his side as they strolled back to their unfinished meal.

"I wish I felt as optimistic as Ray," she said.

The sun was setting behind her head as he turned her to face him. "As Ray pointed out, there're more people rooting for you than you might think. A lot of them would like to see Theo taken out of commission, but they've been afraid to speak out. That's going to change real soon." He untied the ribbon that held her hair back and ran his fingers through the thickness, loving the look in her eyes as her head tipped back.

"I hope you're right."

"I've got a few things to check out tomorrow myself. That clerk in the drugstore—her story's shaky, and she wouldn't look at me the whole time we talked. And I, too, want to talk with the people who frequent the tavern. I'm determined to find someone who left the building around the time of the fire and may have noticed your car sitting there, proving that it was nowhere near the Quincy ranch."

She leaned in to him, allowing his gentle touch to soothe her frazzled nerves. "It's only been a couple of weeks, yet I feel as if we've been preparing my defense for months."

An idea came to him, one that would be good for both of them. "You need a change of scene, to go away where no one and nothing reminds you of all this."

A sigh trembled through Rachel. "*Is* there such a place?"

"Yes. I have a friend who owns a sailboat up near Corpus Christi. We could spend the weekend on it, sail around the bay."

She'd done very little sailing, yet she'd loved being out on the sea, the freedom of open water. "Sounds wonderful. Will there be a problem with the sheriff about my leaving town?"

"I don't see why. Corpus Christi's within jurisdiction of the court."

"How do you know your friend's boat is available?"

He thought of Phil, of the trouble he'd gone to, protecting him years ago in Dallas. "It'll be available. He owes me." Justin looked down into her lovely eyes. "Did you ever spend a night on a boat anchored in a private cove and let the waves rock you to sleep?"

"No." But the thought had her smiling in anticipation.

"Let's do it. We'll drive up Friday afternoon. I'll settle Katie with Pop."

Maybe that was what she needed, a lazy time when she could just let her mind drift. "It's a date."

Justin glanced in through the back screen and saw past the kitchen archway that Katie was seated in front of the television in the living room. "I can hardly wait," he said, as he gathered Rachel closer and covered her mouth with his.

Rachel had almost forgotten how it felt to be carefree. On board the expensive sloop, she basked in the simple pleasure of emptying her mind and concentrating on nothing more complex than the sun on her face and the sea wind tossing her hair about.

Slowly she felt the strain slip from her features and the tension slide away from her taut muscles. The sky was a deep blue, the clouds few, the air warm and smelling of salt. Rachel drew in an intoxicating breath and felt her cares disappear one by one. Temporarily, she knew, but she would settle for that.

Out here on a golden afternoon, no sheriff was looking over her shoulder and no Quincy could harass her. Out here, glancing back at the foamy wake chasing them and tossing her head to laugh into the exhilarating wind, she felt free. Accusations, intimidations and obligations were set aside for a few brief hours as she watched Justin skillfully navigate them past other boats out on the bay.

As they'd cast off, he'd adjusted the sails, and Rachel had assisted him in stretching the flapping canvas. Now she leaned along the shiny mahogany railing as he took the tiller, his hand steady and sure. He'd removed his shirt and wore only a pair of faded trunks, his bare feet planted in a casual stance, looking in command and at ease.

Brushing back her flyaway hair, she studied him as he adjusted their course. He had a good body, lean and hard. She remembered what it was like to be held close to that masculine chest, to feel his heart beat beneath her hand. So exciting, to make a man's heart pound for you, only for you.

On the drive up to Corpus Christi, he'd kept her close alongside him on the seat of his van, boldly stating how much he was looking forward to being alone with her in some sleepy lagoon where they could make love all night long. Even more boldly, he'd slipped his large, rawboned hand along her thigh and kept it there. The hint of arrogance in Justin's manner had oddly fascinated her from the beginning. Perhaps because she knew it was tempered by an innate kindness.

Passion. It was a word that sprang to mind when she just looked at him. She'd never dreamed of passion the way Justin had taught her it could be. She'd been wanted first by boys and then by men as far back as she could remember. Their looks, their need to touch her, had frightened and sometimes repulsed her. So she'd built up an icy reserve, a studied indifference. But Justin had broken down her defenses. Now, she wanted, she desired, she felt passion.

Turning back toward Rachel, Justin stretched out an arm. "Come up here," he coaxed over the sound of the racing wind. "I need to hold you."

The sensual pull of his suggestion washed over her. He seduced by words as well as touch, she thought as she moved to his side and felt his arm encircle her. "You were right," she told him. "I was ready for this."

Justin's hand tangled in the long, loose top she wore over her bathing suit. "It's too hot for this. Take it off. You could use some sun."

She hesitated a moment, studying his eyes, then tugged the top over her head and tossed it onto the seat.

She wore a conservative one-piece suit, yet he found the hidden temptations more exciting than if she'd worn a skimpy bikini. His eyes skimmed her curves appreciatively as his hand wandered to her shoulder strap. "You have a beautiful body, but I'm not comfortable with the thought of men staring at you."

"That makes two of us."

The wind was scooting them along nicely; Justin relaxed his grip on the tiller. "I'd prefer only one man look at you—me. Perhaps later, when we're all alone, we won't need our suits."

"Perhaps." She'd never dressed to please a man before, but rather to keep men at bay. She'd certainly never *undressed* for one until recently. She'd have to get used to the thought of swimming without a suit. Justin, she had learned, had a way of introducing her to new things and letting her discover she liked them. A rare thing, a man who didn't push, but rather allowed her to sample and decide for herself.

They passed the paddle wheeler *Flagship,* all three decks crowded with tourists, returning to the bay area after a swing along the coastline. The narrator's voice describing the sights bounced across the water. The sun was moving lower in the sky as Justin let the sails fill and gather speed. He wanted to find a secluded spot to anchor where peace and privacy would be theirs for the taking. He hadn't had nearly enough time alone with Rachel.

Skimming along, his arm laid loosely across her shoulders, Justin felt at peace with the world. This was how it should be, two people in love just enjoying being together. This was how it *could* be, if only Rachel's trial would begin and end quickly with her acquittal. Yet perhaps then an even harder struggle would begin, convincing Rachel to stay among people who'd given her little enough reason to want to remain.

He'd lived in Schyler long enough to know that basically the residents were good people. Perhaps this trial would vindicate Rachel in their eyes once and for all. Then, acceptance and even a healing welcome could begin. He badly wanted Rachel to feel good about the town. And about herself.

Spotting a quiet cove in the distance, Justin slowed, showing her how to handle the tiller. "We're going to tack in that direction. Just work with the wind while I grab the lines."

She'd done this only once before, but it came naturally to her. Calmly she managed to keep them upright, then took a seat while Justin secured the lines. It was late afternoon and the fishing boats had long since gone in. Where they anchored was devoid of humans for what seemed miles around. For a couple of days, they could be just a man and a woman adrift on the sea, answering to no one. Heady with the thought, she smiled at Justin as he joined her.

"Are you hungry?" she asked. "My mother packed enough food for a week's stay."

"Then let's stay a week," he said, reaching to touch her hair turned golden by the sinking sun. "Maybe, when this is all over, we'll take some time and go off for a while, alone or with Katie."

The mention of his daughter's name brought a smile to her. "Yes, with Katie." If only she would be free to go, to live her life in peace, she would ask for nothing more, Rachel thought in a fierce prayer that had her eyes closing.

"Is something wrong?" Justin asked.

Abruptly she stood, slipping off her boat shoes. "I need to exercise. How about a swim?"

He saw the tension in the stiff way she held herself, so he agreed, hoping the seawater would calm her thoughts. Rising, he offered a hand to assist her, but she ignored it, slipping over the side smoothly. Quickly he followed.

She was a powerful swimmer, he noted as she struck out. The afternoon they'd spent on North Padre Island with Katie, Rachel hadn't gone in the water, hadn't even removed her coverall. But that was before they'd made love. Slowly today, she was relaxing with him. He fully intended to relax her even more.

Hanging back, Justin let her wear herself out. He waited until she slowed, then came alongside as she turned, treading water, her hair flowing behind her, wet and sleek. "Do you swim much in Bakersfield?" he asked, impressed by her stamina.

"We have a shared pool in my condo community. I often swim in the evening when it's mostly deserted."

"But you learned to swim around here?" Shifting to his back, Justin floated.

"Mom used to take the boys and me on Sundays—her only days off—to Baffins Bay and occasionally down to Laguna Madre. We'd swim and picnic while she'd read in the shade of a tree."

Some questions had been circling in his brain, and perhaps she could provide a few answers. "Were you and your brothers close?"

Rachel dipped her head back, then righted herself as she considered that. "I suppose. I remember growing up feeling quite maternal toward them. In their teens, they both grew up to be such big boys that they easily passed me. Then they sort of looked out for me. I still can't believe Orrin's gone."

He angled his head so he could look at her. "The night that Tyrone died, where were the boys?"

"I don't know. I suppose it came out at the trial, because they questioned every one of us, but I can't remember. Sometimes one or both of them would meet me at the school and walk me home. But that evening, unfortunately, neither one showed up. Then again, maybe it's a good thing. Curt was a fighter, but Tyrone could have beaten him easily. And poor Orrin wouldn't have known what was going on." Slowly she filtered water through her fingers in lazy circles. "What made you ask?"

Justin spiraled upright, treading water until he was closer to her. "As I mentioned, I've been reading the transcripts of that old trial. Haven't you wondered how it was that Theo just happened along that night?"

Rachel frowned thoughtfully. "I'm not sure I know what you mean."

"I mean that Theo and Tyrone as twins were probably close, right? Isn't it possible that they both planned to intercept you on your walk home, that Tyrone lay in wait for you and that Theo was supposed to join him after an allotted time had passed?"

"You think they were both going to... to..."

"To rape you, yes. Only their timing got screwed up and someone knocked Tyrone in the head before Theo came running in. Or is it possible that, while you were unconscious on the ground, Theo came in and they quarreled.

Maybe Theo killed his own brother. Sometimes twins can be rivals, for Daddy's affection, for Daddy's money.''

"I must admit, that's one I've not thought of."

"Maybe they even diverted your brothers on their way to meet you. Orrin could have easily been distracted with a minor errand. But not Curt, probably. That's why I've been wondering where he was at the time. There's no testimony from Curt in the trial transcript."

"That's odd. I thought the sheriff had questioned Curt extensively." She stared up at the sunset-streaked sky, trying to remember. "I wish we could get Curt home. For a lot of reasons."

"Ray's filed a request with the Navy Department."

"Think it'll do any good? They wouldn't let him home for Orrin's funeral."

"But his presence might make a difference in a court case, and that has to be a serious consideration."

Suddenly Rachel's mind shot ahead and her eyes widened. "You're not thinking that Curt may have killed Tyrone? No, he couldn't have. Curt's gentle and loving."

He reached out to calm her. "I'm not suggesting any one individual, Rachel. I'm examining possibilities. And I'm wondering why Curt wasn't questioned when everyone remembers that he was constantly fighting, trying to protect you and your mother and even Orrin."

But Rachel was agitated. "I don't like where your mind is going on this, Justin. I don't want Curt brought into suspicion on that old trial. Let them all think I did it and that I got off on a technicality. I won't have my brother implicated. The Hathaways have had enough to deal with in this town."

He let his legs brush against hers, let his fingers twine with hers. "We're just discussing, Rachel. It's not my intention to harm Curt or anyone else in your family. I hope you believe that."

She blinked the moisture from her eyelashes, uncertain whether it was seawater or the tears she had trouble containing lately. "I believe you. Please don't mention this conversation to Ray. Promise me."

"I promise you." He watched her struggle to accept this. "I didn't mean to upset you. Rachel, I'm trying to help clear you."

"I know." She shivered, feeling a sudden chill, and turned to face the boat. "I'm going back." She took a deep breath and set out with long strokes.

He would excuse her touchiness, Justin told himself, as he followed close behind. She had a right to a case of nerves, preparing for a court case, trying to hold her head up high while many in town still regarded her suspiciously. His own nerves were a bit on edge.

She'd already pulled herself over the side when he reached the boat and dropped onto the deck. Letting the water drip from him, he watched her grab a towel and rub her hair dry, avoiding his eyes. She was still annoyed with him. He would let her set the pace, Justin decided, as he picked up his own towel.

"I suppose we should eat," Rachel said without enthusiasm. Moving to the stairs, she ducked down into the small cabin. Bending to the refrigerator, she gazed inside, wondering what had happened to her appetite.

Reaching past her, Justin pulled out a bottle of wine, one of several chilling. "Let's start with this," he said, searching the single drawer for a corkscrew. Perhaps a bit of wine would mellow the mood.

She found glasses and held them out as he poured. Cool and tart, the wine slid around her tongue and slipped down her throat. Closing her eyes briefly, she decided she was worrying unnecessarily. Justin wouldn't hurt her or those she loved. Turning, she saw he was quietly sipping, the towel hanging loosely around his neck, his gray eyes guarded.

She searched for a neutral topic to restore the good feelings between them. "Nice," she said, indicating the wine. "Your friend not only lends you his boat but stocks it for you as well. What kind of favor did you do for him that he's so generous?"

Justin leaned a hip against the counter. "I went to jail to protect him."

Rachel's eyes widened. "You're serious?"

"I never joke about jail. I was working on a Dallas paper and investigating construction fraud on several local government buildings being built. Phil Ambrose worked for his father-in-law at the time, in his construction firm. Phil got me the evidence I needed to break the story about bid tampering. When the case came to trial, they put me on the stand and asked me to reveal my source. I refused."

"So they put you in jail?"

"For two days. There was a lot of hoopla, constitutional rights and all that. My publisher paid the fine and got me out. But the next day, he fired me as being too controversial for his conservative newspaper's image." Justin sipped his wine, feeling the heat drift downward.

"How unfair. What did you do?"

"Picked the best of three offers I suddenly had. Newsmen believe in being protective of their sources, and so I had a lot of support. Phil's father-in-law didn't fare quite so well. He went to prison, and eventually Phil bought out his company. Today he's a very rich man."

"I can see why Phil feels he owes you."

"He really doesn't. I didn't do it as much for him as for something I believe in. Protecting the innocent when it comes to journalism. But Phil feels differently. He's always offering me things, and this is the first time I've ever accepted. However, I told him the only way I'd take the boat is if he let me rent it.''

Rachel found herself admiring that. ''In case you ever have to write another story about his operation?''

''You've got it. It's best for a newspaperman to turn down favors and keep his nose clean. Which brings me to another point.'' Noticing that her glass was nearly empty, he poured more wine for both of them.

''What's that?''

''I'm letting Pop write the copy for the *Gazette* when the trial begins.'' He stepped closer to her in the small galley. ''I'm a bit prejudiced toward the defendant.''

She felt his hand settle on her shoulder. She'd been listening so intently that she hadn't noticed a strap had slipped down. Rachel felt her pulse skitter as his long fingers toyed with the damp material. She set down her glass, realizing she'd probably had enough wine.

''I think perhaps the defendant is a bit prejudiced toward you, too.'' Reaching up, she took hold of the ends of the towel draped around his neck. ''And I'm still not sure it's the best thing for either of us.''

Justin set aside his wine and tugged her other strap down over the curve of her shoulder. ''Do you always do the best thing?''

''Apparently not, or I wouldn't be in the mess I'm in. You, on the other hand, went to jail for a noble cause. It's you who should be having second thoughts.'' She felt his fingers trailing along her skin, felt a quiver of anticipation begin low in her abdomen.

''I'm still dealing with my first thought—my only thought right now—and that's how perfect you feel right here with me.'' Aligning the lower half of their bodies into close contact, Justin inched her straps fractionally lower, teasing them both. "Last chance, Hathaway. Jump ship now, or take your chances. I intend to ravish you."

Heart thudding, she smiled up at him. "Mmm, I've always wanted to be ravished. Permission granted, Wheeler."

He accepted the challenge gladly. His eyes stayed on hers as he inched her suit down, letting it gather at her waist. Green turned to jade as she sucked in a sharp breath just before he bent to press his mouth to one rosy tip. He felt her knees waver, then her head fell back as she sighed his name.

The scent of the sea perfumed the air. Her skin tasted of salt and the heated essence of woman. Slowly, his hands lingering, he pushed off her suit. Her fingers, as eager as his, slid his trunks from him. The bunk was narrow, the light filtering in dim and hazy. They stood a moment, looking their fill, satisfied with what they saw. Justin held out his hand, and she took it. Gently he drew her onto the bunk with him.

It was where she'd wanted to be all day, every day since the last time she'd lain with him. To lose herself in her passion for this man, to let him take her to places she'd only imagined in her dreams, to meld with him, and to do the impossible—make two become one. Rachel reached to bring his mouth to hers.

The corduroy spread beneath her was taut yet welcoming. He eased her onto her side and she opened her eyes to gaze into his. Words between them seemed unnecessary. For long moments, they lay like that, sharing a look of recognition, of delight. *Yes,* their eyes told one another. *You are the one I've waited for. You are my love.* Silently they spoke to one another with a lover's brush of hands, mouth pressing to mouth, letting the ache build.

It had taken Justin some time to get her to trust him with the gift of herself. Now she seemed to be handing him the gift of her feelings. He would treasure the one as much as the other and know she'd not given either lightly. He nibbled along the fragile underside of her breasts, then moved lower and felt her fingers dig into his back. His lips traveled over her sensitive skin, offering her layers of pleasure to store away for the uncertain days ahead. She arched to meet him, and he continued relentlessly, teasing, invading. Outside the window, a gull called out as he dived past; at the same moment he heard Rachel make a sound deep in her throat.

A fierce need to make her his, really his, drummed through Justin as he rose above her. Before she could truly catch her breath, he was inside her, driving her up again, higher, faster.

This time when she cried out in completion, his sigh of satisfaction joined with hers.

Chapter Eleven

Justin's van hummed along the highway Sunday night as they drove back to Schyler. In the seat next to him, Rachel stifled a yawn. She couldn't remember the last time she'd spent two such mindless days lying in the sun, swimming, eating far too much. And, she added, as she angled her head to look at Justin, making love. A blush started low on her throat and moved upward as she thought of the many ways they'd found to pleasure each other over the past forty-eight hours.

And she'd also had a good deal of time to think. Most of her thoughts had been troubled, despite the tranquil respite. The trial would begin soon, but the outcome was still uncertain.

If she was acquitted, then perhaps a life with Justin and Katie would work out. But what if she wasn't? Justin would be angry, but Katie would be devastated. They'd become very close over the past weeks, and Rachel didn't want the child, who'd never really had a mother figure in her life, hurt if she had to go to prison.

Perhaps, until the decision was in, she should pull back and not spend much time with either Justin or Katie. It would be hard on her now, when she needed their support, but harder still if later she'd have to leave them. The last thing she wanted, Rachel thought with a worried frown, was to harm the two people she'd come to love so completely.

Justin glanced over at her. "Weekend-after regrets?" he asked, wondering why she was looking so distressed.

"Not a one," she answered and meant it. "And you?"

"Ditto." He eased the van into the left lane, passing a slow-moving pickup truck. "I wonder if Ray's got any news for us."

Back to harsh reality, Rachel thought. "Like what?"

Justin's mind raced through a variety of possibilities. "Like, did we get the judge we want assigned to our case? Have we got a trial date set yet? What happened when he visited that ranch up north to check on the mustangs? If we can prove Theo's a horse thief, the judge's more apt to believe he's involved in other criminal activities."

Rachel stretched out her legs. "Ray said we'd be getting together this week, and he'd go over the material in preparation for the trial. I wonder if he plans to put me on the stand."

"Probably. Don't worry about it. Just answer his questions as honestly as you know how and trust him." Justin hit the turn signal, indicating he'd be taking the next exit.

She shot him an annoyed look. "I've answered everything honestly, and I do trust him. Why do you feel you need to remind me?"

He edged toward the off ramp. They were nearing the outskirts of town and she was back to being testy. Justin was feeling a little testy himself. They'd had such a peaceful weekend that he hadn't brought up the big question that had been nagging at him for a long while, mostly because he hadn't wanted to get her riled again. However, it was information that Ray should probably know about, and therefore he had little choice but to ask.

Pulling to a halt at the stop street, he turned to look at her. "Are you sure you've told Ray and me everything, that there's nothing you're holding back?"

Fighting a quick surge of anger, Rachel sat up taller. "What are you getting at, Justin?"

Turning left toward Schyler, he scowled out the windshield at the evening sky. "Several times now I've seen you with that bearded man. You've told me he's someone you once knew, yet he keeps reappearing. I asked you about him before, and you got upset. I can't help but wonder who he is."

She drew in a deep breath, reaching for control. She'd had the feeling a couple of times when she'd caught Justin studying her that there was something on his mind. At last he'd come out with it. "If I tell you that he had absolutely nothing to do with any of this—not my first trial nor the one coming up—will you believe me?"

He felt his jaw tighten. "If he has nothing to do with either trial, why do you refuse to discuss him?"

"The only time you've asked me was at the county fair when I hardly knew you. You haven't mentioned him since. I had no idea you were roaming around, spying on me."

Justin gripped the wheel until his knuckles turned white. "I haven't been spying on you. I happened along when you were hugging him on the sidewalk across the street from the *Gazette*. Why are you protecting this man?"

She crossed her arms over her chest. "I think there's more at issue here than him. I find it odd that almost daily, you ask me to trust you. Then you ask me a question, I tell you that it isn't important, yet you don't believe me. Is trust a one-way street with you, Justin?''

He turned onto Edgewater Drive and slowed as they neared Gloria's apartment. "I *do* trust you. I just want to know what this man means to you."

She would be reasonable if it killed her. "He's someone I knew years ago, but never romantically. He's nearly old enough to be my father. I came to you as a virgin. What more assurance do you need?"

Justin pulled the van to a stop alongside the tavern and threw it into park before turning to her. "It's not jealousy. It's just that I—"

"It's just that you don't trust me, not really." Rachel felt a heaviness settle in her chest. Maybe it was better this way. Her anger would keep her isolated from him. Then, if things didn't work out at the trial, having to leave him permanently wouldn't be such a shock. She opened her door. "I've done nothing wrong, and I'm tired of being made to feel that I have. If you can't take me at my word, then perhaps we don't have as much between us as I thought." Grabbing her overnight case, she stepped out. "Thank you for a very enlightening weekend."

"Rachel, wait!" Damn stubborn woman, he fumed. But by the time he stepped out, she was up the stairs and hurrying inside. A middle-aged couple, about to enter the tavern, stopped to stare at him. Irritated with himself and Rachel's unreasonableness, Justin climbed back behind the wheel.

How the hell had a simple question turned into all-out war?

Justin spent a very long, very miserable week before the trial. Rachel hadn't returned to work at the *Gazette,* having called Pop to explain that Ray wanted her free for consultations. That she hadn't called him personally had told Justin loud and clear that she was obviously still angry.

He'd phoned her several times, but always Gloria had answered, saying Rachel was out or she was resting. He would have liked to question Rachel's mother further, but his private nature kept him from spilling his guts to someone who might very well offer an unsympathetic ear. Blood was still thicker than water.

Pop had eyed him curiously, determined quickly that something was wrong, but had kept his thoughts to himself, along with any unsolicited advice, a fact for which Justin was grateful. He was finding it difficult enough to explain to Katie why Rachel wasn't around anymore. Despite several attempts, his feeble explanations hadn't brought the smile back to Katie's face. He hated knowing that his daughter missed Rachel, yet he simply didn't know how to change things.

His conversations with Ray hadn't pleased Justin, either. The trial was to begin Monday morning in circuit court in Corpus Christi, with Judge Colin Thomas presiding. Despite every attempt, they hadn't gotten Judge Powell. Judge Thomas was fairly new, and his leanings unknown to Ray. That fact alone was enough to make Justin nervous.

Then there was the business about Rachel's brother. The attorney had subpoenaed Curt Hathaway through the naval sub base at Point Loma in San Diego, but as yet hadn't had a reply from the captain of operations. Ray had been told, however, that authorization to transfer Curt from the sub would depend on how vital the review board considered his testimony in his sister's trial to be. Justin had this nagging hunch that Curt might have some answers, but Ray only halfheartedly agreed with him.

More bad news. After traveling up to Stamford and popping in on Theo's old college buddy at his ranch, Ray had found not a trace of a single Spanish mustang. Evidently information had been leaked, and Theo had warned his friend. Another dead end.

"So what have we got?" Justin asked Ray on the phone on the Sunday afternoon before the trial.

Ray ticked off their pluses. "We've got three character witnesses for Rachel, all solid citizens. And I've just heard from one of her old teachers who'd moved away, read about the trial and offered to come testify on her behalf. I've talked with nearly everyone in town, and I believe many feel Rachel's innocent. But there's a wait-and-see attitude. Quite a few are planning to attend the trial and watch carefully."

"That sounds promising."

"I think so. And we've got Matt's testimony putting Theo at the point where evidence was found against Rachel. Plus we've got several questionable acts committed by Theo that should prove to the court that he's not the sterling character he pretends to be."

Justin wondered how Ray always managed to sound positive. "And that's it?"

"Well, there's also the fire insurance Theo took out just before the incident, the lab reports on the gas can and tablet, which came up inconclusive, and the fact that I hope to show cause to doubt the drugstore clerk's story. And there's Willy Madigan."

Justin could hear the smile in Ray's voice now. It was terrific that someone could look at all this with good humor. "Who the hell's Willy Madigan?" The name sounded only vaguely familiar.

Ray sighed. "Willy lives in a run-down shack out near the cemetery. It seems he's a regular customer at Gloria's tavern. I questioned all her regulars, and Willy's the only one who recalls seeing Rachel's car parked right next to the apartment the evening of the fire.''

"You don't sound enthusiastic.''

"Probably because Willy's known as a bit of a drinker, and I have a feeling the prosecutor's going to cream him. But we're still going to sober up old Willy, stick him in a clean suit and try to make him sound credible.''

"Wonderful, Ray.''

"You got any better ideas?''

"Yeah. Give me about fifteen minutes in a closed room with Theo Quincy. I'll have a signed confession for you.'' Justin felt as weary as he sounded. Perhaps he'd feel differently if Rachel would at least talk to him. He'd finally bumped into her outside Edna's Diner yesterday. Very cool, very polite, she'd said hello, then hurried on home.

He hadn't gone after her. Begging had never been his style.

Ray had been quiet a long moment. "Justin, do you remember when we first talked, and I mentioned how your personal involvement might be a detriment to our case?''

"Relax, Ray. I'm not going after Theo. But I'd like to.'' He paused a moment, then swallowed his pride. He wasn't sure how much Ray knew of the rift between Rachel and him, but her attorney had to know something, closeted with her nearly daily in preparation. "How's Rachel holding up?''

"She's fine, stronger than most people think. Always has been.''

"I'm glad. Listen, will you tell her that... Never mind.''

"Give it time, Justin. She's got a lot on her mind.''

"Don't we all? See you in court, Counselor.'' Justin hung up the phone and picked up his baseball hat, jamming it on his head. Maybe he'd go to the ball field and hit a few. He badly needed to vent some of his energy.

Rachel tied the belt of her robe more tightly and reached for her comb, running it through her wet hair. She'd spent the entire long day inside the hot apartment in front of the fan that seemed only to rearrange the humid air. She felt a little better after her shower. Of course, part of her discomfort could well be nerves.

Her trial was to begin tomorrow.

Leaving her bedroom, she walked to the kitchen for still another glass of iced tea. She'd practically been living on the stuff this past week, her stomach roiling at the thought of food. Maybe later, she'd try a soft-boiled egg. Or a—

Her head shot up as she heard the sound of someone knocking at the door. Gloria had gone downstairs to check things out at the tavern. Carefully Rachel peered around the corner of the kitchen.

Through the screen, she saw Katie standing there, looking hesitant. Was Justin with her? She hoped not, for she wasn't in the mood for another confrontation. Hurrying over, she held open the door. "Katie. Are you all right?"

Katie nodded as she walked in. "I had to come see you."

"I'm glad you did. Does your Dad know you're here?"

Katie looked up at Rachel, her blue eyes huge in her small face. "No. He's at the ball field. I told him I was going to my girlfriend's house." Her lower lip quivered slightly. "It's only a little lie. I miss you, Rachel."

Rachel's arms slid around the child, closing her eyes on a rush of warmth as she gathered the slender body to her. Staying away from Katie had been so very difficult. "I've missed you, too."

She burrowed into Rachel's softness. "Daddy says you're mad at him, that he said some things that hurt your feelings."

Rachel drew her over to the couch and sat with her. "Yes, he did. But my being upset with your father has nothing to do with you and me. I didn't come by because I didn't want to put you in the middle of our argument, you know?"

Solemnly Katie nodded. "Is it ever going to be all right again?"

Rachel hugged her close a second time. "I hope so, honey. It's a rough time for us all right now, with the court trial." There'd been no keeping that from Katie since the whole town was talking of nothing else. "When it's all over—well, we'll see."

"Pop says that sometimes Daddy says things he doesn't mean."

"*All* of us do that occasionally, Katie."

"Does that mean you haven't stopped caring about us?"

"Of course I haven't. I just need a little time right now." She sat back, trying for a level of normalcy so that Katie would lose her anxious look. "So tell me, how have you been? Is everything going well at school?"

She listened to Katie's ramblings, inserting a comment here and there, but her mind was on Justin. He hadn't sent his daughter to her, of that she was certain. Justin wasn't sneaky. However, seeing Katie, she had to admit that despite her need for distance from Justin, she still loved them both. And she missed them like hell.

But she'd decided to put her relationship with Justin on hold for now. She had a trial to get through, and she needed all her energy for that. If and when it turned out all right, she'd face her feelings about Justin. Perhaps they could talk it out. Perhaps not. She hadn't had much experience with love, but she felt strongly about one thing. Without trust, love wouldn't last.

Realizing that Katie had evidently asked her a question, Rachel turned to her. "What was that, honey?"

"I asked if we could go look for a puppy. You haven't forgotten, have you?"

"No, but finding the right one is going to take some time. In the meantime, I have an idea." Rachel rose and stepped into her bedroom, returning in moments. "I wonder if you'd want to keep Rufus for me until we can get a real dog. He was given to me when I was younger than you. He gets pretty lonely just sitting around in my closet."

Katie gave her a gap-toothed smile and reached out for the scruffy dog. "It looks like you've loved him real hard." She wiggled his floppy ears.

"I have. Will you take care of him for me?"

Katie hugged the stuffed animal to her and nodded.

"Great. I've got some lemonade in the fridge. Would you like some?"

"Yes, please."

In the kitchen, she poured lemonade into a glass and found two oatmeal cookies. "You can have these while I get dressed. Then I'll walk you home."

Holding Katie's hand, Rachel strolled along Barlow Road and saw Justin's house come into view as they rounded the bend. Her heart skipped a beat as memories washed over her. The night she'd first been inside, watching Justin develop the film in his darkroom. Then moving to his bedroom for a glorious night of loving. The afternoon she'd waited, so distraught and upset, sitting on Katie's tree swing. And when he'd arrived, she'd all but ripped his clothes off in her need to be one with him.

Swallowing hard, Rachel stopped halfway up the path to the door and looked down at Katie. "Do you have a key?

Will you be all right until your dad gets home?'' They'd stopped at Pop's, but he hadn't been home, either. ''Maybe I should walk you over to your friend's house instead.''

Katie shook her head. ''Daddy said he'd be home by dinnertime. I'll lock the door and watch TV.''

Rachel checked her watch and saw it was nearly five. She didn't want to run into Justin, yet she felt uncomfortable leaving Katie alone. Her conscience made her choice for her. ''Tell you what, let's sit on the porch steps until we see your dad coming. I'd feel better. Maybe we could play a game.''

Pleased with that, Katie skipped up the steps, went inside and got her checkers and board. Keeping a watchful eye on the road, Rachel set up the game when she returned.

They'd just finished the second round when Rachel heard a sound and looked up to see Justin, wearing a baseball cap and swinging a bat, turning the bend. Quickly she stood.

''Are you going to tell Daddy I lied?'' Katie asked, looking suddenly worried.

Rachel ran a hand down the child's long braid. ''Not this time, but I don't want you to do that again, Katie. Lies have a way of hurting the person who tells them.''

''I won't. But please don't stay away so long.''

Giving her a swift hug, Rachel left the porch. There was no avoiding Justin, but she could make the inevitable short and cool. They reached the end of the walk at the same time. Squaring her shoulders, she met his eyes. ''Hello, Justin.''

He'd been surprised, then delighted to see her sitting on the porch with Katie. Yet now, close up, he saw that she was unsmiling and reserved. ''It's good to see you, Rachel. I've been worried. Are you all right?''

"Yes, fine. I...I missed Katie. We talked awhile and played some checkers." She saw him narrow his eyes thoughtfully. A hard man to fool, but she stood her ground.

Adjusting his cap, Justin took a chance. "You missed just Katie?"

He looked so damn good that her hands trembled with the need to reach out and touch him. Instead she shoved them in her jeans pockets and took a step back fighting the pull of memories as she looked off into the trees without answering.

Justin watched a variety of emotions reflect on her expressive face. He had his answer. "I've missed you," he said softly.

Coming to a decision, Rachel frowned. "After the trial, Justin, we need to talk. I have to concentrate on that right now."

Almost casually he lay a hand on her slender shoulder, wishing instead he could pull her into his arms. But she was as tightly wound as a spring. "I hope you know I'm here for you if you need me."

She nodded. "I know." It was too hard, being this close to him yet feeling she shouldn't be, since her life was still such a mess. She couldn't begin to rebuild their relationship until she was back on track. If she ever would be again. She started to walk around him.

"I love you, Rachel."

That stopped her. She swung back and raised troubled eyes to his. "I love you, too. But I'm not sure if love is always enough." She tore her gaze away, turned and hurried down the road toward home.

Justin watched her walk away with a sinking heart, wondering what he could do to make things right between them again. Love, not enough? She was wrong. He'd never loved like this before. It had to be enough.

He would find a way to prove it to her.

From the back row of the visitors' section of the courtroom, Justin rubbed his hand across his tired eyes. The afternoon of the first day—and things were not exactly going swimmingly.

The prosecutor, Boyd Cadell, was a man Justin thought of as one of "the good old boys." He was third-generation Texan, a big blustery man who smoked cigars and wore a tan suit with a red vest buttoned over a paunch he patted affectionately from time to time as he paced the courtroom. It was a known fact that Boyd had tipped a few with Roy Quincy from time to time. And he was a man who liked to win better than he liked to play poker, which was saying quite a bit.

The morning had been taken up with opening statements. Then Boyd began by calling on several technical witnesses to provide information for the record on the fire and its likely cause, as well as lab experts on the evidence. The prosecutor had scored a few solid points for his side. However, Justin thought that Ray's cross-examination had also made a few gains.

The visitors' section was packed with Schyler residents, most with guarded expressions. They were listening and watching intently, and only a few wore openly hostile expressions. Now, as Boyd finished with Anna Mae Robinson, the drugstore clerk who'd so far stuck to her story, Justin leaned forward to hear what Ray might come up with.

"Mrs. Robinson," Ray began, as he walked over to the slender gray-haired woman seated in the witness box, "you and your husband live out on Grodin Road. Nice stucco house, is that right?"

Glancing toward Theo in the front row of the viewers' section, she swallowed nervously before answering. "Yes, sir."

Ray glanced down at a paper he held. "And what lending institution would hold the mortgage on your home?"

Mrs. Robinson shifted her seat. "We bought it on a land contract."

"Objection, Your Honor," Boyd Cadell said, rising. "This lady's here to testify about selling the defendant some drugstore items, not to discuss mortgages or land contracts."

"Your Honor," Ray said, approaching the bench. "I believe there's definite relevance to the Robinsons' financial arrangements, and this lady's testimony."

Judge Thomas fingered his white mustache thoughtfully. "I'll allow it, but get to it, Counselor."

"Thank you, Your Honor. Mrs. Robinson, who holds the deed on your property? Who is the person you make payments to?" Ray heard the woman mumble something but couldn't make it out. "Speak up, Mrs. Robinson."

"Theo Quincy," the woman spit out.

"I see," Ray commented. "Mrs. Robinson, are you aware of the consequences of committing perjury?"

Defiantly the woman tipped up her pointy chin. "I saw what I saw, and that woman over there bought a home permanent and a tablet. Mr. Quincy's a fine man, been awful good to my husband and me since Henry lost his job. Ain't no one going to hurt Mr. Quincy if I can help it."

"No further questions." Ray walked back and seated himself.

Justin leaned back, allowing himself a moment of satisfaction. He'd been watching the judge's face, and it seemed as if Ray had planted a seed of doubt in pointing out that the woman had a perfect reason to lie for her employer.

Next, Boyd called Sheriff Duncan up and walked him through the investigation, slowly and methodically. When it was time for Ray to cross-examine, he had only one question for the sheriff.

"Tell me, sir, who called to tip you off that there might be evidence in the Hathaways' shed?"

Duncan shifted restlessly, his eyes on the floor. "Uh, it was Theo. He told me that, since he'd seen Rachel's yellow Toyota leaving his drive, maybe I ought to check out her backyard for clues."

As the sheriff was excused and stepped down, he sent a nervous glance at the judge, who was studying him intently. Justin couldn't help wondering if the judge was thinking the same thing he was, that Quincy money had kept the sheriff in office.

Finally Boyd called Theo to the stand. Justin swung his gaze to Rachel. Seated next to Ray, wearing a severely cut black suit, he saw her square her slender shoulders. Gloria Hathaway, seated a row behind her daughter, wore a navy dress that seemed too large for her small frame. But she sat tall and straight with a hint of defiance to the set of her shoulders.

Swaggering and confident, Theo answered his attorney's questions in an obviously well-rehearsed manner, occasionally using words that Justin guessed the man hadn't used since leaving college, if then. He smiled benevolently toward his parents and wife seated in the front row.

After having Theo describe the fire scene, Boyd also tried to slip a fast one by. "Have you had trouble with the defendant before, Mr. Quincy?"

"Yes, sir. She killed my brother ten years ago."

"Objection, Your Honor." Ray was on his feet. "Calling for a conclusion of the witness. Inflammatory."

"Sustained," Judge Thomas said, frowning at Boyd. "You know better, Mr. Cadell."

Looking not the least chagrined, Boyd bowed to the judge and turned to Ray. "Your witness."

"No questions at this time, Your Honor. Reserve the right to cross-examine later."

The prosecution rested its case. The judge checked his watch, then informed them that the defense could begin tomorrow morning at nine. With a pounding of his gravel, he announced they were adjourned and left the courtroom. News reporters covering the trial rushed out through the double doors, followed more slowly by a packed gallery of the curious.

Justin tried to reach Rachel's side through the people crowding the aisle. But after a whispered consultation with Ray, she took her mother's arm and quickly stepped out a side door before he was even near. Dejectedly he approached Ray. "Not going very well, is it?"

"It's early," Ray answered noncommittally, as he stuffed papers into his worn briefcase.

"How do you plan to begin?"

"Slowly, with character witnesses that hopefully will convince the judge that Rachel's a good person incapable of such a crime."

"Are you going to put her on the stand?"

Ray snapped his case shut and sighed. "Probably, unless we get a miracle. What else have we got, really, except a soft-spoken woman—a teacher of children—who will quietly tell her own story?"

"I'm working on something," Justin confided. "Not a miracle, but rather a long shot. Still, it may pan out. I'll know more tomorrow."

The last to leave, Ray swung into step with Justin. "Fine, but I need you here tomorrow as a character witness and for moral support."

He was beginning to doubt that Rachel even knew he was in the courtroom. She'd glanced back his way occasionally, then quickly turned around. "I'll be here, at least in the morning, not that she seems to care."

At the double doors, Ray stopped. "She cares, more than she lets on. Cut her a little slack here, Justin."

"Yeah, all right." He walked out, determined that tomorrow he would get a few answers. He fervently hoped they were the right ones.

Rachel felt as if a hive of busy bees had taken up residence in her stomach. Seated next to Ray on the second day of the trial, she was nervous, headachy and nearly rigid with tension. Even the fact that the first two witnesses this morning, Edna and Pop, had made her sound like a warm and wonderful human being who wouldn't hurt a fly, hadn't managed to lift her spirits. Boyd Cadell's insidious attempts at trying to trip them up hadn't budged her two loyal friends.

Glancing back at the gallery, she saw a solid group of the good citizens of Schyler who had journeyed the thirty miles to Corpus Christi to sit in on the trial. Some of them were friends of the Quincys or worked for them. Yet there were others who looked at both Roy and Theo with speculative frowns. And there were even a few who'd sent her hesitant, encouraging smiles. Could Ray be right? Could support be shifting to her?

Roy had walked about earlier, glad-handing in the manner of a generous Texas founding father. Muriel Quincy sat quietly in the front row between her husband and son, looking small and pale compared to the two robust men.

Her eyes seldom lifted from her hands, worrying a hankie in her lap. Rachel wished she could see into the woman's mind.

As she wished she could read Justin's mind. He was sprawled in the last row as he had been yesterday, his eyes hooded, his expression unreadable. She was better off if she didn't turn to look at him. If indeed the judge ruled against her, she couldn't help wondering what Justin's reaction would be. If he couldn't take her word about the man they'd been discussing, how could she trust that he believed her about the fire? Yet if he didn't, why was he here?

She rubbed the spot between her eyes where the headache was throbbing and tried to pay attention to the prosecutor. He was attempting to shake Matt Russell's eyewitness account placing Theo at the Hathaways' backyard. Matt's girlfriend, Annie, had already testified and had told the same story, even though she'd looked frightened at being in the courtroom.

Realizing he was getting nowhere with Matt, Boyd dismissed him. Matt stepped down from the witness box and winked at Rachel encouragingly as he passed on by. She gave him a weak smile.

She heard Ray call their next witness, Hugh Stoller. Now, she thought, turning back to glance at Justin as Hugh entered the courtroom. Now perhaps Justin would have reason to believe her.

He was tall and slim, wearing an expensive doublebreasted suit and a neat brown beard flecked with gray. He walked slowly and carried himself with dignity. After being sworn in, Hugh was asked to explain who he was. "I used to teach at Schyler High. I moved to northern Texas about ten years ago."

"And what is your connection to Rachel Hathaway and this case?" Ray asked.

Hugh's soft brown eyes moved to Rachel's face and he smiled. "I was one of her teachers. I spotted her potential early and encouraged her to pursue a career in teaching. When I read in the paper that she was being accused of arson, I called you and offered my assistance as a character witness."

Ray was aware that behind him, Theo Quincy was whispering across his mother into Roy's ear. Fingering his bright green suspenders under his open jacket, Ray chose his words carefully. "Mr. Stoller, are you now or have you ever been involved with Rachel Hathaway?"

"Not in the way you probably mean. A long time ago, she came to my defense when I badly needed support. Although it did little good, I've never forgotten." Hugh crossed his legs and leaned back.

"How did that come about?"

"The school board fired me. Rachel burst in on one of their meetings and tried to convince them to keep me on."

Ray angled so he could see the faces in the gallery. "And why were you fired?"

Hugh's gaze was unwavering. "On the basis of a morals clause in my contract. They discovered I was gay." He became aware of the restless whispering in the visitors' section but chose to ignore it. "Certain people made it impossible for me to remain in Schyler. I relocated and applied for another teaching position, but the board members had sent letters around."

"Your Honor," Boyd said rather loudly, "I fail to see where this is going, and what it has to do with our case."

"Make your point, Counselor," Judge Thomas directed.

"Right away, Your Honor. Mr. Stoller, why did you come forth now, when it must be difficult for you to bring up the past?"

Hugh allowed himself a small smile. "I knew she wouldn't ask me to. But I wanted to tell the court what a fine woman Rachel Hathaway was then and is now. When nearly everyone avoided me, though there'd never been a single incident to indicate immoral behavior in or out of my classroom, she believed in me. After I moved, she wrote to me and even called me on the phone when she knew I was struggling to make a new start. I've met few people in my life as good as Rachel, as nonjudgmental. She would never hurt anyone, nor set fire to an anthill."

"Thank you, sir," Ray said. "Your witness."

As Boyd slowly rose and strolled to the front, Rachel chanced a look at Justin. He sat slumped in his seat, gazing intently at Hugh through his steepled fingers. She wondered what he was thinking.

"Mr. Stoller, are you still a practicing homosexual?" Boyd asked, a look of distaste on his flushed face.

Hugh looked amused. "It isn't something you turn on and off."

"And what line of work are you in now?"

"I'm in city management in a large metropolitan city, fiscal planning. I manage a staff of some forty people."

"And they don't care if you're gay?"

Hugh ran a hand over his chin. "Let's just say I find that some small towns and the people who run them seem to embrace their chosen prejudices and often ignore serious flaws among themselves, such as dishonesty, thievery, adultery, whereas folks in a larger city seem more tolerant of their fellow citizens."

Rachel smiled. That was telling them. She listened as Boyd tried valiantly to discredit Hugh, but the prosecutor soon discovered he was dealing with an unshakable witness. Hugh's manner was quietly self-assured, albeit hard won, and his answers painfully honest, though filled with obvious disdain for his questioner. At last, Boyd returned to his chair, ignoring the angry glares he received from both Quincy men.

Rachel glanced at the gallery, surprised and pleased to see no expressions of derision as the visitors watched Hugh leave the courtroom. Instead some were looking at him with admiration for daring to say what many of them had felt but been afraid to utter out loud. Had Schyler finally learned to live and let live? Rachel wondered.

The judge signaled that they'd break for lunch. Swinging her eyes to the rear, Rachel looked for Justin.

His seat was empty.

Chapter Twelve

Seated at the defense table, Rachel shifted nervously in her chair. It was midmorning of the third day, and Justin was nowhere to be seen. She lowered her head to stare at her damp hands twisting a tissue.

He'd left sometime during Hugh's testimony yesterday afternoon. Why? If anything, hearing what Hugh had to say should have answered the questions he'd been asking her. What had he heard or seen that had caused him to get up, walk away and not return? Her biggest fear—that the love they shared wouldn't be strong enough to sustain them through this difficult, emotional time—was becoming a reality. And there wasn't one thing she could do about it.

Realizing that Ray had returned from taking an important call, she looked up. "Everything all right?" she asked.

"Stop worrying," he directed. "He'll be back."

She'd been afraid her astute attorney would notice her distressed state and guess the reason behind it beyond the trial itself. "Do you know where he is?"

"I just talked to Justin. He said he had a hunch and had to check it out. You know newspapermen." Ray glanced at his notes. "However, I was going to put him on the stand as a character witness, but now we'll have to skip him and go right to you after Willy. Can you handle that?"

Rachel took a deep breath. "I guess I'll have to."

Ray patted her hand, then rose to call Willy Madigan.

The suit was cheap but obviously new, as was the haircut on the thin, lanky man who ambled up to sit down. He wore the expression of a puppy eager to please as he blinked at Ray through thick glasses. Listening to her attorney try valiantly to have his witness seem like an upstanding citizen whose observations could be trusted, Rachel felt her spirits sag even further.

The morning had started out with Gloria testifying that Rachel had been home with her and Katie Wheeler at the time the Quincy fire had been started. From somewhere, Gloria had found the strength to sound firm in her statements, but the prosecutor had hammered away at her frailty, at her loyalty to her daughter, at her questionable occupation as a tavern owner. Dressed simply in a lavender linen dress, Gloria had answered politely despite his insinuations, though in her eyes had danced a fire that Rachel hadn't seen in some time.

They'd had a long talk last evening, she and her mother—a good one. Rachel had been so wrapped up in her own problems that she hadn't noticed until Gloria had drawn her attention to it that her mother had stopped smoking the day the trial had begun.

With her husky voice stronger than Rachel had heard it in years, Gloria explained that if Rachel could go through another trial after the first had so radically changed her life, then the least her mother could do was have the same measure of courage. The withdrawal she was going through was awful, the craving causing her hands to tremble and her face to bead with sweat regularly. She wasn't sure if she could do it, Gloria had confessed, but she was taking it one day at a time. Tears streaming down her face, Rachel had hugged her mother, telling her how proud she was of her.

And she'd been equally proud of the way she'd handled herself on the witness stand. After Gloria's testimony, they'd listened to a handwriting expert on the note found tacked to the tree. Nothing he found indicated the block letters had been hand printed by Rachel, the man testified, after making extensive comparisons. Of course, Boyd had also gotten him to admit that it was also possible that she had written the note. A stalemate.

Now, Rachel could only imagine what Boyd Cadell would do to poor Willy. And then it would be her turn.

She hadn't realized how much she'd been subconsciously relying on Justin's solid presence, even though she'd scarcely spoken to him. Ray had said Justin was following a hunch, which had to mean he was trying to help her. Which also had to mean he still believed in her. Yet, if he didn't return soon, it would all end right here today.

Putting her on the stand involved some risk, Ray had explained last evening. But the pluses outweighed the minuses, he felt. She would tell her story and pray that Boyd wouldn't somehow break down her fragile composure. Then they'd all leave and wait for the judge's decision.

Pressing her lips together to keep them from trembling, Rachel again looked toward the back row.

Hurry, Justin. Please hurry.

The courtroom was packed. The number of reporters covering the trial seemed to have doubled since the lunch recess. Perhaps because the news had spread like wild-fire—the defense was putting that Hathaway woman on the stand this afternoon.

Rachel raised her right hand to take the oath, trying to keep from shaking as she spoke the familiar words. Sitting down, her eyes automatically scanned the back row. Still no Justin. She swallowed and concentrated on her attorney.

Gently but firmly, Ray asked about her life in California as an elementary school teacher, her involvement with the children as a baseball coach, her quiet existence. Next, he led her through the day of the fire, guiding but allowing her to tell her story in her own way. She kept her gaze fastened on him, knowing that to gaze at the Quincys, to see that remembered hatred on their faces, would shatter her control, such as it was.

Finally Ray stood back and looked at her. "Rachel Hathaway, did you set fire to the Quincy property on the night in question?"

"No, sir, I did not."

"Thank you. Your witness." Ray walked back to the defense table.

Slowly Boyd Cadell rose and strolled to her. His smile, Rachel was certain, was intended to disarm her, to make her relax before he moved in for the kill. But she'd been through this before, at a far more tender age, and the memory of that time and that trial burned in her brain as she strove to be calm and cool.

Boyd began innocuously enough, asking about her early life in Schyler, her father's abandonment, her home above the tavern. When he hinted that Gloria had been a less than perfect mother who left her children unsupervised a great deal of the time, Ray objected. But the judge ruled that Rachel's upbringing was relevant to the woman she'd become, one who was now accused of a serious crime. Despite Rachel's insistence that she'd been raised in a loving home, she was fearful that the judge already thought otherwise. Hands locked together, she braced herself.

"Now then," Boyd continued, "in high school, you were a good student and, as we heard Hugh Stoller testify, you planned to go on to college and become a teacher. Is that right?"

"Yes."

"But you didn't attend college in Texas. Why was that, Rachel?"

"Objection, Your Honor," Ray called out. "Irrelevant."

"Overruled. I'll allow her to answer," Judge Thomas ruled.

"I decided to move to California and go to college there," Rachel replied uneasily, worried about this line of questioning.

"Just like that, up and moved, at the tender age of seventeen. My, my." Pacing in front of her, Boyd patted his bulging belly. Suddenly he swung back, narrowing his eyes. "Have you ever been convicted of first-degree murder in this county?"

Ray leaped to his feet as the gallery began buzzing with excitement. "Objection. Inadmissible, Your Honor."

"Overruled," Judge Thomas said in a loud voice. He turned to Rachel. "You may answer."

Ray stepped forward angrily. "Objection, Your Honor. Motion for a mistrial." Behind him, newsmen were whispering among themselves as were many of the visitors.

Judge Thomas bristled as he banged his gavel twice. "I will have order in my court, or I will clear it." He swung his dark gaze back to Ray. "Motion denied."

Just barely, Ray kept a lid on his temper. "Let the record show my objection for purposes of appeal, Your Honor."

"So noted." He swung back to Rachel as Ray reluctantly resumed his seat. "The witness will answer the question."

Trying to keep from looking smug, Boyd walked closer to Rachel. "Do you want me to repeat the question?"

"No," she said, staring straight at him, striving to appear calm.

Slowly Boyd moved close to her, all but blocking her view of the courtroom. "Are you sure?"

A muscle beneath her eye twitched. "I was acquitted," she told him firmly. Then, as Boyd moved back and she saw Ray shake his head, she realized she'd said too much. In rehearsing her, her attorney had emphasized that she must never offer information, but just answer the question. She felt moisture trail down her spine as she sent Ray an apologetic look.

"Tried and acquitted," Boyd repeated. "And what was the name of the victim?"

Fire leaped into her eyes, despite her best attempts to contain her temper. "What difference does it make?"

Boyd smiled, all friendly like. "Humor me, little lady."

Little lady. It seemed like the beginning of the end to Rachel. She'd been worried that they'd introduce her former trial, to try to imply her guilt despite the acquittal. But Ray had assured her it would be most difficult to do. Yet this posturing prosecutor had managed to maneuver her into saying what he'd wanted to hear. She had little choice but to continue. "Tyrone Quincy."

"Uh-huh. And now you've come back to try to get rid of Tyrone's twin brother, Theo." Ray again jumped up, objecting, but Boyd kept on. "You set fire to his garage and barn and hoped it would spread to the house and kill all the Quincys. Didn't you, little lady?''

The judge pounded his gavel, finally acknowledging that Boyd had gone too far. ''Mr. Cadell, that will do. We're trying an arson case here, not attempted murder.''

No sooner were the words out of his mouth than the double doors at the back swung open and two men walked in. Her eyes on them, Rachel almost cried out. Gloria, seated behind Ray, allowed her tears to flow freely as she gasped aloud.

Ray, too, gazed at the newcomers as the officer at the back checked their ID, and the gallery whispering resumed. ''Your Honor,'' Ray said, turning to the judge, ''the defense requests a twenty-minute recess due to the fact that an important witness we'd subpoenaed has just arrived.''

It was Boyd Cadell's turn to interrupt. ''Objection, Your Honor. There's been no disclosure of a new witness.''

''His name was on the list presented to the prosecution,'' Ray explained. ''Petty Officer Curt Hathaway. Due to Navy red tape, he's been unable to join us sooner.''

Standing next to Justin, Curt sent his sister an encouraging smile.

''That being the case,'' Judge Thomas said, ''we are in recess. Twenty minutes, gentlemen.'' He rose and left the courtroom, his robes billowing behind him.

Hurrying from the stand, Rachel rushed past Roy, Theo and Boyd huddled together in conference at the prosecution table. She saw Ray grab both Curt and Justin and maneuver them toward the private office off the courtroom that they'd been using to confer in. She stopped only long enough to take Gloria's arm, then walked quickly after them.

She had no idea what kind of hunch Justin had acted upon. She only prayed it would work.

Justin's arms were wrapped tightly around her, and, for a moment, Rachel allowed herself to believe everything would once again be right in her world. She'd already hugged Curt and stepped back now to watch Gloria tearfully and lovingly touch her son's face.

"I can't believe you're here," Gloria said, her voice quavery.

"We can thank Justin," Curt said. "They weren't going to authorize my leave, until he intervened and convinced them that my testimony here was vital."

"But how did you get here?" Gloria asked. "I thought the submarine you were on wasn't going to surface for another couple of weeks."

Holding her arm, Curt led her to a chair at the conference table. "It wasn't easy. The captain of operations in San Diego is always in contact with my sub through satellite navigation. When Justin finally got clearance, they did a vertical lift, sent a helicopter from a carrier, then transported me to shore base. That was early this morning. Justin was waiting, and we grabbed the first plane here." He grinned around the table. "Talk about your eleventh-hour arrival."

Standing, Ray checked his watch. "Lots of time for your reunion later, folks. We don't have much time, and I need to go over some things with Curt." He opened the connecting door and glanced inside, nodding when he saw it was empty. "Let's go in here, Curt. Did you bring the box?"

"Yes, sir," Curt said, moving to the doorway.

"Why can't you talk in front of us?" Rachel asked.

"Because I believe it's best if you learn of this information at the same time the judge does, that he sees your face." Ray sent her a sincere appeal. "Will you trust me on this, Rachel, please?"

Her eyes swung to Justin. There was that word again—trust. He was back, and perhaps he'd saved the day. She'd doubted him there for a while, just as he'd doubted her earlier. Maybe they'd both learned an important lesson. "I trust you," she said to Ray, knowing both men got the message.

"Good. Justin, you come with us. We've got about fifteen minutes." Ray scooted the two men into the connecting office and closed the door.

Gloria wiped her eyes and reached into her purse for a cigarette. For a long moment, she fingered the rumpled package in her shaky hands. Then, with determination, she shoved the pack back into her purse.

From her stance by the window, Rachel witnessed her mother's struggle and smiled her approval.

Gloria smiled back. "Everything's going to be all right, Rachel. I just know it is."

"Finally, I think so, too, Mom."

"The defense calls Petty Officer Curt Hathaway to the stand," Ray said, as the trial resumed.

Rachel sat at the defense table alone, wishing Justin could be next to her. Running her tongue along her lips, she tasted the residue of the kiss they'd shared in a private moment just before they'd both walked back into the courtroom. With luck, they'd share more tonight.

The press and the visitors seemed to lean forward as a group, wondering what this new witness would have to say. Judge Thomas had warned them again as he'd sat down that if they didn't conduct themselves in an orderly fashion, he'd clear the courtroom. Curiosity was also running high about a rather large box that had been placed at the end of the defense table right before the judge had returned.

After Curt was sworn in and had stated who he was in relation to the defendant, Ray began his serious questioning, very aware that Theo and Boyd were watching him carefully. "Will you tell the court, please, Curt, if you were living here at the time that your sister, Rachel Hathaway, was accused of killing Tyrone Quincy?"

"Objection, Your Honor." Boyd stood, obviously having been expecting this line of questioning. "This trial deals with an arson charge. That murder trial took place ten years ago, and I believe Ms. Hathaway was acquitted."

Judge Thomas folded his hands in front of him. "Funny, that's what I was trying to tell you earlier, Mr. Cadell. However, you introduced the previous trial and made it part of the record. Since you opened the door, I'm going to allow the defense to question this witness, provided it's relevant to the arson case. Is that where you're headed, Mr. Brewster?"

Ray nodded. "Yes, Your Honor. The prosecutor earlier today accused my client of setting fire to the Quincys' garage and barn with the hope that they would all be killed, inferring that she's holding this ten-year grudge against the entire family. I intend to prove that not only did someone else kill Tyrone Quincy, but that Rachel Hathaway's only wish has been that the Quincys stop harassing her."

"Proceed, Counselor," the judge said with a wave of his hand.

Listening, Justin concluded that perhaps Judge Thomas wasn't as prejudiced toward the prosecution as he'd first assumed.

Ray turned back to Curt and repeated his question.

"Yes, I was living above the tavern with my mother, my sister, and my brother, Orrin, back then," Curt stated.

Justin leaned back, silently cheering Curt on. He'd gotten the call yesterday afternoon from San Diego that clearance for Curt was imminent. He'd flown to meet him, praying his hunch would prove right, and Curt could provide the answers they needed. They'd conferred most of the way back on the plane, and to Justin's utter delight, Rachel's brother could clear her. Some hunches paid big dividends. He focused again on the witness box.

"And do you have any information about the death of Tyrone Quincy that you've never revealed before?" Ray asked.

"Yes, sir."

"Would you tell the court, please, in your own words."

Justin watched Curt take a moment to gather his thoughts. Tall and lean, his blond hair cut Navy-regulation short, he resembled his sister a great deal, except his eyes were a blue-green. Justin's glance shifted to Rachel who was listening intently. *Soon,* he thought, *it'll all be over soon, honey.*

"My family was really broken up during that trial," Curt said. "We were awfully worried about Rachel, even though we knew she didn't do it. Even after she was cleared, not too many people in town seemed to think she was innocent." He let his eyes skim over the Schyler visitors, then slowly across the row where the Quincys sat staring sullenly at him. "People were pretty cruel."

"Go on," Ray urged.

"Rachel decided to move to California, to get away from everything. I hated to see her go, but I knew how she felt."

"How old were you then?"

"Fifteen. And Orrin was a year younger. We used to sit and talk nights—we shared a bedroom—about how rotten it was that Rachel was forced out of Schyler. One night, a couple of months after she'd left, Orrin told me what had happened out there in the woods that day. That he killed Tyrone Quincy."

The whispers turned into exclamations, and the gallery was thrumming with sound. Gloria stifled a sob, and Rachel turned even paler, as the judge pounded his gavel and demanded order.

"Objection," Boyd shouted. "Hearsay."

But Ray was already moving to the bench. "It's an exception to the hearsay rule, Your Honor, as an admission against interest made by the declarant."

Justin silently cheered Ray on. They had discussed this tactic earlier—a seldom-used exception, it would allow the judge to accept a confession by the dead man.

For a long moment, Judge Thomas stroked his mustache. Finally he nodded. "I'll allow it. Proceed."

"But, Your Honor..." Boyd insisted.

Frowning in annoyance, the judge turned to the prosecutor. "Sit down, Mr. Cadell."

Justin let out a breath he'd been holding too long. A close one and now they were almost home free. He kept his eyes on Ray.

Clearing his throat, the attorney approached his witness again. "Tell us what your brother told you, Curt."

"The two of us took turns walking Rachel home from school when she stayed late because she liked to cut through the woods, and we knew it was dangerous. See, Rachel's always been real pretty, and guys were always after her." He took a moment to glare in the direction of the first row. "Especially the Quincy twins."

Before Cadell could object, Ray raised his hand. "Stick to what happened, Curt."

He shifted on his chair. "Well, that afternoon, I couldn't meet her 'cause I was over at Reed's Grocery interviewing for a summer job, so Orrin said he'd go. Orrin was retarded, you know, but he could tell time. Somehow that afternoon, he got a late start, and Rachel was already on the path in the woods. Orrin told me that as he walked through the trees, he heard shouting—a man and a woman—so he ran in."

"Describe Orrin for us, will you, Curt?"

"He was big for fourteen, about five-nine, and weighed about one-sixty. Anyhow, when he reached the path, he saw Rachel struggling with Tyrone. He saw Tyrone hit her real hard, and she fell to the ground. Then Orrin saw Tyrone unzip his pants and pull up her dress."

Again, the gallery began to murmur, but Justin saw the judge glower at them, and the noise died down. In front, Theo leaned forward to whisper in Boyd's ear, but Cadell shook his head and waved him away.

"Orrin told me he was scared, but he grabbed a tree branch he found on the ground and ran over. He hit Tyrone as hard as he could with it. Tyrone fell down, the back of his head all bloody, and he didn't move. Rachel wasn't moving, either. Orrin was really frightened by then, so he ran out of the woods and home. He still had the stick in his hand. At first, he hid it under his bed. But later, he threw it into an old cardboard box he found in our basement and shoved it behind the furnace."

Ray walked to the defense table. "Is this the box?"

"Yes, sir. I picked it up from our basement before coming here today."

"Is there anything else in the box besides the tree branch?"

"Yes. A pair of shoes with tire-tread soles that belonged to Orrin. Footprints made by those shoes had been found at the scene of the crime."

Ray looked skeptical. "How did Orrin, who was retarded, know enough to hide his shoes?"

"Orrin worked at the *Schyler Gazette* back then, running errands for Pop Wheeler. He listened and heard a lot. One day he heard they were looking for a man who wore shoes with tire-tread soles in connection with Tyrone's murder, and that scared him. So he threw them into the same box."

Ray strolled back. "During that investigation, all the area shoe stores were questioned about tire-tread shoes. How is it that no one remembered selling those shoes to Orrin or your mother?"

Curt sent an apologetic glance to his mother. "We didn't have much money. Mom used to drive us to the Goodwill store in Kingsville. We got those secondhand."

"After Orrin told you all this, Curt, did you tell your mother?"

"No, sir."

"Who did you tell?"

"No one, not until today. I wanted to tell Rachel, but I didn't figure it would do any good. She'd already been acquitted, and I knew if anyone found out, they'd send Orrin away. He wouldn't have been able to handle that." Curt looked up at the judge. "He was a good kid. He was only trying to protect his sister."

"Your Honor," Ray said, as he walked back to the box, "at this time, I move to admit into evidence this box containing the stick and shoes and request a one-week adjournment so that the crime lab may examine them."

"Your Honor," Boyd began, getting to his feet, "that evidence is irrelevant to *this* case."

"No, sir, it is not," Ray interrupted. "Theo Quincy has been trying to smear my client from the day she returned to Schyler until today. We want to prove to the court that Rachel Hathaway did not kill Tyrone Quincy, holds no grudges, and therefore had no motive to start a fire at the Quincy ranch."

"Mr. Cadell," the judge said, "I remind you that you introduced Rachel Hathaway's previous trial. I believe the evidence should be examined. So ordered. Case is adjourned one week." He banged his gavel.

"No! You can't do this!" Theo Quincy lurched out of his seat, shouting. "You can't let her get away with this. She lured my brother into those woods, and then Orrin killed him. She set that fire. She—"

"Mr. Quincy," Judge Thomas said, "you are out of order. Sit down."

But Theo was out of control. "No! She set that fire."

"No, she did not. You did." Slowly getting to her feet, Muriel Quincy walked to her son's side, her shoulders sagging with defeat, her eyes weary. "I saw you, Theo. You thought I was asleep, but I wasn't. I was looking out my bedroom window, and I saw you set the fire, then get into your Cadillac with that gas can and drive off. Just like your daughter saw you hang her kitten. You tried to blame Rachel for that, too." She touched her son's arm. "You're filled with hate, Theo, just like your father. It has to stop. Today, right here."

"No, Mama." Pitifully Theo brushed a tear from his cheek. "Don't say no more."

"I've got to. This has gone far enough." She swiveled toward her husband who, surprisingly enough, was watching her in shocked silence. "You started all this by letting those boys do anything they wanted and made sure they got away with it. I don't know how many girls you paid off that they got in trouble. Well, one of your sons is dead, and the other's a sick man." Muriel sent a sad glance at her daughter-in-law. "The Quincy women never stand up to their men, right? Well, this one does today."

Justin watched Muriel turn to face Rachel, including Gloria in the look. "I apologize for all the grief my family's caused you both." She looked up at the judge. "Theo set the fire, Judge, and I'm deeply sorry."

Judge Thomas nodded to Muriel. "Bailiff, please take Theo Quincy into custody. The charge is arson and perjury. Arraignment to be set within statutory time period. This case is dismissed, and this court now stands adjourned."

Pandemonium broke out in the gallery, the noise loud enough to drown out the sound of the final gavel striking. Reporters shoved toward the doors while visitors exchanged shocked comments. But Justin managed to push his way to the front.

He wasn't really certain everything was all right until he had his arms around Rachel and his lips on hers.

But after that moment, it was nearly midnight before his lips were back on hers, really back. Holding her close, his body language saying he never wanted to let her go, Justin kissed her hungrily. Finally he smiled into her wonderful green eyes. "I thought we'd never be alone again."

"Mmm, me, too." Rachel kissed him, then sighed. "What a day this has been."

They'd stayed in the courtroom long enough to see Theo Quincy escorted off to jail. Sadly they'd watched his broken parents and his weeping wife walk away, arm in arm.

But if Rachel thought the day's surprises had ended, the most astonishing event was still to come. Several Schyler residents who'd sat through the trial had come over to hug

Gloria and to shake Rachel's hand. With the Quincys shaken and defeated, the townspeople acknowledged by those gestures that perhaps their loyalty had been misplaced. Justin watched Rachel hesitantly accept the good wishes, knowing it would take time for her to trust them. Fortunately they had time—the rest of their lives.

Then the celebrations had begun. They'd all driven back to Schyler, and for the first time in her memory, Rachel was glad to be in the tavern, glad to be a part of a festive atmosphere that included her mother and Curt plus all the regulars and, of course, Ray and Pop and Edna. But most especially, there'd been Justin and Katie.

They'd eaten, they'd drunk, they'd recounted, and they'd smiled a lot. It had been a long time coming, but victory had been sweet indeed.

Then Gloria had coaxed Curt upstairs for a long-overdue visit, Ray and Edna had said good-night, and Pop had taken one look at Rachel and Justin and persuaded Katie to spend the night at his house. Finally alone with Justin in his home, Rachel found herself drawing deep breaths, feeling free, feeling vindicated at last. And only one man was truly responsible.

However, she still had a few nagging questions as she turned to Justin. "What did you think of Hugh Stoller?"

He'd thought she'd ask. "Seems like a good and loyal friend. I'm sorry I doubted you."

"I guess we both had some doubts. But that's in the past." She paused thoughtfully. "What do you think will happen to the drugstore clerk who lied for Theo?"

"She could be facing perjury charges."

"And Theo?"

"Arson is a crime, even if you set fire to your own place, especially if it's heavily insured. And perjury's no laughing matter. I think the man needs counseling as well."

"I think you're right. I felt sorry for his mother." She frowned. "Tell me, what made you think Curt held the key to all this?"

"I'm not really sure. Hunches are unexplainable. It just seemed in reading the transcript over and over, he was the one name never mentioned. Yet, according to everyone, he'd been a bright fifteen-year-old back then." Justin shrugged. "Sometimes I get a funny feeling I can't explain, and I have to act on it."

Setting down the glass of champagne he'd insisted on pouring her, she leaned down to him and nuzzled his neck. "Thank goodness for your hunches. Whenever you have another, I'll give you free rein."

Justin looked up at the ceiling. "I think I'm getting one now."

She angled back and raised a suspicious eyebrow. "Oh?"

"It indicates that you're going to marry me and Katie, and very soon. And that we're going to live happily ever after."

"What a wonderful little hunch," Rachel said with a smile, as she moved into his embrace.

Epilogue

"You don't think this is just a shade corny, a white picket fence?" Rachel asked, as she swiped at her itchy nose with a paint-speckled hand.

Justin leaned back on his haunches, critically examining the board he'd just finished painting. "Nope. If Gloria wants a house with a white picket fence, then the least we can do is give it to her." He propped the brush on the top of the bucket and sat back in the grass. "She's come a long way in the three months since the trial, and I think we need to encourage her all we can."

Rachel glanced down the length of the fence Justin had built around the perimeter of his house. "I have to admit she deserves a reward of some sort. I understand it's harder to quit smoking than almost any other addiction."

"So I've heard. And getting her to agree to move into this house will eliminate all that stair-climbing." He leaned to place a soft kiss on her lips. "Maybe once she's moved in here, you'll stop worrying so much about her."

"I'm not worried, exactly. Just concerned. There's no reversing her condition, you know."

"But you can stop the progression of the disease, and she's done that. Having you back has helped her emotionally. And in another week, Curt will be out of the Navy and living upstairs at the tavern, so Gloria can relax, knowing someone's keeping an eye on her little saloon." Justin flopped back on the grass, pulling her down with him. "Your family's okay. Now you concentrate on your *new* family."

Rachel flipped to her stomach, easing herself onto his chest, her hands touching his face. Never would she tire of touching this man who'd become the center of her world. "I thought I *was* concentrating on my new family. I've spent nearly every day for a month out at that big ranch house you insisted we need, redecorating so we can move in. I've gone shopping with Katie for new school clothes, and I'm housebreaking her puppy. Did I miss anything?"

He brushed a lock of hair off her face with the back of his hand. "Yes. It's been nearly an hour since I've had a kiss—a real kiss."

"Justin, it's broad daylight. People walk by here all the time and—"

"Let them watch. Besides, who wants to stare at married people kissing on their front lawn?" He drew her nearer and took her mouth, pleased as always at her quick response, the eager way she returned his kiss. Long moments later, he studied her face. "Are you happy, Rachel?"

"You know I am."

"You're sure you want to turn down the school board's offer?"

Probably the largest sign of vindication she'd experienced since the trial had been the call from the Schyler School Board offering her a job on their teaching staff. Roy Quincy had tendered his resignation, and the other members had lost their narrow-minded viewpoint, it would seem. But Rachel had lost interest.

She smiled down into Justin's serious gaze. "This is what I've always wanted—a home and a family of my own. Maybe one day I'll return to teaching, and I am pleased that the board's changed its position. But for now, I have plenty to keep me busy with the new house and Katie. And you. Always you."

Justin slipped his hand between their bodies, his long fingers caressing her flat stomach. "And the baby."

Rachel felt the warmth spread, from his touch and the reminder. Only this morning she'd been to see Doc Tremayne, who'd confirmed what she'd suspected for several weeks now. The news had delighted her and thrilled Justin. "Yes, the baby."

"I can hardly wait to see Katie's face when we tell her."

"Think it'll be even better than getting her puppy?"

Justin smiled. "Uh-huh. She's been pestering me for a baby sister since she was about five."

Rachel sent him a mock scowl. "So, that's why you married me?"

But Justin grew serious. "I married you because I can't imagine a life without you."

How did he manage to always know the right thing to say? "Nor I without you." And she lowered her head to kiss him.

* * * * *

THE DONOVAN LEGACY
from Nora Roberts

Meet the Donovans—Morgana, Sebastian and Anastasia.
They're an unusual threesome. Triple your fun with double
cousins, the only children of triplet sisters and triplet brothers.
Each one is unique. Each one is...special.

In September you will be *Captivated* by Morgana Donovan. In
Special Edition #768, horror-film writer Nash Kirkland doesn't
know what to do when he meets an actual witch!

Be *Entranced* in October by Sebastian Donovan in Special
Edition #774. Private investigator Mary Ellen Sutherland
doesn't believe in psychic phenomena. But she discovers
Sebastian has strange powers...over her.

In November's Special Edition #780, you'll be *Charmed* by
Anastasia Donovan, along with Boone Sawyer and his little
girl. Anastasia was a healer, but for her it was Boone's touch
that cast a spell.

Enjoy the magic of Nora Roberts. Don't miss *Captivated*,
Entranced or *Charmed*. Only from
Silhouette Special Edition....

Silhouette Special Edition®

Linda Lael Miller

Beyond the Threshold

Two stories linked by centuries, and by love....

There and Now

The story of Elisabeth McCartney, a woman looking for a love she can't
find in the 1990s. Only with the mystery of her Aunt Verity's necklace
can she discover her true love—Dr. Jonathan Fortner, a country doctor
in Washington—in 1892....

There and Now, #754, available in July 1992.

Here and Then

Desperate to find her cousin, Elisabeth, Rue Claridge searched for her in
this century . . . and the last. She found Elisabeth, all right. And also
found U.S. Marshal Farley Haynes—a nineteenth-century man with a
vision for the future....

Here and Then, #762, available in August 1992.

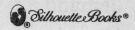